I0676527

SEEKING A COMMON THREAD

A novel based on a True Holocaust Story;

Book One of the Trunk Trilogy

Susan Spielvogel

Copyright 2015 by Susan Spielvogel
All rights reserved
Common Thread Press
ISBN: 0692464905
ISBN 13: 9780692464908
Library of Congress Control Number: 2015909190
Seeking a Common Thread, Bridgewater, NJ

ACKNOWLEDGEMENTS

The Author's father, Samuel, was an eyewitness to the Anschluss and the rise of the Nazis in Austria. *Seeking a Common Thread* is based on his testimony. The narrative interweaves original letters from the time period.

The Author would like to thank Samuel Spielvogel, Elsa Singer, and Etka Felsenstein for their testimony.

The Author also wishes to thank her mother Rosalind Spielvogel for her contribution to the chapter, "Snooping Around."

All letters printed in *Seeking a Common Thread* from Jakob Spielvogel, Florence Hobson and Itzhak Handel are authentic and original. Letters from Jakob Spielvogel were translated from the original German by Samuel Spielvogel.

The Author would also like to thank her cousin, Dalia Singer who has acted as tour guide through Vienna and Antwerp.

Front Cover: Photograph of the Spielvogel Family taken in Sniatyn, Poland circa 1934. Photograph taken by Zaklad Art Photography, R. Scharfa, Photographer. Jakob Spielvogel – second row; first on left. David Spielvogel, the author's grandfather, second row; third from left.

(Photograph: Collection of the Author)

Seeking a Common Thread is dedicated to the memory of Lusia and Jakob Spielvogel

And dedicated to the memory of D. Ann Lindbeck, who made me feel a part of the Hopkins School strand.

For more information and illustrations to accompany the Trilogy, please visit the author's website at http://www.SusanSpielvogelAuthor.com/ and her facebook page at www.facebook.com/SusanSpielvogelAuthor.

PROLOGUE
HIDDEN IN PLAIN SIGHT

Hidden in plain sight in the dining room of our apartment was an old trunk. That was before we moved out to the suburbs. It stood in the corner underneath a faded remnant of green cloth as a sort of an impromptu table for our record player.

One day, when I was in Kindergarten, I pulled back the green cloth to reveal that what I'd always thought was a table was really an old trunk made of grey canvas with wooden spines and metal brackets reinforcing its corners. That night, I dreamt that the trunk was a pirate's treasure chest, holding riches so dazzling it would blind the eye. In my dream, I opened it up to reveal gold doubloons, pieces of eight, strands of pearls, and diamonds, rubies, and sapphires; riches beyond anything that anyone could ever imagine.

As I grew older, I became aware that the trunk had once belonged to members of my father's family who had perished in the Holocaust. Not knowing what else to do with it, my father had inadvertently become the trunk's permanent caretaker. Perhaps he was holding on to it with the hopes that his relatives might someday come back for it, even when reason dictated it was something he should have discarded long ago. Like the remnant of green cloth my mother had thrown over the trunk, the trunk itself was the last remaining remnant of my father's relatives who had perished. To throw it away would have meant discarding any remaining connection my father held to these loved ones.

I'd never known what the trunk held inside, but I have a photograph of me with it when I was eight years old. I am with my sister and one of her friends; the three of us are dressed up as fairy princesses. We are all wearing striped stockings on our heads and dancing around the trunk. Youthful and carefree. Unaware of the Holocaust and the trunk's secrets.

November 19, 1957

                                        Carnalea, County Down, Ireland

Dear Susan,

    I have a very bad conscience about you and this silver spoon that has been laid aside for you, and every day for the past year I've reminded myself that I should write the accompanying letter. That has kept me thinking of you incessantly and now you are one years old. If I don't hurry up now you will be grown up and I past writing at all.

    I wish you could see my very beautiful cream coloured golden retriever. Honey by name and nature. She has never had a fight or quarrel in her life and is now nearly four years old.

    Thank your daddy for his letter which I was glad and to hear you are well. His letter eased my conscience a little.

    This is about all at the moment and tomorrow I shall feel a stone lighter having written at last!

                       With love to you all, Florence

CHAPTER 1
"TURNING FIFTEEN"

New Haven, Connecticut   November, 1971

Luck's on my side. No one can convince me otherwise. I've finally mastered the macramé knot I've been trying so hard for weeks to perfect. It's been maddening! After so many, many hours of knotting and pulling out knots, I've finally gotten the hang of it! If any macramé purists out there had witnessed me, they would have been furious! The knot I've perfected isn't even a true macramé knot, so please don't write or call. I've actually invented my own way of knotting. I don't like following instructions in how-to books. I'm more comfortable doing it my own way.

My knots follow their own path.

⇒⇐ ⇒

As I turn fifteen, my mother promises me that among the gifts I will be receiving will be a new pair of blue jeans. She thinks it's time that I get a new pair since all my other jeans are hand-me-downs from my sister.

I really shouldn't complain. All I ever wear are blue jeans, anyway. Back when I was in public school in junior high, my school district changed the dress code to allow girls to wear pants. From that moment on, I went cold turkey. I stopped wearing dresses or skirts to school altogether. For years, the prep school I now attend, Hopkins Grammar School, founded in 1660, whose motto is dedicated to the "breeding up of hopeful youths," used to have a school uniform consisting of a blue and black plaid woolen skirt with a white button-down shirt. Fortunately for me, this uniform was dispensed with the year before I began attending the school, leaving me the freedom to wear jeans every day. For now, my birthday blue jeans will remain new and intact for a little while. It's only a matter of time before the knees will go. The knees are always the first to go. And then the rest of the pants will disintegrate.

On top of everything, I always wear the same grey wool jacket to school that I received as an old hand-me-down from the daughter of one of my mother's friends. It's got these silver buttons we sewed on from my mother's sewing kit. I don't know what happened to the original buttons. For all I know, my fellow classmates whisper about my ancient jacket behind my back. That jacket must be at least as old as I am.

I feel different from the rest of my classmates. I don't really fit in with them. I can't even pinpoint why I have this feeling. They all dress well. They have that preppie, tweedy look. I follow my own personal style. In a way, I have no choice. My mother, Rosalind, who grew up in Brooklyn, says they are saving up money for college, so there isn't much money left for superfluous purchases such as fashion. My father, Samuel, who grew up in Vienna, says that his parents were very frugal and taught him to be frugal, too. They rarely spent money on clothing. One pair of shoes and two pairs of pants a year was all his parents gave him. In addition, he constantly reminds me about the single wooden truck he had to make do with as the only toy he played with throughout his entire childhood. For years, I've inherited my wardrobe from my sister who is three years older than I am.

Since my mother is an only child, I really don't have much of an extended family around me except for my maternal grandmother, whom we call Grammy, who lives in Brooklyn, and she rarely criticizes my clothing choices.

I am open to wear whatever my heart tells me to.

My fashion follows its own path.

⪥⪤

After dinner, my father pushes an envelope in my face. "Florence sends you greetings from Ireland on your fifteenth birthday. She says she can't believe you're turning fifteen! I can't believe your turning fifteen, either. I remember it was a year after you were born when Florence finally sent you a present in honor of your birth. She apologized for having taken a year to send it to you. Remember the silver spoon she sent you?"

I look over at my mother, whose concept of a fashion statement is a black polyester pantsuit. I can tell by the expression on her face that she does not remember Florence's silver spoon, either.

"No, I don't remember anything about it," I shrug. "I was a year old at the time. Have I ever seen this spoon?"

"Perhaps you have. Maybe you don't remember it, after all. She did send it to you a long time ago."

"Where is it, anyway?"

"It's over here in the china cabinet."

My father trots over to the corner cabinet to grab the silver spoon from the drawer and holds it out for my inspection. I glance at the tiny, now hopelessly tarnished ladle. I definitely do not remember that spoon. I do, however, remember who Florence is. Her exact relationship to my father is a bit of a puzzle because he was originally from Vienna and she lives in Ireland.

"How is that we know Florence, anyway?"

"It's a long story. She's almost like a member of the family, though. She rescued me. She saved my life. If it hadn't been for her, I wouldn't be here, and you certainly wouldn't be here, either."

The profound words of my father fail to seep in. I am more concerned with present matters, my upcoming birthday for one.

⤙ ⤚

The next day, I travel with mother to Cole's Country Casuals at the Amity Shopping Center to buy my new pair of blue jeans. At the store, I look for just the right size, a task which for me can be met with extreme difficulty. The challenge is to get just the right fit. My legs are short and thin, and my waist is very narrow. For some reason, jeans manufacturers apparently do not take my body type into account. Without any further ado or ruffles and flourishes, I pull three pairs of jeans off a rack and drape them over my left arm. I want to buy a pair of jeans that fit me well to avoid the fashion *faux pas* I made last year when visiting my sister in college in Saratoga Springs. We were at a hippie boutique called Sunshine Sparkle, and they were having a sale. I made the mistake of buying a pair of white jeans with thin blue stripes just because they were greatly reduced in price. Sure, they were just the right length, but they were very, very loose at the waist. I compromised by holding them up with a belt, but it bulged out too much in the front. As a result, I began to wear loose-fitting sweaters to compensate. After that experience, I swore that I would never buy a pair of pants that didn't fit right just because they were on sale.

I pull the curtain of the changing room, thinking, "if only I could have inherited my sister's old pair of blue jeans this time, I would not be going through this humiliating ritual of having to try on one pair of jeans after another." None of which I know will fit me. The first pair is too tight at the waist but are the right length.

The second pair fits at the waist, but the legs are too long. The third pair is just too big all over. Now, I am forced to put my own pants back on, put each pair back on its original hanger, and trudge back out into the bright, blinding fluorescent store lighting to search for three more pairs. None of which I am sure will fit me, either.

As I am about to emerge from behind the curtain with three pairs of jeans all lumped over my left arm, my mother shouts, "It's getting down to the wire. We have to leave soon to pick your father up from the office!"

I rush past my mother and randomly grab three more pairs of pants, which I now drape over my left arm, and trudge back towards the dressing room.

Under pressure for time, I try on the three pairs of jeans, the last of which finally fit me perfectly. I emerge triumphant from behind the curtain like a victorious Roman general carrying the trophies of war captured from the enemy. Just in time for my mother to pay and rush us off to pick up my father from his office in downtown New Haven, where he works as a city planner.

My father's mother, my grandmother, whom we call Omi, short for Omama, currently lives in Vienna with my father's sister, Elsa, and her family. They escaped from Vienna to Israel in 1939 and returned after the War to reclaim the family business, the lumberyard which had been left in the hands of Herr Schumacher, a Nazi sympathizer. They reclaimed their lives, re-established their business, and re-established themselves in the city from which they had once fled. Elsa has two daughters, my first cousins, Dalia and Silvia. They live in the Margareten District. Onkel Ernst now runs the lumberyard. Life goes on.

My father never speaks of these ghosts, these invisible relatives and their children who will never be able to come to my birthday parties. They have long since vanished off the face of the earth. It angers me that all my friends have cousins close to their own age and aunts, and uncles at whose houses they are able to spend their holidays. Had any of my father's other relatives lived, they might have had children my own age. It's bad enough I'm separated by an ocean from the two first cousins that I do have. Living in Vienna, they are too far away to stop by for a piece of birthday cake.

Although I'd like to learn more about these lost family members, it upsets my father to discuss anything about them. I was never told a single thing about my ancestors, who they were in life, what they were like.

A sense of separation sweeps over me.

If ever I've felt disconnected from my family, it's now.

I don't feel as if I'm part of the thread of my family.

There's been a break in the strand.

I don't even have names to go with faces.

Or faces to go with names.

I have nothing.

CHAPTER 2
"COWBOYS AND INDIANS"

Beheimgasse 21   Vienna, May, 1930

Lusia knows Jakob loves her. He indulges her every whim when it comes to her love of fashion. But she knows he'd draw the line at, say, a bright-purple hat with an ostrich plume. Jakob lavishes Lusia with everything she's ever wanted: a nice wardrobe and a nicely decorated apartment with brightly colored curtains and decorative table coverings. She wants for nothing.

Yet something is missing,

⇌ ⇌

The apartment house on Beheimgasse 21, in the Seventeenth District of Vienna, stands three stories tall. Jakob shared in the purchase of the building back in 1920 along with his brothers David, Leo, and Simon, and their sister, Chajce. With the exception of David, the other siblings remain in Sniatyn. Simon, David, Jakob, and Chajce were all named on the building's deed. Leo's name was left off because of his proclivities for gambling, and there was a fear that he might gamble the entire apartment house away in some midnight poker game.

The third story of the apartment house remains uninhabited. Lusia's sister-in-law Eva has taken to using that level to dry her laundry on lines stretched across the length of the floor. Typical of Viennese architecture of 1900, Beheimgasse 21 had been built long before the Spielvogel family took occupancy of it. David's lumberyard office is situated on the first floor. Originally structured to accommodate horse stables and a carriage, the space formerly occupied by the horse's stall is now being used as a space to store David's lumber. This is where the green, newly cut boards are left to dry out. In the corner, David keeps a metal cabinet in which he stores exotic woods, such as teak, ebony, and zebra wood, used for special orders by his customers for inlay work.

Located in the center store of the ground floor, Ferdinand "Ferry" Nemeth has set up his coffinmaker's shop. On the second floor, David and Eva occupy the middle apartment with their ten-year-old son, Samuel, and six-year-old daughter, Elsa. Herr Nemeth lives in the apartment to the right of David and Eva with his mother and his German Shepard, Fritz. To the left of David and Eva live Frau Mayer and her husband. A busybody, Frau Mayer always noses her business into the activities of others. Her curtained window looks out onto the hallway and affords her a view of her landlord's comings and goings. Samuel always looks out for Frau Mayer's peeping eyeball peering through the curtain as he passes on his way to and from his family's apartment.

The third tenants are Frau Neckar and her family. Frau Neckar raises canaries, which she sells to local pet stores. Herr Neckar earns his living by sewing boy's coats, which he sells to several of the larger department stores in Vienna. Their son, Karl, works as a waiter at a nearby restaurant. Their daughter, Helen, is a teenager who mostly keeps to herself. Of all the members of the family, Samuel is the one Frau Neckar truly warms up to. She always invites him into the apartment to watch the newly hatched canaries as they flutter about in their cages. Every December, Frau Neckar invites Samuel into her apartment to see her Christmas tree all lit up with real candles. Every candle blazing, they bring the brightest light this modest apartment will see all year.

David and Eva's apartment has a kitchen, a living room boasting an upright piano, a master bedroom, and the *Kabinett*, the cramped bedroom that Samuel and Elsa share. The *Kabinett* has been furnished by Eva's cousins, the Siebold Bothers, who are master cabinetmakers who create furniture in the Bauhaus style. The built-in cabinets with orange upholstered beds are made of highly polished walnut.

Lusia and Jakob's apartment is located on the ground floor. The front of the apartment faces the street, while the rear of the apartment faces David's lumberyard separated by a glass window.

Through this window, the stock of lumber piled floor to ceiling is clearly visible.

For now, these are comfortable living quarters with a kitchen and a living room, but it is far from Jakob's own lumberyard near Hardtmuthgasse. Since it is a long commute every day, Jakob contemplates moving somewhere closer to his business on Hardtmuthgasse in the Tenth District.

⇒⊢ ⊣⇐

In a way, Lusia's nephew Samuel has become like a surrogate child to her. She is fond of him and has begun to think of him almost as though he were her own son. Lusia reassures herself that it will only be a matter of time before she will have a baby. The fact that Jakob spares no expense on doctors for her infertility has lulled her into a sense that one day she will have a family of her own. She dares not think otherwise.

In a way, Lusia misses her native Stanislau and her mother. She is happy to be in a big city, so full of many more possibilities than there ever were back home. Her father's leather luggage factory Express was an exciting place to visit when she was a little girl, but eventually, she tired of watching the leather tanners or seamstresses stitching. It was boring to observe the workers doing their same tasks over and over, for each and every piece of luggage they made. After that, Lusia made a vow to herself to always do something new each and every time. Never repeating the same design over again.

Not ever.

Lusia's mother first introduced her to the art of embroidery when she was ten and had placed a needle and thread in her hands. Then and there, Lusia vowed to herself that since some of the embroidery is in and of itself a repetitive business, she would concede to repeat a pattern within the same piece of cloth, but never to duplicate the same design ever again on the next project.

At the age of ten, Samuel is just old enough to take himself to the local Kino to sit in the darkened theater by himself. He gazes up at the screen as the star of American cowboy films, Buck Jones (which he pronounces "Book Yonas"), dressed in white, vanquishes villains all dressed in black. During each fight scene, Samuel shifts to the left and then to the right with every punch. When he gets home from the Kino, he acts out these cowboy scenes when he thinks that no one is looking.

One day when Eva is not at home, Samuel is there, alone and unaware that the door has slowly been opened. Lusia has come upstairs for a visit. Out of the corner of her eye, she spots her nephew standing in the kitchen as he gestures his fingers in a way that she does not understand. Samuel is shooting his fingers off into the air, making shooting sounds at the same time.

Pow! Pow!

Suddenly, he turns around and pretends to shoot at an imaginary villain lurking behind him.

Pow! Pow!

Lusia dare not make her presence known. Not at this moment. She doesn't wish to embarrass her nephew. His imaginary play amuses her. Still, she finds his actions curious. A smile forms on Lusia's lips as she finally recognizes that Samuel is imitating the American cowboys and Indians he has seen in the silent movies at the Kino.

CHAPTER 3

"SNIATYN"

New Haven, Connecticut   December, 1971

"I haven't the vaguest idea which relative that trunk belonged to," my mother says as she sets the table in anticipation of a visit from my father's cousin Etka, his only relative living in America. "You know that your father never tells me anything about that period of his life."

The trunk that had once stood in plain sight in our old dining room back in our garden apartment in New Haven has now been relegated upstairs out of sight to the spare room off of my parents' bedroom when we moved to the suburbs in 1967.

Upon her arrival at our house, Etka rushes in through the front door, past the Irish linen panel Florence had sent to us depicting the characters from the *Canterbury Tales* that my mother had proudly hung on the foyer wall. Etka follows fast on the heels of my mother, as the two of them fly past the images of the characters from Chaucer.

I've never really been quite sure just how Etka is related to us. All I know is that she's related to my father somehow. I have been told that, like my father, Etka was born and raised in the *shtetl* of Sniatyn. Unlike Etka, my father was born in Sniatyn but had moved with his family to Vienna when he was still very young.

My mother settles Etka into the seat at the end of the dining room table. That's usually my spot, but, whenever visitors come over, it's used for the guest of honor. Now that I've been displaced, my mother relegates me to a seat on the side of the table.

Etka begins to speak in her heavy, Yiddish-Polish accent. "Everybody knew everybody in Sniatyn. The town was that small. And everybody was a relative. Even distant cousins were considered as close family. Not like it is today in America, where nobody knows anybody…"

"Would you like another piece of spiced apple cake, Etka?" my mother offers.

"Why, thank you Roz," Etka smiles. "As I was saying, Sniatyn was a small town surrounded by the Carpathian Mountains in the region called Galicia. My family's home overlooked the border between Poland and Romania. By then, it was Poland, no longer Austria. As you know, it became part of Poland with the collapse of the Austro-Hungarian Empire at the end of World War I. It was beautiful there; everything was green. Not like this pollution we have in Queens. Of course, you live out here in the country in Connecticut. You shouldn't know from pollution."

"It is pleasant here," affirms my mother.

"Here it is more like Sniatyn than Queens is like Sniatyn with those mountains behind your house."

"Etka, would you like some more coffee?" my mother offers.

"No, thank you, Roz. I'm fine. Susan, come sit next to me. I want to tell you about how your great-grandfather, my Uncle Joachim, and his wife Brance lived. He had five children. David, the oldest, was your grandfather. Then there was Simon, Leo,

Jakob and their sister, Chajce. It is through my Tante Brance, your great-grandmother, that we are related. She was a Linder, I was a Linder. Come here, Susan, I must tell you so that you should know..."

I obligingly move my chair closer.

"Have you ever gone back to Sniatyn?" I innocently ask, not knowing what emotions I might elicit from such a question.

"A Sniatyn to go back to, you ask?! I haven't been back since I was a teenager, just before it all happened. In 1935 I went to Palestina to study. Then, I went back to Sniatyn just before I came to America in 1938, after I'd finished my studies. A friend of mine insisted that I come to America with her because she wanted my company. Together, we worked in a stocking factory. I said my goodbyes to my parents and my two brothers and sister back in Sniatyn. I came to New York where I married my husband David and that was that. Everything changed with the war. There's no more Sniatyn to visit. At least, not the way your father or I would have remembered it. Whatever family members once lived there either fled or were killed in Auschwitz. Besides, the place is now in the Ukraine, behind the Iron Curtain. I couldn't go back there even if I'd wanted to..."

"That's too bad," I shrug, not finding any other words to say.

"Let me first tell you that your great-grandfather Joachim's world was one of superstition," Etka continues. "It's embarrassing for your father and me to talk about such things now. You see how Samuel is smiling. I know he agrees with me. But these were very superstitious people. Now that I have lived in the United States these thirty-four years. I understand the difference. Back then there was a very strong belief in the evil eye, the *ayin hora*. Joachim believed that a simple clove of garlic could ward off evil. Always he had braided strands of garlic hanging from the ceiling of his kitchen. How well I remember it! As your father will tell you, Joachim always insisted that everyone should carry a clove of garlic around with them in their pockets. He convinced us this would be a protection against evil."

A smile of recollection crosses my father's face.

Etka sighs as she continues to recall the town of her youth. "The people of Sniatyn lived in the isolation of the *shtetl*. They feared the outside world. Your father's family's world rose and fell around Joachim's strict vision. He was a follower of the Veitzener Rebbe, the leader of a sect of ultra-Orthodox Jews. Joachim was determined that his children should be equally as devout even as the world around him was becoming modernized. Joachim and Brance lived in a one- story house made of wood with a straw roof. It was covered on the outside with long ivy vines. There was no running water, no electricity, no central heating. Instead, there was a wood-burning stove in the kitchen that was used for cooking. The house was located on the *Wihode*, the open field up in the Carpathian Mountains in the town of Mikulence. Sniatyn was the larger city at the foot of the mountains. The region had once been a colony of the Roman Empire. When we lived there, Sniatyn served as the administrative center for the smaller surrounding towns. Most Jews, if they emigrated, went to Vienna. Not many wanted to come to America. After all, Vienna had been the capital of the Austro-Hungarian Empire. And then there was some interest in the community to immigrate to what was then called Palestina. In 1898, a number of Galician Jews established a colony there called *Mahnayim*."

"When I was a little boy," my father begins to speak in a soft voice, "I used to spend my summer vacations visiting both sets of grandparents back in Sniatyn. We took the *Schnellzug*. Looking back, the *Schnellzug* was something of a joke. It literally means 'fast train,' but it took twenty-four hours to travel from Vienna to Zalutia, the town closest to Sniatyn. Grandfather Joachim would always insist that I wear a *kippah* and *tallis* as long as I was visiting under his roof. It's true he insisted that I place a clove of garlic in my pocket to ward off the evil eye, Etka is right. We, in Vienna never believed in such superstitions, but I felt compelled to practice what my grandfather preached, at least while I stayed in his house. I wanted to please him no matter how archaic his ways seemed to me."

I turn to my father, "Weren't you raised with the same superstitions as Etka had been in Sniatyn?"

"I was two years old when my family moved away. Things were much different in Vienna. My sister and I weren't exposed to these superstitions. The big city diluted any sort of fervor as far as my mother and father was concerned. We lived in a world surrounded by modern amenities. In Vienna, we had automobiles, trams, telephones, and running water. In contrast, my grandfather lived his life up in the mountains, the way his father and his father's father had. There were only a handful of Jewish families living in our neighborhood in Vienna, called the Hernals District. Once my parents moved from the *shtetl* to the city, they left behind whatever superstitious beliefs they may have had. Still, my father remained religiously observant. He and I walked to Telemann Schul every Friday night for *Mincha* and *Maariv* services and again on Saturday morning for *Shacharit* services. After services, we'd walk home for a lunch of fish or stew. Then we'd return to *schul* in the afternoon for *Musaf* services."

"In Sniatyn, houses were lit with kerosene lamps," Etka adds, "Cooking was done over wood -burning stoves in the kitchen. *Shabbos* was a quiet time for families to gather together. I can recall looking out the window of our house on Friday nights and seeing all the homes with their candles in the windows. I can still recall the image of how their bright lights dotted the mountainside, piercing the nighttime darkness. At Chanukah, we could see the menorah with all their candles burning in each menorah in each window was especially wonderful. *Accchh*, it's a world we've lost forever. We can never go back to the way things once were. So many relatives lost. The loss of the children was the most profound. The future of our family was nearly squashed forever."

At that moment, my father falls silent. Regaining his composure, he goes over to the built-in hutch in the corner of the dining room. From the drawer, he pulls out an old sepia photograph that shows a group of people. It appears to be a family portrait of some kind. Instantly, Etka recognizes the faces in the photograph.

"Ah yes, I remember that event well," Etka sighs. "This picture was taken shortly after Brance's death in 1934. All the family members who could make it to the funeral came to pose for the portrait. Some came from Vienna, some came from Sniatyn, some came from Zalutia…"

"Just who are these people?" I ask as I stare into the faces of my ancestors for the very first time.

"If you must know," Etka begins, "that man in the center in the back row is your grandfather, David. He owned his own lumberyard on Beheimgasse in Vienna. The man on the left in the back row with the mustache and striped tie is his brother Jakob. He lived in Vienna with his wife Lusia. Like your grandfather, he, too, owned his own lumberyard. Next to him is Simon. He lived in Zalutia. He had a wife named Feige. Unfortunately, she was a sickly woman and could not make it to the photographer's studio, but his daughter, Elsa, is standing over here in the left hand corner. She's the one wearing the summery dress with the flower print. Next to your grandfather is Leo. He lived in Sniatyn and ran his own lumberyard. This is his wife, here in the front row. She's the one wearing the pearl necklace. Her name is Genia. Their son, Bronus, is the baby who sits on your great-grandfather Joachim's lap."

"That man in the center is my great-grandfather?" I ask. I gaze upon the face of an ancient man in black robes with a broad-brimmed hat, grey hair with *payis,* and a serious look in his eyes. Joachim looks like the type of person who must have been a strict disciplinarian. I can tell by the black robes he wears that he must have defined himself by his garments. His identity and his religion were intertwined with the clothing he wore. Instantly, I realize that perhaps he wouldn't have approved of how we live now in America, or more specifically, would never have approved of me as a teenager in modern America. And certainly, he wouldn't have approved of having great-granddaughters who wear blue jeans.

"Yes," says Etka. "What is it you are thinking?"

"Well," I reply, "Joachim looks so serious and so old-fashioned. You can tell that he must have been very religious."

"Yes, he was a very observant man," responds Etka. "As you can seem he had a beard and *payis*. Always he wore that hat and his long black robes. He was a *Chasid,* a pious Orthodox Jew."

I look at the faces of the clean-shaven sons. "But his sons don't have beards. Did Joachim permit that?"

Etka sighs. "He must have accepted it. They, too, were all religious, but as you can see, more progressive than their father."

"And who were the rest of the people in the photograph?"

"That man to the right of Leo was Baruch Auerbach. He was married to your grandfather's sister, Chajce. He ran a paint and hardware store in Sniatyn. Chajce is that woman with the flower on her dress. She is sitting in between her two children, Muniu, her son is standing on her right. He's the one with the long hair, wearing the white shirt. Elsa is the little girl in the dress who is standing to the left of Chajce."

"As a matter of fact," my father adds, "that little girl Elsa is now a grown woman and lives in Austria with her family. If we ever go back to Vienna, we can visit her."

I am amazed that someone in the photograph has survived, but I dare not ask about the rest of those who pose in this picture. I glance into the faces of these relatives. Their eyes gaze back into the camera as though they are staring at me. The fashions they wear must have been what were in style at the time the photograph had been taken, but to my eyes, they seem so out dated. As I gaze from one face to the next, searching for clues, I try to figure out just which one could have been the owner of the trunk. It is the shorter man who stands in the back row next to my grandfather? Is it the woman sitting down in the center wearing the elegant thirties-style dress with the pearls? Or is it the woman who sits between the two little children? I cannot tell, not by looking into their faces. I don't even know if the trunk's owner is pictured in this portrait.

"What about that man in the back?" I point to the image of the tall man with the mustache who wears a striped tie.

"That's Jakob," affirms my father. "He was married to Lusia who came from Stanislau. She's not in the photograph."

"Tell me more about them," I say, hoping to hear clues that might link them to trunk.

"Well, Jakob came to Vienna with Lusia in the early twenties from Sniatyn to start a lumberyard of his own located near Hardtmuthgasse. For a time, they lived in an apartment on the first floor at Beheimgasse 21 until Jakob grew tired of the commute to his place of business. That's when they moved to a corner apartment on Hardtmuthgasse in the Tenth District, called the Favoriten District."

"Tell me more about Lusia." I say, fishing for more clues.

"She came from Stanislau," my father adds. "The marriage was a match. All the marriages from your grandfather's generation were arranged ones."

I look at the photograph again. "Why isn't she in the photograph?"

"For whatever reason, she was unable to make it to Sniatyn to be in the photograph."

"Who was Genia?" I ask Etka. Of all the people in the photograph, she seems the likeliest candidate to have been the trunk's owner.

"Oh, Genia. She was such a sweet and *sympatische* woman." Etka begins. "She and Leo had a son named Bronus. The three of them lived under Joachim's roof. It was supposed to be a temporary measure, until Leo could earn enough money to buy a house of their own. But that was never to happen. Genia's parents had not approved of her marriage to Leo. Herr and Frau Schmerler knew of Leo's reputation as a gambler. In addition, the Schmerlers thought Joachim was too provincial and out of touch with the modern world. Coming from Stanislau, a much larger city, they viewed Joachim as something of a throwback.

"To prove himself a responsible businessman, Leo would go up the Carpathian Mountains to supervise the cutting of the trees for his lumber. He would watch the newly cut logs as they floated down the Czeremosz and Prut Rivers into Sniatyn. Then he would dry out the green wood on the special racks behind his lumberyard.

"After the marriage, it became customary for Genia and Brance to prepare the *Shabbos* meals together. Working side by side, they each had their own tasks, which they accomplished in a near ritual manner. That way, there would be no bickering between the two over who would do what chore. The workload was shared and that was that. Over time, Genia became used to this primitive home of Joachim's. It was after the birth of their son, Bronus, that she became more relaxed and felt all the more a part of our family.

"Every Friday night before sunset, Genia would light the *Shabbos* candles over by the sideboard in the kitchen. She was careful to let them burn all the way down to the base of the candlestick. According to superstition, it was considered bad luck to blow the candles out.

"Poor little Bronus. He would complain to his mother that his father was always at work and never at home. Genia would have to explain that he was away at the lumberyard in order to earn money to provide for his family. Over and over again, Bronus would complain, 'Mama, I want to play. I want Papa to come home from work before it gets dark outside so I can play with him...' Then Genia would begin to clap her hands in rhythm. She began to sing. 'There were two cats together. One was grey. One was black.

One cat runs to catch a mouse. And the second one rocks Bronus in the cradle.'"

We continue to listen in silence as Etka continues with her reminiscences.

"And the holidays! We celebrated the holidays like nowhere else! Especially for all the children, even little Bronus! They had the most fun! One Purim, when Bronus was three, just before sunset, Leo took him by the hand and walked the two miles down the mountain to the synagogue in the village. The wooden building lit up the night by candlelight. All of Sniatyn's population of small children sat on their father's laps, all holding wooden gragers, the noisemakers used during the Purim service, their little hands poised in anticipation of hearing the name 'Haman.' Boys dressed as girls. Girls dressed as boys. Bronus dressed up as Mordechai. He did his best not to wipe the shoe polish moustache from his upper lip, even though it tickled his nose.

"During the reading of the *Megillah*, the sounds of the *boos* and *hisses* made by the children when the rabbi said the name 'Haman' shook all around the wooden building, echoing outside into the mountains. After the service, the children proceeded to march door to door to the local houses where they were given *Hamantaschen*, home-baked poppy seed filled pastries. Ah, yes, my dear Susan, that is world we've lost forever."

Etka sighs and looks down at the table.

"Another cup of coffee, Etka?" my mother interjects.

"Oh no thank you, Roz, I'm fine." Etka forces a smile.

Etka takes a final sip of her coffee. "So, Sam, how is your sister Elsa?"

"She's doing well, although she writes us that this winter was a bit harsher than the last."

"And what news do you have of your mother, Eva? I suppose the girls call her Omama," says Etka.

"We call her Omi," I chime in.

"Omi, of course!" smiles Etka. "How is she doing?"

"She's doing well," replies my father. "She likes to sit on the bench in the park with the fountain that's right in front of the apartment house and watch the people pass by."

"And Elsa's daughters, Dalia and Silvia, how are they doing?"

"Very well, thank you. Dalia is now twelve years old and Silvia is going on ten."

"I hope someday they will visit us," I add.

"Perhaps they will," says my father. "Elsa writes us that Ernst can't get away from his lumberyard anytime soon. He is short on helping hands. Otherwise, they would love to all come to the U.S. for a visit."

Etka looks around our dining room; her gaze catches a piece of glassware on display in the cabinet at the top of the built-in hutch where my father had stored the family photograph.

"So, Sam, what news do you have from that woman in Ireland, the one who rescued you? She still lives in Belfast, doesn't she?"

"Yes, Florence still lives at the same address in Carnalea, County Down, as she had when I first knew her thirty-three years ago. Beautiful countryside."

"I'm glad to hear she is well," says Etka.

"Florence still writes to us," my father adds. "Do you know that she just turned ninety this year and she's going strong?"

"Ninety!" exclaims Etka.

"Have you ever thought about going back to visit her?" I ask.

My father lets out a sigh. "Not anymore. Right now, Belfast's a war zone. I'm afraid if I did go back there, I'd be killed by a car bomb. Florence writes us about the "Troubles." She says that their political troubles continue and that she believes them to be a disgrace to any community. As a Quaker, she's opposed to all the violence and says extremists on both side keep the pot boiling. In a recent letter, she wrote us saying that the situation in Northern Ireland is not improving and does not look like it's going to improve because there's no logic anywhere. She never knows from day to day what will happen next. In her letters, she writes that the extremists on both sides are trying to make it impossible for the government to rule and they cannot be allowed to go into anarchy."

"Such as shame people can't live in peace," Etka sighs.

"When I first met Florence," adds my father, "I had left Vienna behind with Nazis crawling out of the woodwork. Soon thereafter, the war broke out. Back then, Ireland was a country at peace. Unfortunately, today, it's reversed. Today, I can easily return to Vienna without fear, while I find it impossible to return to Belfast."

"Florence recently sent us a beautiful Irish linen tablecloth," my mother chimes in. "It's printed with the characters from the *Canterbury Tales*. We've put it up in the front hallway…"

"Yes, yes, I saw that on my way in," says Etka. "It's very nice."

My mother continues. "It's got Canterbury Cathedral in the center, surrounded by all the characters riding on horseback. There's the Wife of Bath, the Ploughman, the Yeoman, the Good Parson, the Nun, the Lady Prioress, and even Chaucer the poet, himself."

"Very nice," repeats Etka.

There is a lull in the conversation. I sit and stare into space for a brief second, unsure of what might be said next.

Etka breaks the silence. "By the way, Susan, are you still making jewelry?"

"Yes, I'm working on some macramé necklaces with beads. They're called sand beads, but actually they're made of glass."

"You should show me."

"Everything's over there in the corner." I point to the corner table between the two couches. "That's where I do my work." I get up from my seat at the table and bring out some pieces still tacked to a piece of corkboard. "These are some of the necklaces I've been working on, and these two pieces are wall hangings…" I hold up my work for Etka to see.

My father chimes in. "In fact, I'd written to Florence about Susan's interest in arts and crafts. And do you know something? She wrote back that she was amused and interested in her handcraft efforts, saying she was very handy-crafty herself. She writes that at ninety, she can still sew and hold a needle and thread. She wrote recently that she made a project out of a fur glove. Her dog had eaten the other glove, so she decided to make something out of the mate. According to Florence, the project was a success."

"Susan's work is very nice," smile Etka. "Back when I was young, girls were taught to embroider. You must know that back then, Sniatyn was a center for embroidery. There was a factory, well, not a factory in the modern sense; it was really more of a cottage industry. As soon as a girl turned ten, a needle and thread were placed in her hands, and so she was taught to embroider. But that was not what interested me. I never wanted very much to learn how to embroider."

"Why not?" I interrupt, not understanding why Etka wouldn't want to learn a craft.

"I was more interested in books, like my brothers. Embroidery was for girls. I wanted an education."

Throughout her visit, I want to get Etka alone to ask her about the trunk. It isn't until she is standing in the hallway about to leave that I have my opportunity. As she whisks past the Wife of Bath, the Monk, the Oxford Scholar, and even Chaucer, himself, I try to get her attention before it is too late. I need to ask her those questions out of earshot that I dare not ask my father, before my parents run out to say their goodbyes.

As Etka hurries towards the front door, I rush to pull her aside. "What about the people who owned the trunk?" I ask breathlessly.

"Trunk? What trunk?" Etka furrows her brow as she buttons up her black woolen overcoat. "I've never heard anything about a trunk."

"Didn't it belong to Genia, that woman in the photograph who was wearing the pearl necklace?"

"Genia? No, she never owned such a trunk. She never had enough money to buy enough possessions to fill a trunk."

"Or was it Chajce, the woman with the little children?"

"No, Chajce never owned any trunk, not that I've ever heard of."

"I know that it didn't belong to my grandmother. I'm sure of it."

"Where is this trunk anyway?" Etka frowns.

"It's upstairs in the spare room off of my parents' bedroom. We've always had it. For as long as I can remember. Even when I was little. It used to be in our dining room in our old apartment back on Whalley Avenue. It had belonged to somebody in Europe. But I don't know just who…"

"Why don't you ask your father?"

"It upsets him too much to speak of these things."

"Of course! It's upsetting! Very upsetting! It's been very upsetting for all of us. I came from a family of four. I'm the only one left. Over the years, I've learned to live with the fact that my parents and my brothers and sister are no more. Even though I was living in New York City when I got married and I was far away from the Nazis, I still decided never to have any children because I never knew what might happen to them. You never know what can happen in the future."

I pause for a moment, letting what Etka has just told me sink in. "My father has never spoken about the trunk's owners. I thought you might know who they were."

"But he's never told me of such a trunk."

"It's a very big trunk."

"Could be…but I don't know anything about it."

"I'm not even sure whether it was owned by relatives from Sniatyn or from Vienna. All I know is that the trunk is now upstairs in the spare room."

"Do you know what's inside?"

"No. we've never opened it up."

"I'm sorry, but I can't help you out. I know nothing about it. Must have been a relative from Vienna. From the other side of the family, maybe. I left for America in 1938. Several years later, I got word from surviving relatives that my entire family had been massacred. Maybe the trunk comes from relatives in Vienna from your father's mother's side of the family; I never knew them very well. I wish I could tell you more, but I can't. I'm sorry…one thing you should know, you should be proud of your grandfather. You have nothing to be ashamed of. He was a successful businessman, respected in his community."

"I was never told very much about him."

"Ask your father; he should tell you."

"Yes, I'd like to ask him. But how can I find out about the trunk without upsetting my father too much?"

"If it's something you want to know, then ask him."

Just then, my mother rushes ahead of my father into the front hallway to say their goodbyes. I move back toward the hallway, out of the way. I feel very small at this moment. And even more baffled than ever!

CHAPTER 4
"DRESSMAKER'S DUMMY"

Beheimgasse 21   Vienna, April, 1930

Lusia sits on Frau Ingber's couch in her atelier on Renngasse in the First District. The seamstress's atelier is located in the vicinity of the Graben just steps away from the Pestsaule, the monument that is dedicated to the plague of 1679. Patiently, she waits as the seamstress takes the measurements of another client. Lusia nimbly pushes the needle containing heavy, twisted embroidery thread through the circular white linen tablecloth she is stitching. It is to go on the round table by the window, the one with the legs carved to look like lion's claws. After she embroiders a large blue flower with a Lazy Daisy stitch, she turns the cloth over and knots the end of the thread. Expertly, she moves the hoop over to the location where another blue flower is to be embroidered.

Lusia looks up momentarily from her stitching to watch as Frau Ingber transfers her client's measurements to re-shape the dummy to suit Frau Schmidt's body type. She continues, eyes on her embroidery, reflecting back on her appointment earlier in the morning with Vienna's premiere fertility expert, Herr Doktor Porges. Will the doctor give her good news when she returns to him for her next appointment? After many years of marriage, Lusia is anxious to please Jakob, who wants nothing more than for her to present him with a son.

And nothing more.

The new dress, she has decided, is to have bright pretty blue flowers and short sleeves. Lusia stares at all the bolts of cloth on the seamstress's workbench, searching for just the right print.

Stitching the next blue flower along the garden path, Lusia continues her wishes for good news from Herr Doktor Porges. As though to hold her breath will ensure a positive test result. As if to make a wish as she threads her needle will lead to her ability to conceive a child.

Is it to be a boy or a girl? A boy would please Jakob very much. But if I had a girl, I could dress her up in frilly little dresses, brush her hair, buy her pretty little patent leather shoes. I could teach her how to embroider. A daughter would be more of a companion to me than a son. But how Jakob longs for a son!

A baby's smile, that's all I long for!

Stitch. Stitch. Knot. A blue flower is created. A baby's smile is imagined.

Lusia pushes some more of the blue thread into the white linen. She pulls it taut.

Greta was married the same year as Jakob and I. Last month, she delivered their third child. How proud her husband Franz was!

Lusia winces as this thought passes through her mind, her face resembling a woman who has just sucked on a lemon.

What if all the money Jakob has lavished on medical specialists is for nothing? Suppose that after all this poking and prodding is done with, it turns out that nothing can be done to assist us in starting a family?

Lusia tilts her head as though this bad thought could be drained out of one side. She stitches another blue cross-stitch. She smiles at the superstitious notion of her father-in-law Joachim back in Sniatyn, who believes that a clove of garlic can ward off the evil eye. To her, such a belief is old fashioned, out of date, out of touch with what she holds to be modern reality. She believes, instead, in the rational and the scientific methods of Herr Doktor Porges. She reassures herself with the thought that Jakob is sparing no expense when it comes to her medical tests and treatments for fertility.

A fleeting thought sweeps over Lusia like a swift arrow. What if all this time, their assumptions have been wrong? Suppose the problem does not lie with her, but instead lies with Jakob? That thought passes out of her mind as swiftly as it had come. She dare not think such thoughts. And even worse, she dare not relate them to Jakob, He would never forgive her for thinking that he could possibly be the one to blame for her inability to have a baby.

"*Keyn ayin hora*, no evil eye!" mutters Lusia *soto voce* to herself. Then she wonders aloud, "Did I really say that?"

If I were superstitious like my father-in-law, I'd say that I was being cursed by the evil eye. I'm so glad that Jakob does not share in his father's superstitious ways. He'd blame the evil eye for my predicament!

A stitch.

A wish.

A stitch.

A prayer.

As though a stitch could become a prayer made real,

As though to pray would make a wish concrete.

I pray I have a baby. Please make it be soon. I don't care if it's to be a boy or a girl.

I don't care if Jakob only wishes for a son. I pray I have a baby. I pray it will be soon.

Frau Ingber pulls the cloth tape out of her tape measure as she walks forward towards Lusia. As Lusia pulls down her tablecloth onto the couch and rises for her fitting, her thoughts do not remain on the new dress with the floral print for which she is about to be fitted. They remain stuck on that doctor's appointment she had earlier in the morning.

Will it be wonderful news or news which will lead to a lifetime of disappointment?

Frau Ingber's dressmaker's dummy is now ready to be rearranged with Lusia's own dress measurements just as Frau Schmidt puts on her lightweight spring coat and prepares herself to leave the atelier.

"A new fabric has just arrived! Let me show you," beams Frau Ingber as she pulls the measuring tape out from its sheath. "It's called rayon. It was developed by scientists to replace silk. It's very popular and in great demand. It has been perfected for the open market and is now available. Here it is. Feel it!"

Lusia holds out her hand to feel the smooth cloth wrapped on the bolt, "Yes, it does feel like silk. Yes it does!"

"It's half the cost of silk and much more durable. So much more modern," smiles the seamstress. "Here are the selections of fabrics in rayon. Take a look."

Lusia gazes over at the bolts of cloth, each one with a pattern more attractive than the next. "I don't know, Frau Ingber, each one is so pretty. Which one shall I choose?"

"Well, Lusia, with your complexion, I'd select the cloth with the black with the blue and yellow flowers."

"I like the print with the red and white flowers better. Perhaps you are right. I'll go with the print with the blue and yellow flowers."

"You've made a wise decision. I'll begin work on the dress right away."

Lusia smiles back at the seamstress as her thoughts remain not on her new dress but on that expensive fertility expert.

A stitch.

A wish.

A stitch.

A prayer.

CHAPTER 5

"SNOOPING AROUND"

New Haven, Connecticut   January, 1972

Perhaps in the back of my father's mind, he had been saving the trunk on behalf of these nameless relatives in the hopes they might have possibly survived and one day would be reclaiming their possessions.

Shortly after Etka's visit, I walk into the living room where I notice that one of the drawers of my father's desk is opened slightly to reveal what looks to me to be some old photo albums. I slip closer to pull the drawer open just a tiny bit further to see that there are three photo albums, each one with faded covers stamped with gold designs and brown rope tassels.

As I pull put a small album marked "Photographs," I see that inside are small photos mounted on black construction paper with black photo corners. Just as I am about to grab the album out of the drawer for a better glimpse, my father suddenly walks into the room.

Catching me with my hand inside the desk, he shouts, "Hey, keep out of there!"

"Who are those photographs of?" I boldly ask, not believing I have actually summoned up the courage to ask such a question.

"None of your business!"

What little courage I'd mustered is rapidly draining out of me. "Why can't I have a look?"

"Stop snooping around where you don't belong!"

"Why can't I see the photographs?"

"It's not polite to snoop around into other people's business," he affirms. "Keep out of my desk drawer!"

"Okay, okay, I'll keep out!" I say, holding my hands up in an 'I surrender' stance. "I promise I won't go snooping around anymore."

⊷⊶

My mother catches my glance. "It's almost time for dinner," she smiles. "You'll have to put down your macramé and come to the table."

I smile back. Then I stop smiling. "Mom, you were born in America and lived through the period of the Holocaust. Back then, did you know anything at all about what was happening in Europe?"

My mother's facial expression turns to one of concern. "We only knew about the refugees when they came to America because of the Nazi persecutions. We never heard about all those people left behind in Germany who had no ability to escape. Americans were unaware that people were being killed in the concentration camps. I personally didn't know until after the war was over that so many people had been killed. Nobody knew. The count of six million trickled out slowly over a period of time. It wasn't until after that the Red Cross had come out with the number of six

32

million. Certainly, we Americans knew of Germany's discrimination against the Jews and other minorities. We knew what a racist Hitler was. But at the time, we never dreamed that his racism would translate into mass murder."

"Surely some news of what was going on must have leaked out. Hadn't anyone from the outside world noticed that Jewish citizens were disappearing from their homes?"

"German citizens were not allowed to speak out against Hitler. If they did, they would have been jailed for it…or worse…"

"Like shot?"

"Yes, shot on sight, no further questions asked."

"Weren't Americans of certain events? Kristallnacht for one?"

"I turned thirteen on November 9, 1938. If I was typical of any American, I was busy with my own life on that day. That afternoon, Grammy threw a party for me at A&S, the big department store in downtown Brooklyn. A&S was a favorite shopping mecca where one could find everything for the good life right there in Brooklyn. There were many who rarely ventured forth into New York City because every necessity was there was available in their own snug borough.

"It was a time when, except for certain few local politicians, we rarely questioned their motives or had any idea of term limits. We loved and trusted our politicians from the president on down: Franklin Delano Roosevelt, Herbert Lehman, governor of New York and especially our beloved mayor of New York, Fiorello LaGuardia. And we had Ebbets Field. A child could walk or take the trolley or subway alone from one area to the other. It was a comfortable life.

"My thirteenth birthday party was held in the dining room of A&S with large screens that had been made from worn sheets stretched over wide aluminum tubes. Those screens separated the children from those shoppers of a certain age who combined the resting of their feet with the eating of their lunch. The broad windows of the dining room had been washed in the center, leaving their edges thick with the encrustation of the downtown soot. But all was serene.

"For my party, there had been much serious discussion as to the type of ice cream we should order until finally my mother chose the perfect Breyer's in the shapes of flowers and fruits. Although it was a Wednesday afternoon, my entire class converged in small groups on the unsuspecting building. The boys all wore their first good woolen suits with long pants or knickers. The girls all wore their patent-leather Mary Janes and standard pastel dresses. They wore their hair either long or short in corkscrew curls.

"The adolescents, as we were called back then, tried at first to act as they thought would be expected of them. They ate their food, played their games. The boys and girls giggled at each other. Although the class was co-ed and they had known each other from early childhood, this was an awkward social situation. Gradually, the boys and the girls separated. As if by a secret signal, the boys broke away and started to chase one another around the table, much to the chagrin of the few parents who had volunteered to keep order. They had foolishly thought it would have been an easy job. The boys separated the screens and made a dash for the escalators. At first, they were content to the use the up escalator to go up and the down escalator to go down. But egging each other on, they did the inevitable. They began to compete with one another to see who could go up the down escalator or down the up escalator, occasionally jostling the shoppers in their desire to beat their classmates coming in the other direction. The party planners had never thought of such a glorious entertainment! What a time! What freedom! How snug and comfortable it was to be growing up in Brooklyn.

"It was Wednesday, November 9, 1938. We were all going about our lives as usual, but across the ocean, it was Kristallnacht."

"The world should have known then that something was wrong, that they should take action." I shrug, perhaps feeling myself a bit too self-righteous. "Shouldn't that have been the wake-up call?"

"Hindsight is always 20/20. If my own life was any indication of how little Kristallnacht affected us in our daily lives, it was no wonder that the horrors continued. We were too involved in our own lives. Historians now refer to that night as the beginning of the Holocaust. At the time, though, what could we in America have done?"

"But, Americans did know about the refugees from Germany who were coming to this country…and they knew specifically why they were coming here."

"Yes, we knew it was bad, but we didn't know just how bad it really was. Hitler made sure that his camps of mass extermination remained a secret. I'm not sure at the time if all those German refugees who came to America even knew about what went on in the concentration camps."

Having listened carefully to my mother's words, I am even more baffled than ever. If people had known, even if they'd only known only about the discrimination and not the mass murders, why hadn't anyone ever spoken out or protested?

All my classmates and I are against the Vietnam War. And that's happening far away from us. Yet we're still concerned about it and want to protest against it. Shouldn't someone, anyone in America who had known something, spoken up? And if anyone had spoken up, why hadn't anyone listened?

CHAPTER 6
"CHAJESREALGYMNASIUM"

Beheimgasse 21   Vienna, June, 1930

"So what's the news?" Lusia puts down the china tea cup with the delicate flowers across the rim as Samuel walks into his family's apartment. His school bag hangs from his shoulder.

"Samuel is to go to the Chajesrealgymnasium, the Jewish school in the Second District," responds Eva as she pours herself a second cup of tea. "It's located at Castellezgasse 35. We've just received word from Herr Kellner, the school's director, that he's passed all his entrance exams. He's just been accepted."

"And it's a good thing, too," adds Lusia. "He's not so safe at *Die Volksschule* with those anti- Semites. I remember the day he came home when he had first started at *Die Volksschule* when he was six. He came to me in tears, crying, 'Tante Lusia, you won't believe what just happened to me. I was walking home from school when this older boy accosted me. I never knew that the name Samuel was something bad."

Samuel chimes in. "This nine year-old-boy named Josef Brinsky came over to me and asked me my name. I told him it was Samuel, not knowing what response I'd get. He shouted back at me, 'Hey, wait a minute, isn't Samuel a Jewish name? He then called me a 'Jew-pig.' I told him I wasn't a 'Jew-pig.' Suddenly, he and three other boys grabbed my schoolbag. Since I was new and this was my first day of school, my only concern was that my mother would be mad at me for getting my brand-new schoolbag dirty. After Josef pulled the bag from my shoulder and threw it to the ground, I quickly scrambled to pick it up. My arm successfully connected with the loop of the shoulder strap just in time for me to flee. As I was running away, I could hear them chanting 'Jew-pig, Jew-pig' all the way until I was two blocks away."

Lusia lets out a sigh. "I suppose it's a good thing then that your father has decided to send you to the new school. Who knows what this Brinsky boy will say to you in the future now that you are older."

"But Mama, Tante Lusia, the new school is too far from home."

Eva jumps in, "I know you will have to get used to it. Right now, your school is only eight blocks away. Now you'll have a forty-minute tram ride each way every day. But I know you'll get used to it."

Better he should have a forty-minute tram ride every day than to have to put up with the likes of Josef Brinsky," Lusia reassures her nephew and her sister-in-law. As she speaks, Lusia recalls the sting of the needle as it jabbed into her skin for the latest fertility test. In her mind is the fleeting image of the glass vial as it filled with her red blood. Her blood to be tested to determine whether or not motherhood is in her future. Another image appears. The crisp white linen of Herr Doktor Porges's sleeve of his doctor's coat when he drew her blood. Lusia had stared at the blinding white sleeve, then looked away just as the needle was about to pierce her skin.

Lusia's mind goes back to her discussion with Eva. She had been so lost in her own thoughts that she could not focus on the discussion of her nephew's schooling. Yes, she is glad for Samuel, but at the same time, she feels the twinge of disappointment. For the very first time, she is jealous of her sister-in-law.

If only I could have had a son of my own. If only he were the one attending such a school.

Eva is ecstatic. "This will be a wonderful opportunity for my son. I know that when the time comes, he'll adjust to the long commute and be happy that his father made the right decision."

CHAPTER 7
"POLKA DOTS"

Beheimgasse 21   Vienna, June, 1930

Crackling static emits from the radio. A Strauss waltz barely audible breaks through the crackle. Lusia dresses up in her black and white polka-dot dress Frau Ingber created for her two months ago. Polka dots for luck. In the hopes it will bring good news from Herr Doktor Porges's office. A phone call with news of the last rounds of her infertility tests is expected at any moment. In her mind, as silly as it sounds even to her, she believes that the wearing of this particular dress can change her fate.

⇒⁙ ⁙⇐

Later in the morning, the long-anticipated phone call comes from Herr Doktor Porges's office with the test results. The doctor gives Lusia the option to come into the office and hear the results in person, but he tells her it won't make a difference.

A fibroid tumor in her ovaries is the culprit.

It is definitive.

Doktor Porges can offer no cure. No surgical procedure is available to reverse this condition. Nothing that the doctor can do will enable Lusia to have a child.

Nothing!

Expectations!

Throughout her married life, Lusia held expectations that her husband will provide her will every comfort she desired. A tailor-made life, her dresses tailor-made to suit her down to the selection of fabrics, and an apartment furnished with every modern convenience. Why couldn't the rest of her life be that way, too? Why couldn't she just give God her dimensions and He could craft a life for her? Why couldn't Herr Doktor Porges provide her with the solution to her fertility problems she so desired? It's as if she'd given God her measurements and He couldn't add them up.

⊷⊷

Located in the First District in a block-long alley off of Rotenturmstrasse is Frau Grauen's thread shop. It's just around the corner from the Ankeruhr, the mechanical clock that spans from one side of the street to the other. The clock chimes every hour with a figure from Austrian history appearing hourly until noon or midnight, when all twelve figures walk across the bridge. At one o'clock, Kaiser Marcus Aurelius makes his appearance; two o'clock, Kaiser Karl der Grosse; at three, Herzog Leopold VI; at four, Herr Walther con der Vogelweide; at five, Konig Rudolph von Hapsburg; at six, Meister Hans Puchsbaum; at seven, Kaiser Maximillian; at eight, Burger Andreas von Lieberberg; at nine, Graf Rudiger von Starhemberg; at ten, Prinz Eugen von Savoyen; at eleven, Kaiserin Maria Theresa and finally, at twelve, Joseph Haydn.

It is now three o'clock and the bronze figure of Herzog Leopold VI materializes and glides across the bridge. The clock plays the music of *Das Nibelungenlied,* and as it does so, it chimes three times.

Lusia walks beneath the clock's bridge, making her way towards the thread shop. Frau Grauen's shop is as ancient as the cobblestoned street on which it is set. The shopkeeper's finished work can be seen hanging in the shop's window display. Lusia has always admired Frau Grauen's knitting prowess, especially her scarves and sweater. Not good at knitting, herself, she has always stuck to embroidery, a craft which she has occupied herself with ever since she was ten years old.

Lusia sets off the bell as she enters the glass door of the thread shop. She looks up at all the balls of wool lining one wall. On the opposite side are boxes of thread piled higher and higher towards the ceiling. Thread samples of each color are tacked to the outside of these boxes, revealing what hues are to be found inside. To Lusia, it appears as though there are hundreds of different sizes of knitting needles set on top of the glass counter, although it is more likely to be twenty or so. Against the far wall, she sees familiar wooden embroidery hoops lined up in descending sizes.

Frau Grauen emerges from behind the simple brown cloth curtain that separates the back room from the shop, where she keeps herself occupied by knitting when she has no customers.

"*Gruss Gott,*" Frau Grauen greets Lusia, knitting needles still in hand. "What can I help you with today?"

"*Gruss Gott,*" returns Lusia, "I'd like to start a new embroidery project. What do you suggest?"

"These placemats just came in from Bavaria. Have a look."

Frau Grauen leads Lusia over to the table with the placemats pre-stamped with designs. Lusia rummages through the pile until she finds just the right design that suits her. Her eyes fall on a particular set of mats with a floral border.

"I'll take this set of four," Lusia tells the shopkeeper, pointing to the white cloth rectangles with the tiny flowers printed on them in pale blue ink.

"Very well," smiles Frau Grauen. "Another lady bought the very same design just last week. She showed me part of what she's completed so far. They're so *verliebt!*"

"Well, I hope mine come out just as nicely. I'm still not very good at French Knots, you see. I do keep practicing, but I've always found it so hard to get them just right!"

"I've always warned my customers about French Knots. Most of the time, knots are not meant to be seen on the front of the cloth. French Knots are different. They are to be seen from the front, so it's especially important that you do them neatly. There is a trick to them, shall I show you?"

"Yes, yes, please do," smiles Lusia.

"I'll get a small square of cloth to use in the demonstration. Give me one moment."

Frau Grauen goes to a corner table behind the counter, from which she pulls a small white square of cloth. "I have a needle with some thread." She holds up a needle already threaded with some red thread. "You see, you knot the end of the thread and push the needle through the cloth as you would normally do, but in the front. Knot the thread first, then turn the cloth to the reverse side and push the needle through at the spot where you want to place the knot on the other side. Then hold the thread down with your left thumb, take the needle, and wind the thread twice around it. While still holding the thread firmly, twist the thread and pull it. Reposition the needle back to the position where the thread came out. Pull the thread taut to the back of the cloth. Knot the end of the thread. It's really very simple. I suggest you practice on your own square of cloth at home until you feel confident enough to embroider the knots on the final placemats."

"Thank you for your advice, Frau Grauen. I'll do just that."

The shopkeeper smiles a deep, crinkly smile. "So what color threads would you like for your placemats?"

"Oh, I suppose bright spring colors-reds, pinks, different shades of blue." Lusia returns the shopkeeper's smile as she gives her thread order. In the back of her mind, though, she is still reeling over the doctor's news, still refusing to believe it.

Perhaps there was a lab error with those results; Lusia desperately tries to reassure herself. *No, I think this is it. Herr Doktor Porges reaffirmed that these were the definitive tests. What do I tell Jakob?"*

The shopkeeper breaks Lusia's reverie. "Very good, then." Frau Grauen smiles, oblivious to the unhappy expression that now crosses Lusia's face. "Give me a moment to add all this up."

Lusia puts her smile back on. She does not want the store clerk to detect her pain. Then she pays Frau Grauen and heads for the door.

"Gruss Gott," Lusia's voice is almost sing-song as she sets the bell off on the door as she leaves.

"Gruss Gott," returns Frau Grauen as she heads back behind the curtain to continue on with her knitting.

Out on the cobblestoned street, the sound of her heels echo with a click-clack off the stones that pave the narrow, block-long street. She passes under one wooden shop sign after another written in Yiddish in gold lettering across a black background. Many of these signs have faded over time, while others appear to be newly painted.

In the past, Lusia had believed that Herr Doktor Porges was the key to giving her hope to unlock the fertility puzzle. Now on this day, after so many specialists and so many tests, her hopes have been dashed. Once she had believed that her black and white polka-dot dress held good luck for her. Now she knows better. She kicks herself for such superstitious thoughts, believing that wearing a particular dress could ever bring good luck.

On the outside, Lusia appears fashion forward in her polka-dotted dress. Neat and tidy, every hair in place, her make-up plain but effective. A little face powder, some red lipstick that is all.

Anyone who saw her on this day would believe that her life must be perfect.

On the inside, however, Lusia begins to feel as though her life were caving in. How will she break the news of Herr Doktor Porges's phone call to Jakob? How will Jakob take the news that his wife will never be able to have children?

CHAPTER 8
"BUT I WANT TO KNOW"

New Haven, Connecticut   January, 1972

"Me and Julio Down by the Schoolyard" plays on the radio as I do my homework for Madame K's French class. I conjugate the verbs *essuyer, ennuyer* and *essayer* and read a chapter of *La Silence de la Mer.*

How do I define myself?

The daughter of a father who escaped from the Holocaust?

The daughter of a mother from Brooklyn who is third-generation American with a grandmother born in Branford to Jewish-Russian immigrants who calls herself a Connecticut Yankee?

A hippie?

An anti-war protester? (Even though my father never allowed me to attend any of the rallies in downtown New Haven.)

A traditionalist?

An artist?

Am I a rebel in bell bottoms and love beads and shoulder-length hair?

Am I a non-conformist?

Or am I really a conformist because everyone else considers themselves to be a non- conformist, too?

⇒⊢ ⊣⇐

I ponder my mother's words about my father's sensitivities very carefully. I think about that old trunk now relegated to the spare room upstairs. All these years, I have never put any pressure on either parent to open it up. Who knows what old wounds it might bring up in my father?

But I want to know!

I deserve to know not only what the trunk contains, but also about the people who had once owned it. Walking into my mother's art studio, I blurt out, "And what of the trunk?"

"What about it? My mother quietly puts down her paintbrush and shrugs. She is painting images of unborn children over a montage of newspaper clippings of headlines shouting about horrific events such as wars, shootings and starvation. Depicting the world into which these innocent unborn children will be born, she is calling it *Matrix of the Unformed*.

"What's inside the trunk?" I demand.

"What's inside? Old *schmatas*…that's what inside."

"*Schmatas*? What does *schmatas* mean?"

"It's Yiddish for rags. The trunk's got old clothing…linens… whatever the people who once owned it had packed away before they escaped."

"Have you ever looked inside it?"

"I've peeked inside once or twice."

"Aren't you even the least bit curious about the contents?"

"It's just some old stuff…nothing much."

"Nothing much? How do you know there isn't anything of value in it? No jewels…no silverware…just some old clothing and linens?"

"I'm sure the most valuable thing inside is probably a set of linen bed sheets. And anyway, whatever clothing is inside would be hopelessly out of fashion by now. Maybe we should just give the entire contents away to the Salvation Army or the Goodwill."

"Why can't we open it up and see just to be sure. Perhaps there is something of value in there, maybe just not in the way you might view an object's value."

"Someday, maybe we will open it up…"

"Someday?"

"Yes, someday in the future."

"And just how far is this 'future'? Is it next week…next month… next year…ten years from now?"

My mother seems definitive in her hindrance of my quest to open up the trunk. I begin to wonder why. Since she has raised me with such a liberal upbringing, I've always been able to ask her anything…sex…drugs…you name it. When I was in eighth grade, I smoked a cigarette in front of her to know what it felt like. Since no one in my family smokes, I'd 'borrowed' a cigarette from a girl in the girl's room before school started. I wanted to experience what it felt like to smoke. I did it once and never did it again. When I was in ninth grade, I asked my mother about sex. She went to the library and checked out scientifically illustrated books on the subject. Whenever I've asked my mother about what happened to my father's family, she tells me that it's a subject she doesn't want me to discuss with him. That is the one taboo subject I'm forbidden to ask about.

Yet, I persist in pumping my mother for information. "Has Dad ever told you about them? Who they once were?"

"No, not really. I'm sorry, but I've no idea whose these relatives were."

"Has he ever told you about those people in the photograph?"

"Only in vague terms. The only person in the photograph I really know about is his father, your grandfather. After all, he was my father-in-law."

"Haven't you ever asked him about any of his other relatives?"

"What is there to ask?"

"You could ask him things like who they were, what their names were, what they were like."

"I try to avoid discussing those sorts of things with him."

"But aren't you taking away from these people's memories not to know anything about who they were?"

"I don't think about these things often enough to ask about them. I have more pressing things on my mind. At the moment, I have to get back to my painting."

"But doesn't it make their murders all the more profound because they are forgotten? Doesn't it make them die twice?"

"Die twice? How can they die twice?"

"It's one thing for them to have been murdered. It's another thing for them to be forgotten."

"I don't know who these people were in the first place, how can I forget them?"

"But not to even know who they were…"

"I don't know which members in your father's family were killed to even begin to ask about them."

"If you begin to ask, you might get to know more about them and who they were."

"Your father is very sensitive about the subject. All I do know is that whenever I did try to ask, it upset him very much."

CHAPTER 9
"WHAT TO TELL JAKOB?"

Hardtmuthgasse 10   Vienna, June, 1930

"The Merry Widow Waltz" plays on the radio.

A new move to a new district, The Tenth, known as the Favoriten District. Now Jakob can be near his lumberyard.

The promise of a new life,

How shall Lusia define herself?

As a woman from Stanislau now living in Vienna?

As a woman who cannot have a family?

As a happily married woman who is content to live her life in the present with her husband with no worries of having to raise children?

Her husband!

Lusia has been so upset by Herr Doktor Porges's news that she has kept it from Jakob for the past two weeks.

What shall I tell Jakob? How will he take the news? I know how upset he will be! I know I can't keep this a secret forever. I must tell him sometime. But it must be when the moment is right.

Lusia goes back to her ironing. Perhaps if she smooths out the wrinkles in Jakob's striped shirts, he will forgive her for everything else.

But life isn't simple like that. God can't iron out our problems for us just like that, can He?

⪧ ⪦

At noon, Lusia stands at the Ankeruhr and stares as all twelve figures march across the bridge. As if to ask each one of them how she shall tell Jakob the untellable. The one thing in the world she knows he would not want to hear.

"But Meister Haydn, what do I tell my husband?" she asks the last of the bronze figures to wobbily toddle across the clock. As if the musician can hear her. This man holding a violin, the one who wears a bronze version of a powdered wig. As if he can grant her wish of having a child. Why not make a wish upon a bronze figure holding a violin? After all, if nothing else has worked, maybe this will. According to the doctor, there are no scientific answers to this problem.

Why not try wishing instead?

Jakob will be curious to know what Herr Doktor Porges's test results show. After all, he has lavished a fortune on one doctor after another in an attempt to solve the problem of Lusia's infertility in the hopes of starting a family.

Curiosity.

Lusia knows Jakob will want answers. He will want them soon. She can't keep the doctor's test results to herself forever.

Still shaking from the news, Lusia climbs the steps of the tram heading back to the Hardtmuthgasse. Self-conscious over her situation, Lusia glares at the others on the tram, inwardly feeling an inexplicable hostility, feeling everyone is staring at her when, in reality, everyone is minding their own business.

Once back in her neighborhood, Lusia takes deliberate strides along the narrow street towards Fortuna Park, a small park down the block. It is a one-block oasis in this working-class neighborhood. Named for the Roman goddess of good luck. Both good and bad. Luck can go both ways. This neighborhood park is not like the parks in the fancier districts, the Stadtpark for one. Here, there are no monuments, no sculptures; an English landscape garden in miniature nestled among these apartment houses. In the center, stands a single tree with a circular stone fence surrounding it, setting it apart from the other trees in the park. Isolating it to make it different. Yes, Lusia is a woman like these other women in the park. But they are mothers. Like this tree with its stone fence, Lusia is isolated, set apart by her infertility.

Lusia walks along the tree-lined path with benches filled with mothers and children--the last thing she wants to see at this moment. Plopping herself down on one of the benches along the winding path, she stares at the tree opposite her. She has come to this park so often that her eyes have been closed to the details of her surroundings. Today, she opens her eyes to discover that this tree has broad leaves with long beans that look like string beans hanging down. It has taken this unhappy news for Lusia to see the world around her in a new light. The sun shines onto the leaves, giving them the appearance of an Impressionist painting dappled with dark and light greens. She stares at these strange strings nestled amidst the elephant-eared leaves. Someday, it will be winter again, and those strings will still be hanging down. The leaves will long gone, but those strings will still be there. Desiccated. Lifeless. Stiff. But for now, Lusia has the pleasure of enjoying the greenery.

Yes, she knows winter will come one day. Yes, she knows one day when it's cold, these leaves will fall. Yes, she knows that there was a possibility that one day Herr Doktor Porges could give her the news that the test results might show that she was barren. She just wasn't prepared for this news on such a green sunny day.

Before today, Lusia had always come here seeking refuge. Always envisioning that one day she could be counted among these mothers. From now on, Lusia will see herself from a different perspective. In a different light. She ponders Herr Doktor Porges's words and still wonders what to tell Jakob.

The finality of it all!

All her life, Lusia had assumed she would get married and have a family. If it were a boy, she would leave much of the raising to Jakob. A father should raise a son, she's always reasoned. But if it were a girl, Lusia could teach her daughter the stitches of embroidery, the way her mother had patiently taught her. And it wasn't so easy. There were many times when Lusia was first learning and made so many, many mistakes that she almost gave up embroidery forever. But her mother insisted she persist, insisted she stick with it. Eventually she would catch on. And she did! All this time, Lusia had likewise persisted in the notion she would one day have a family.

And look where this persistence has gotten her!

She can't patiently stick with it like embroidery and have a successful outcome. In this case, hard work has not paid off. Her mother, too, will not be pleased with this news. But she knows that Jakob will be the one to be even more disappointed.

"Surprise me with the good news," Jakob would say every day when he returned home from work. But day after day, Lusia had no good news for him. Days turned into months. Now, months have turned into years. Never with the good news.

Surprise me with the good news echoes over and over in Lusia's head. Now, for certain, there will be no good news for Jakob.

"But what shall I tell my husband?" she asks this tree with its elephant ears and string beans, as though to ask will grant her the answers that she seeks. She thinks back to all the times she and Jakob had waltzed, enjoying their lives together as a couple at their wedding back in Stanislau.

If only life were as simple as a waltz. To glide through life with the grace of a waltz, with all of one's steps predetermined. All the right moves one is supposed to make. Get married, have a family. But what happens when you are whirling around in a waltz and you miss a step?

Life's dance goes out of kilter.

CHAPTER 10
"ACCIDENTAL HEIRLOOMS"

New Haven, Connecticut   January, 1972

T hose nagging questions will not go away. They just keep in returning. *What is really packed inside that trunk? And just who were those people who had once owned it?*

Now that I'm fifteen, I've given up on that Kindergarten fantasy that the trunk was really a pirate's treasure chest. I've discarded the notion that it might actually contain gold doubloons. Or strands of pearls. Or rubies. Or diamonds. Or sapphires.

Even if all the trunk contains are *schmatas,* as my mother has referred to them, I still want to know what's inside. She's so worried that whatever fashions packed away inside will be so outdated they will be of no use to anyone.

What do I care about fashion?

I break down. It's high time for me to ask some questions. My sister is still away at college; it's up to me to be the one to plead and beg.

"What's inside the trunk upstairs anyway?" I inquire as my father sits there calmly at the Saturday breakfast table eating his eggs and toast.

"It's a complicated story…I can't talk about it right now," my father sighs. A look of sorrow crosses his face. "Maybe someday I will tell you…"

"But I want to know right now!"

As I say these words, my mother draws me aside. "I told you not to ask him about that," she whispers in a low voice, hoping my father won't hear her. Then she drags me off in the direction of the front hallway. We both stand beneath the poet Chaucer and his *Canterbury Tales* companions as she begins to raise her voice to reprimand me. I hope my father can't hear my mother now. "You know your father is really sensitive about these things. You know how much it upsets him to talk about it."

"Isn't it time we opened up that old trunk once and for all?" I protest.

"Maybe…just maybe…it is better that you don't know."

"Well, what exactly did happen to the trunk's owners? How bad could it be?"

"You know very well that it's nothing good."

"Hasn't he ever told you *anything*?"

"Not everything. He doesn't like to talk about it. He will cry every night for a week if you bring up bad memories. Haven't you ever heard him at night? He sobs himself to sleep every time anyone in this family has asked him about his past. And when he does that, it keeps me awake all night in the process."

"Maybe he'd stop crying once and for all if those bad memories were brought out into the open. It might clear his mind if he got it all out of his system. Maybe, just maybe, it might make him feel better to talk about it."

"I don't think so."

"Why not?"

"You don't have the years of experience with him like I have. I'm the one who has to put up with his sobbing all night…I'm the one who's going to lose sleep if you bring it up to him…"

"Why don't we just open the trunk up ourselves? We could do it when Dad's not looking. We could sneak upstairs on a day when he's at the office."

My mother cringes at this thought. "I'm not sure that's such a good idea. He'd be really angry if he found out later on that we'd opened it up without asking him. I think it might be better if we got his permission first."

"But if we never open it, we'll never know what's inside." I continue to beg.

"Oh, all right," my mother finally gives in. I think she's doing this just to shut me up. "Okay, you've convinced me. I suppose once and for all, I'd also like to see exactly what's inside, too." My mother lets out a sigh. "I'll go ahead and ask your father tonight if it's okay with him."

⊱ ⊰

We are finally going to open up the trunk! A waking dream! This is the moment I'd dreamt about all though my childhood. But unlike my dreams, I know I will be able to reach out and touch whatever objects we will find in the trunk. I know they will always be here when I am awake. I won't have to close my eyes and dream. Whatever it is that the trunk holds will still be here with me when I'm awake.

This is real.

This is tangible.

⊱ ⊰

The next morning, my mother and father appoint themselves as the designated trunk movers. Deeming me to be too weak to heft such a heavy object, my father insists that I stand here like a lump at the bottom of the stairs.

"No, wait, Roz," I can hear my father shout from the spare room upstairs. "You hold that side and I'll take this side."

I can hear the muffled noises of the bumping and thumping coming from upstairs as the two of them proceed to lift the weighty trunk and heft it out of the spare room. Whatever it is that's inside, it's weighing the trunk down all the more.

"Better be careful," my father warns my mother, "you don't want to hurt your back. This thing is really heavy!"

I continue to wait in the front hallway as my father and mother twist and turn to maneuver the trunk out the door of the spare room and into the bedroom. Finally, their voices grow louder as they reach the top of the upstairs hallway.

"This thing weighs a ton," my mother sighs as she puts her end of the trunk on the floor with a thunk. "I sure hope this is all worth it."

"Susan wanted to open it up," snaps my father, showing signs of a growing reluctance to go ahead with the exercise.

"And, if I may add," my mother chimes in, shouting at me from upstairs, "whatever clothing is in there is horribly outdated."

My father and mother proceed to carefully move the trunk over to the top of the staircase. Placing it down again gently, the two of them take a moment to catch their breaths.

"Be careful going down the stairs," my father warns. "We'll have to ease it down slowly. We can't just push it down."

Once again, the trunk is lifted up as the two of them gently glide it down and around the bend of the winding staircase. They successfully manage the chest ever so slowly down to the bottom of the stairs.

"Now, let's get this thing into the living room," my father directs. "Susan, could you give us a hand now?"

"What do you want me to do?" I ask as I approach the trunk, no longer a side table for our record player on which we play our 45 RPM records or an imagined pirate's treasure chest. Now it is an object to be opened up.

"Just grab that handle over there and help us lift it into the living room. We'll unpack it over by the fireplace."

"Okay. Do you now know who the trunk belonged to?" I whisper to my mother.

"All I know is that it belonged to a relative; that's all I know." My mother shrugs her shoulders.

For all this time, throughout my life, the trunk had been there.

Taken for granted.

Sealed.

Silent.

Waiting for us to open it up to discover its true contents.

Even before my birth, the trunk had been waiting patiently for its original owners to come back and reclaim it, the objects inside frozen in time, like a time capsule. Ready at any time to reveal how its owners had once lived.

Our family takes a break for lunch. This lull in the action enables our tired and sore limbs to recover from the ordeal. Quickly, we eat our sandwiches as my mother stands in the kitchen slicing some fresh fruit for dessert.

My father remains poker faced. No emotion to reveal his inner thoughts or reveal just who had once owned the trunk.

After the fruit salad, the three of us gather around the trunk again as my father slowly and with great ceremony opens the two front grey metal latches. He lifts the lid and opens the trunk up as the must of the ages hits my nostrils.

Inside, on top, is a large flat tray packed with some smaller items. As my father begins to unpack these items one by one, not once does he utter the names of the trunk's former owners. His silence only serves to keep me further detached from these ancestors. Yet, for the very first time in my life, I know I am coming one step closer to learning about my family's past.

"What's that?" my mother asks as my father pulls out some folded pieces of cloth from the top tray.

"Just a moment," my father begs as he slowly unwraps a bundle of white cloth. "It appears to be embroidery of some sort…"

"Embroidery?" My interest is piqued. "Let me see!"

My father continues to unfold a small piece of cloth before our very eyes.

An irresistible urge comes over me. I can't help but run my fingers across the tightly pulled stitches of what appears to be a hand-embroidered placemat. I can't help but notice how smooth the thread is. It is luminous, like silk, and distinctly different from the sticky, waxy beige macramé cord to which I have lately become all too accustomed.

"How beautiful!" Look at this needlework!" I exclaim as I gaze across at the other pieces of cloth, all of them obviously embroidered by hand. "It must have taken a lot of patience to create these."

My father picks up embroidered cloth after embroidered cloth, each one more colorful than the next. Bold flowers in bright colors, all stitched onto pale pieces of white linen cloth.

The thcrc's a small square, a covering of sorts, that is next to emerge. It has designs in pink and blue with gold lettering in Hebrew. Dots of yellow run across the design of a square, creating the image of a matzo.

"What's this?" I ask.

"Why, that's a matzo cover," is my father's response.

"It's smooth and shiny…what material is it made out of?"

"I suppose it must be silk," he shrugs.

"What beautiful colors," my mother gasps.

With this one statement, we begin the process of distributing the trunk's contents to its accidental heirs.

Next is a series of what appear to me to be some custom-made dresses.

"Let me see…I want to see…," feeling anxious, I try to get a little closer to one dress in particular that I'd spotted from deep within a pile of folded clothing. "I want to see that red dress. That one over there."

My father obligingly pulls the dress out from beneath the pile and presents it to me. On closer inspection, I discover that it's red with tiny green squares.

"This dress is beautiful!" I exclaim as I run my fingers along the cloth. "Look at this fabric! I've never seen such fabric before! Look how it's been woven! And it's got a belt to match."

"What's next?" My mother fidgets. "What's next?"

"Have patience. Give me a moment," objects my father. "You don't want to rush the unpacking of these dresses, do you?" Next, my father unfolds a dress with black and white polka dots. So lifeless in its folded state, separated from its original owner. He gives us no hint about the woman who had once inhabited the dress.

"Look under the arm!" gasps my mother. "There are dress shields sewn in under the arms. That must have been what they used back then to protect dresses from sweat stains."

"Look at this clothing," my mother continues. "Have you ever, ever seen such shiny cloth like this before? I think it must be rayon. I don't think it could be silk or satin."

"What's next, what's next?" I squirm. "I can't wait to see what's coming up next…" My father takes out yet another dress and presents it to us.

"Oh, look at the floral print on that dress," declares my mother. "How beautiful these colors are!"

After having fallen in love with the unusual material of that red and green dress, I am not going to let it out of my hands so easily, I blurt out, "I want that dress, that red and green one."

"Take whichever dresses you want," acquiesces my father.

I spot an emerald green dress in the pile and think of the Emerald City of Oz.

"What's that green dress, under there?" I ask my father. "Could I see it, please?"

Obligingly, my father pulls out a green dress and hands it to me.

Upon closer inspection, I see that it's made of thin, emerald green wool with short sleeves. I hold it up to my chin. It comes down to my ankles.

"This woman must have been tall," says my mother. "Back in the thirties, dresses went down to just above the ankle."

The next items to come out of the trunk are the undergarments.

"What's that?" I ask as my father pulls out a grey woolen slip. "Is that a dress?"

"No, that's a woolen slip," my father admits. "That's what women in Vienna wore in the winter time under their dresses. It gets cold and snowy there, too, after all."

"Colder and snowier than here in Connecticut?" I ask.

"Yes, much colder, and the snow stays on the ground for much longer than it does here," sighs my father.

"I could wear that as a dress," I say. "Who's going to know it was supposed to be a slip?"

Next come what appear to be long pink underpants.

"What are those?" I ask.

"Those arc *gotkas*," declares my Brooklyn-born mother with great authority.

"*Gotkas?*"

"Yes," affirms my mother. "They're underpants with legs that go down to mid-thigh. People still wear those in Brooklyn. Take my word for it."

From the depths of the pile, my father gingerly pulls out what appear to be more undergarments. I can tell by the expression on his face that he is less than pleased to bring these to light. As if they were never meant to be seen by anyone other than their original owner. The pale pink girdles are hand embroidered with the initials "LS" in blue thread.

My father puts these two girdles gingerly aside. "These were not meant to be seen by us," he says in a soft voice.

Next, my father unfolds some long grey woolen undershirts and two hand-crocheted sweaters. One for a man, one for a woman. Both reddish-pink with white flecks.

"Look at these sweaters!" I exclaim. "Look at those pom-poms at the ends of the ties! I suppose you use them to tie around your neck to secure it."

Next to come is the clothing that must have once belonged to my father's male relative. There is a group of striped shirts, presumably of silk, with a "J" monogrammed by hand on each of them. The collars had all been neatly bundled separately. I am so captivated by the excitement of the moment, it never dawns on me that the monograms and the initials on the girdles might be clues to the identities of the trunk's owners.

"What's this fuzzy thing?" I ask as my father uncovers a black fur coat from just beneath the shirts.

My father begins to speak briskly. "That, my dear, is a 'Persianner' coat. It's black lamb's fur. Back in Vienna, it was far more valuable and prized than mink is today."

My father still makes no mention of the woman who had once owned this coat. But since he mentions how prized that kind of fur was back in Vienna, the coat must have meant an awful lot to his relative. Has he replaced his emotions with a material value? As if to mask his emotions by stressing how this kind of fur was prized is more important than mentioning the woman who had once owned this coat.

As my father gets closer to the bottom of the trunk, my attention drifts back towards those embroideries from the top tray. While no one is looking, I pull out a folded tablecloth from beneath the pile of some other needlework. As I proceed to open up the folded cloth, I discover that one half has remained blank, with only the pale blue ink of the pattern stamped on it.

Instantly, I feel a tinge of disappointment. My mother notices my frown. "What's the matter?" she asks.

"Oh, it hasn't been finished," I shrug. "What use is it? What could we use a half-finished tablecloth for *anyway?*"

"Wait, look," my mother says as she points to the skeins of embroidery thread which have fallen to the floor around my feet just as I had opened up the tablecloth. "That must be all the thread needed to complete the rest of it."

I look down. There at my feet are skeins and skeins of thread! All in different bright colors.

I proceed to gather the packages of thread off the ground and gently place them on a nearby coffee table.

Suddenly, I feel sorry for this orphan.

The cloth speaks to me.

As though it needs me.

Just beneath is packed a thick, heavy comforter with a wine-red cotton cover.

"Their *Federdecke*," sighs my father in a quiet voice.

"A *Federdecke*...What's a *Federdecke*? I ask.

"It's a quilt stuffed with goose feathers," says my mother. "It keeps you very warm."

"Stuffed with goose feathers?!" I exclaim.

"I think we can put that on our bed," my mother declares, not asking me whether or not I might want it, too.

My father peers back inside the trunk. "We've come to the bottom," he sighs. "All that's left are the heavy white linen bed sheets and some yellow curtains. Of little use to us. These sheets wouldn't fit any of our beds. And our windows are far too big for these curtains."

My mother adds, "These curtains are such a bright golden color...too bright a color for our house even if they did fit our windows."

"Very well," says my father. "That's it. Now you know what was in the trunk all this time. You can stop bugging me about it now!"

No sooner said, I'm off to the other side of the living room to try on the various dresses I've claimed for myself. Marveling at my new found vintage clothing, I now have retro fashions to wear back to school. I can't wait until my sister comes home from college to finally see what was in the trunk all this time.

Yet, even at this moment, I still do not know the names of these relatives who had been stolen from me. As I try on the "special" red dress with the little green squares, I come to realize that this is the very same cloth that my ancestor had once worn that now envelopes my own body. For a brief instant, I sense a distant kinship.

I don't know why, but I am drawn to this dress like a magnet. It is a color which I can only best describe as rusted red and pea green. An Art Deco pattern of small pea-green open squares with tiny solid squares at one corner covers the entire surface of the fabric. Turning over the skirt of the dress to look at the underside, I discover that the opposite is true. The pattern reverses and is now pea-green with rusted red squares.

⇒⊢ ⊣⇐

This evening, as I sit in the living room, I look around at the entire contents of the trunk we've scattered about in piles on various couches. I am overwhelmed by the sheer quantity of belongings my father's relatives had packed in anticipation of a life free from Hitler's madness.

Although these pieces of cloth have been covered with the must of decades in storage, they serve as a reminder of precious lives cut short. Every piece a treasure. I don't care that my mother may think these are fashions so outdated that I could never possibly wear them.

I pause. If only I could have known the woman who had owned these dresses. If only she could have lived on long enough for me to get to know her. Instead, all that is left behind of her existence are these dresses, these pieces of cloth.

I look on the backs of the necks of these dresses for any hint of a manufacturer's label. There are none. It becomes obvious to me that all this clothing had been custom-made for my father's relatives. Inspecting the stitches on the dresses, I discern that these are not hand sewn but must have been made by a sewing machine.

To touch the cloth is to sense an elegance of a bygone era. On a whim, I decide to try on the blue dress with its simple thirties styling. It fits me perfectly! Next, I try on a simple pale blue nightgown. It is square at the neck with an Art Deco design at the base of the collar. I fold it back up, attempting to match the exact folds my nameless ancestor had made all those years before. To me, these dresses are stunning fashion. This coming from the person who wears the same pair of blue jeans every day. In my mind's eye, I envision "the woman of the trunk" as some sort of glamor queen who must have read every single fashion magazine. I imagine her trying to emulate American movie stars of the day like Joan Crawford and Bette Davis. My imagination is set free to believe whatever my teenaged mind might dream up. I envision her walking along the expensive shopping street in Vienna, searching the windows for just the right accessories to go with her dresses newly created for her by her seamstress. I see her not as a woman from the *shtetl*, but rather as a glamorous big city woman. From her dresses, I discern that she must have been a woman who kept up with the fashion of her day.

I am caught up in this waking dream. The pirate's chest from my childhood has now been opened. I can scarcely believe my eyes! So this is what has been trapped in the trunk all these years. I am awake! I can actually touch the cloth to make sure it is solid. It is real. It's all here in colors so vivid I think I'm still dreaming.

What I had once thought in my childhood's imagination was a pirate's treasure chest now has revealed itself to be the ultimate dress-up trunk. I close my eyes and recall those images I've seen on television documentaries about the Holocaust. Slowly, I put on the black and white polka-dotted dress as I recall the images of all those piles and piles of confiscated possessions taken from concentration camps victims, all separated and sorted out into mounds of shoes, shirts, dresses, toys, and eyeglasses. I realize that I have now inherited what might otherwise have ended up in those many anonymous piles.

I touch the stitches on the half-embroidered tablecloth. Funny how each stitch is a small, insignificant mark of thread. Individually taken, these marks, these stitches, have no meaning. Yet when taken as a whole, each mark takes on its true meaning as it contributes a facet to the entire pattern.

It upsets me greatly that this tablecloth has remained unfinished by its original creator.

CHAPTER 11
"FOR WHAT DO I LIVE?"

Hardtmuthgasse 10   Vienna, July, 1930

A portrait of Lusia. She's a woman in a Vermeer painting. Quietly holding her embroidery hoop. Needle poised at the moment, about to take a stitch. Sheltered in the intimacy of her own space. Using her hands is a way to keep her mind off life's troubles, yet her brow is furrowed.

Etched with concern.

⇌ ⇋

Carefully, Lusia prepares a hazelnut torte, the way she has always done for the past six years of marriage. She sifts the flour, chops the nuts, and stirs the melted chocolate for the topping. Only this time, things are different.

Every day of her marriage, Lusia has shopped for food. Every day she has cooked dinner for her husband. Every day she has embroidered. Lusia's days are dictated by these everyday tasks.

But this day is different.

Her legs begin to quiver.

When is it ever the right time, I wonder? When shall I tell Jakob about this awful news? Will Jakob think of me differently from now on? I will still be his wife, but, oh, how disappointed he will be! Those tests Herr Doktor Porges took were our last hope...Will Jakob ever look at me the same way?

Everything should appear normal when her husband walks through the door. If nothing else, everything must look good on the surface. Even if she is crying on the inside.

As the hazelnut torte is baking, she carefully polishes the silverware so shiny that she can see her reflection in one of her knives. Gently, Lusia puts the knife down and picks up a second one.

Her life now following in slow motion.

With deliberate movements, she sets the table. Slowly, she puts the fork, the knife, the spoon at her husband's place setting. Thinking that if everything is set perfectly in place, everything else in her life will fall into place, too.

But life isn't like a perfectly set table. Her silverware may be in place, but everything else is out of kilter. If only life were as simple as a table setting.

Once the torte is baked, Lusia takes the cake out of the oven and patiently begins to frost it with the melted chocolate she's had boiling on the stove for some time now.

The dinner prepared, the table set, Lusia steps into her bedroom to prepare her own appearance. For this evening, she has decided to put on one of her favorite dresses that Frau Ingber has created for her. It is the flowered dress of shiny rayon. After all Frau Ingber had gone on touting the praises of a modern fabric, of a modern way of life made better through technology, Lusia now realizes this sad irony. Science can create a modern fabric to resemble the ancient fabric of silk, but it cannot help her to start a family.

With deliberate motions, she pulls the dress over her head, and with a single shimmy, pulls it down her body. Buttoning one button after another, her heart thumping with anticipation. How will her husband take this awful, life-altering news? Lusia pulls on her stockings, rolling them first up her right leg, then up her left. She brushes her hair, puts on her lipstick. Powders her cheeks. Checks her visage one more time in the mirror, making sure everything is just right.

Her heart skips a beat as Jakob comes through the door. She turns off the radio just as a Strauss waltz is playing. She had hoped that the music might soothe her mood.

It does not.

Lusia forces her lips into a smile, crinkling the corners of her mouth in an attempt at an upturned direction.

As Jakob sits down for his dinner, Lusia gazes at him with a look she's never given him before. She knows she must choose her words very carefully. She knows that the news she is about to give her husband may forever change the way he views her.

Lusia takes a deep breath.

Will Jakob remain the loving husband he has always been?

Or will he grow cold?

Will he resent Lusia for not being able to fulfill the function as a mother he has always expected of her since their wedding day?

Worse yet, will he want to divorce her and marry a new wife? A new wife who will be able to present him with a son?

For all these years, Lusia has been so desperate to please Jakob. She had cooperated at every turn with every procedure that every fertility expert in Vienna had made her endure. Her eager- to-please personality had always been unaffected. Until now.

As Lusia is about to utter the life-altering words, she does not realize just how much the words that Jakob will say in response will be equally as life altering for her. These words will stay with her and echo in her brain for the rest of her life.

Lusia gets up just enough courage to speak.

"Jakob, I must tell you something. News of the fertility test results finally came from Herr Doktor Porges office. "Even if "finally" is a month after she, herself, has received the results.

"Surprise me with the good news!" says Jakob. A look of concern crosses his face as he takes a bite of his torte. "Well…tell me, is it good or bad?"

"It's final," Lusia breaks down, almost sobbing. "There is nothing the doctor can do to help the situation. It's nature's way…or God's will."

"Is that so?"

"Yes."

Not even a hazelnut torte can soften the blow.

Jakob begins to sob loudly. "Why, God? Why? For what do I live?"

"Can we really blame God for this?" Lusia sighs.

"For what do I live!" wails Jakob. "I have all the money to pay for medical procedures. All for what? I have all the furnishings I can provide for our household. My wife has all the dresses and the finery she could ever want. I've provided her with everything she desires. The one thing I want more than anything is a family. The one thing! And yet, this I cannot have!"

Lusia tries to put her arms around Jakob, but she feels the force of his arms as he tries to push her away. Lusia slinks away as her heart begins to sink. Her good nature begins to change. For all the things she has done for all these years to make Jakob happy, keep a tidy household, cook his favorite dishes, nothing she has done could have prepared him for this moment.

Her hopes dashed, Lusia does not know how to feel. What should she feel? She is numb. So numb that she does not know who has been more affected by this news, she or Jakob. On the one hand, he has held all the hopes and dreams of having a son, to carry on the family name. A son, after all, has always been the traditional prized possession through many generations of his family. Lusia, on the other hand, had not cared whether or not it was a boy or a girl. To her, a girl would have been a perfect companion.

Someone to fill her days. Someone to teach the art of embroidery stitches the way her mother had done for her.

But now, that will never happen. She and Jakob will never have a little one of their own.

No one to pass the family name to.

No one to teach embroidery stitches.

How empty Lusia now feels inside!

Now, she must forever live in her solitude, alone with her stitches.

And no one else to share them with.

Not even a hazelnut torte can soften the blow.

Or even a lifetime of disappointment.

CHAPTER 12
"THE DRESSES"

New Haven, Connecticut   January, 1972

My "new" birthday jeans are ripping a tiny bit at the right knee. I knew it was only a matter of time before this would happen. I'd always known that the knees would be the first to go. The bad thing is that I know I won't be getting a new pair of jeans anytime soon. Once these pants wear out, my mother will be hesitant to buy me a replacement pair. I might just have to think up a creative way to repair them. And I'll have to do that sooner than later if the knee continues to tear at this rate.

I look at the Indian bedspread that covers the fraying upholstery on the other couch in the living room. My mother is too lazy to re-upholster it, so she's thrown a cover on it instead. It's got hand-blocked images of elephants dancing along the border in blue, green, and black. According to my grandmother who lives in Brooklyn, only elephants with their trunks turned up are lucky. The trunks of these elephants (thankfully) are turned up!

The dresses from the trunk appeal to my following my own path of fashion. The red and green dress of rayon has cloth-covered buttons that fasten down the front. A matching belt half green and half red has a button closure. A "V" piece of fabric folds up at the end of each short sleeve, attached by a button revealing the opposite pattern of green and red. The black and white polka-dot dress buttons down the front with six mother-of-pearl buttons. There is a matching belt to go around the waist. The third dress is of a shiny satin-like material with a print of yellow, red, and white flowers and green leaves against a black background. It zippers up the front with two pulls to tie at the neck. There is a blue and white dress of woven material with white, which has five cloth-covered buttons down the front. Another dress with white, yellow, and red flowers outlined with black lines against a black background has ruffles dropping off a V-neck collar. There is an emerald green dress of what appears to be finely woven wool with short sleeves. It buttons all the way down the front of the dress with cloth-covered buttons and looks like what a citizen of the Emerald City might wear. Finally, there is a heavy grey woolen dress with long sleeves, which has five cloth buttons down the front.

Now I have a bunch of dresses that I have no idea what to do with. I have no place to wear them. And so far, I have no face to go with the owner of these dresses, either.

My mother was right, though. Compared to Hot Pants and the Midi skirt, these dresses may be considered retro, but even for retro, they do seem to be hopelessly out of fashion.

On the other hand, there's nothing to say that I can't make these dresses my own fashion. We don't live under a fashion dictatorship. I'm not forced to wear the exact same clothing as everyone else around me, am I? No force of physics can tell me I will fall off the face of the planet if I were to wear one of the dresses from the trunk to school. And if I wait long enough maybe, just maybe, these dresses will come back into fashion again.

I gaze at my selection and decide to try on the red and green dress first. After buttoning up the dress in front, I tie on the matching belt in the hopes that by wearing this dress, I will somehow find the answers to all my questions about my ancestors. As if the truth will seep into my body through the very cloth I am wearing. I remind myself just how tight-lipped my father had remained about its original owners as we were unpacking the trunk. I know it had taken a lot out of him just to open up the luggage, and I don't want to take any more chances of upsetting him further by badgering him about the relatives he's lost.

After I come home from school, I stand in the front hallway gazing at the Canterbury Tales tablecloth. "I want to wear the dresses from the trunk to school," I blurt out to my mother as she comes down the stairs.

"What?" asks my mother. I don't know whether or not she's heard me or doesn't want to hear me.

"I'm going to wear one of the dresses from the trunk to school."

"But what will the other kids say? I'm afraid they might make fun of you for wearing clothing so badly out of style."

"I don't care what they say. I like these dresses. I like the style. Who says everybody has to wear the exact same thing at the exact same time? We don't live in a society of uniforms."

"But you might get teased."

"I don't think so."

"We live in the suburbs. As much as you hate to think this, people conform here."

"People may conform, but there's no town ordinance against dressing differently." "You were teased a few years ago for dressing like a hippie in tattered jeans when all the other kids were wearing tweeds and plaids."

"That was seventh grade. I wore bell-bottom jeans splattered with white paint because that's what I thought was in fashion. I had been painting a picture with white acrylic paint and after a while, the paint just wouldn't come off the denim. It wasn't my fault that the other junior high kids didn't realize that what I was wearing was the height of fashion. At least, I know it was what was in fashion for college kids at the time."

"But at your school, everyone else was wearing woolen tweed and houndstooth jackets with pants to match. Why didn't you want to dress like them?"

"Did I own any houndstooth or plaid tweed clothing?" "You have some hand-me-down woolen clothing from your sister. As I recall, you have her old black and white houndstooth jacket. And I did at one time buy you two pairs of pants on sale from Cole's Country Casuals. Wasn't one pair blue and white houndstooth and the other pair red, white, and black plaid? You can wear those to school."

"I think I outgrew those years ago."

"And you have that red plaid woolen skirt with brass buttons that had once been your sister's. You know, the one with the suspenders?"

"Yeah, I wore that woolen skirt to class and someone came up to me and asked if I'd bought it last year at the school's 'Nearly New Sale.'" Even though I don't care about other people's opinions, I still felt embarrassed over the comment.

"What about that nice grey shirt and skirt I bought for your sister two years ago at Macy's? That should fit you now. I don't think she took that with her to wear at college."

"I really don't think that's my style."

"What, I thought you made anything your own style."

"Very funny."

"Then there's that blue woolen mini skirt you and your sister shared. Didn't your sister hem it to make it shorter?'"

"Yes, but she made it too short."

"Didn't it bother you that you were being teased by the kids at school when you were wearing those tattered jeans?"

"That was their problem! I was wearing what hippies were wearing. I was ahead of my time. Eventually those tweedy kids caught up with me, and I'm sure they're finally beginning to wear tattered jeans, too."

"You may have been ahead of your time, but it seems like it takes an awfully long time for other people to catch up with you. It seems to me you're always out of sync with everyone else when it comes to fashion."

"I don't mind. Eventually people will catch up with me and see that I'm right."

I look at what my mother is wearing. It's a black polyester jacket and pants with a button- down shirt with a splashy paisley print. She's not conforming to what I think everyone else her age is wearing in the suburbs, either.

"And just why would you want to wear the old style of clothing from the trunk, anyway?"

"I heard somewhere on T.V. that vintage clothing is 'in' right now."

"Vintage fashion is one thing. Those dresses are ancient."

"Wouldn't they have been what were in style when you were a little girl?"

"Yes, but I was a little girl a very long time ago."

"I think my classmates won't care one or another. In seventh grade, I was going to the public school. Now that I'm at Hopkins, I think my classmates will be different."

"You think so, do you?"

"There's only one way to see, and that's by me wearing one of the dresses to school and see what the reaction I get. I'll bet no one will even care."

CHAPTER 13

"JUST AN IDEA"

Hardtmuthgasse 10   Vienna, June, 1932

*F*or *what do I live?* For the past two years, Jakob's words repeat over and over again inside Lusia's head. As if in a never-ending loop. Even though it has now been a long time since Herr Doktor Porges determined that Lusia would never have a family of her own, the fact that she is barren hits Lusia every day like a freshly made flesh wound. *Doesn't Jakob love me for me? Surely our marriage is strong enough to survive not having any children. Surely a strong marriage can overcome anything.* What Jakob had wanted more than anything was a family, and her infertility has stood in the way of that. It was all her fault, wasn't it? At least that's what specialist after specialist had led her to believe.

Jakob's threats of divorce prove to be fleeting.

As she gazes out her corner window at a little boy down the street at play, an idea suddenly comes to Lusia. She will run this idea by Jakob when he returns home from work.

———

Lusia sits on the couch with her feet crossed, trying to relax, listening to the radio. Crackling. Static. An almost inaudible Humoresque plays as Jakob enters the apartment. He forces himself to smile at his wife, although in the back of his mind, he knows that he will never be happy with Lusia's infertility. He will never come home to a son rushing to greet him with open arms as he comes home from a long day at the lumberyard. Putting on a major façade, Jakob greets her with a kiss on her cheek, the same as he always has every day of his marriage. But the words *for what do I live?* still repeat over and over in his mind all these years later. Jakob does not want to further offend his wife by uttering these words aloud ever again. But he knows with such profound sorrow over this unacceptable situation he may never be able to stop himself from uttering them. Even if were only in front of family members.

But it is too late.

These words have already stuck in Lusia's head.

And will stay in her mind forever.

Around the apartment, Lusia searches for answers. Wanting to demonstrate to her husband that she is an adequate wife and that, despite her infertility, she reassures herself that she is keeping a proper home for him. As she looks around, however, all she sees are the material possessions, all the finery with which Jakob has provided her. Everything in her life that she owns is visible to her eyes. She knows she can never show her husband just how much she appreciates his gifts. Yes, she is grateful. At the same time, she resents him for his disappointment. Naturally, she, too, had wanted a family more than anything. Yet, her pain, possibly more profound than his, is based on her own frustration that there is nothing she can do to change his mind.

Suddenly Lusia gets up the nerve to speak her mind to her husband. "Jakob," she begins hesitantly, "I was thinking earlier today, why don't we invite Chajce's son, Muniu, to come live with us in Vienna? We could raise him as our own. We could educate him here. After all, education in Vienna is superior to the schools back in Sniatyn. What do you think?"

Jakob hesitates. He is struck by her enthusiasm. "Maybe you've got something there, Lusia. But first, I'd have to convince Chajce and Baruch. It's true that the schools are better here, but would my sister want to be separated from her son? He's young, still. Only five years old."

"Yes, he's young, but this would be the perfect time to approach your sister while he is still young. He can come here to live with us; we can educate and mold him. We could send him to Chajesrealgymnasium, the same school where Samuel is going. Raise him the way we would have if we had a child of our own."

"I don't know what Chajce and Baruch will say."

"Please, Jakob. Now would be the perfect time!"

"I wouldn't want to impose on my sister. Suppose she said 'no,' then we'd forever resent her for it."

"There's no time like the present. Why not ask her now?"

"Maybe we should wait until he's older. If we ask now when he's too young, it may upset Chajce to think that her son will be taken away from her at too early an age. If we ask when he gets a little older, she may be more likely to agree to the arrangement."

"But, Jakob, if we ask and say it's not for now, but for when he's older, then maybe, just maybe, she might agree. This way we'll know for sure that he will be coming to live with us. When the time comes for him to stay with us, everything will be settled, everything will be arranged. Don't you see? This is what's best for the boy. After all, Vienna has better educational opportunities. Muniu can go to school here; there are museums and the theater here… they do not have these things in Sniatyn."

"You've convinced me. Now all I have to do is convince my sister and her husband."

"Why don't you write them and ask. It couldn't hurt to ask. It would be nice to have a boy around the house. Even if he weren't really our own. We won't know if Chajce is in agreement unless we ask. It couldn't hurt to ask…"

"Fine, I'll go ahead and write Chajce. Since it takes such a long time to get a letter to Sniatyn, the sooner I write the letter, the sooner we will get an answer."

"I don't see any harm in it. I don't see how your sister could ever resent us just for asking."

Lusia smiles to herself. Yes, perhaps she could be redeemed in the eyes of her husband if she took in his nephew and raised him as her own. If only Chajce and Baruch will give their blessing.

Just that thought of taking Muniu into her home has restored her belief in herself. Now, Jakob will have something to live for, to raise and educate his nephew in Vienna. The simple notion in her mind that Muniu may be coming to Vienna for her to raise as if he were her own son gives Lusia that same sense of elation she had felt when Jakob had first married her and expected to raise a family. A renewed faith in herself.

"Come, *Liebchen,*" says Jakob as he motions to Lusia, "come, let's go out for a bite to eat. It doesn't hurt to celebrate even when I still have yet to ask my sister about our proposal. I'm sure that once we ask my sister, one day, maybe she will come around to our idea."

As they walk out of the apartment house, Lusia breathes in the air. Suddenly, her world has been transformed back to the way it had been before Herr Doktor Porges's shattering news. Restored back to her genial self,

Silently, Lusia makes a wish that Chajce and Baruch will be amenable to their proposal. She shuts her eyes tight and prays that even though her first wish to have a family has fallen through, at least this wish might come true. Her childhood ritual of making a wish every time she ties a knot whenever she embroiders has always brought her luck. Maybe it will again.

A prayer.

A wish.

Lusia feels as though the cadence of life she'd experienced after she was first married has returned. Back to that notion of motherhood, even if it isn't a child of her own. The rhythm of a waltz goes through her head. What would Vienna have been without Strauss?

As they walk along Hardtmuthgasse towards Braunspergengasse, little by little, bit by bit, Lusia begins to feel like her old self again. As she looks up towards the stars, questioning the nature of her universe, Lusia feels reassured things are not so bad after all. There still may be hope for a family.

CHAPTER 14
"PERSIANNER COAT"

Hardtmuthgasse 10   Vienna, October, 1935

The crowd at the Café Schwarzenberg is all dressed up for an evening of lively dining. Their conversations drone in hushed tones, all bubbling together as if in a unified dirge. Couples dressed in heavier suits, dresses and winter coats reaffirm the crispness in the autumn air. A string quartet plays a piece by Bach.

The high mirrored walls with gilt embellishments reflect the faces of the happy diners. Thinly hammered sheets of gold cover the wood of the mirrors' frames carved with wooden flowers. A baser material masking its humble worth with golden material fit for a king. As she gazes up, the high vaulted ceilings make Lusia feel so small, so humbled. Looking down, she finds the white tiling on the floor more soothing. Looking towards the glass display of pastries reminds her of good things to come.

Jakob and Lusia are seated by the waiter in his crisp white linen shirt and neatly pressed black jacket. A cleanly pressed towel drapes from his arm. Lusia orders her usual *Wiener Schnitzel* and *Gemischter Salat*. Jakob orders *Leberknodelsuppe* and *Rindsgulasch*. While they wait for their dinner to be served, Lusia ruminates over her disappointment that Chajce and Baruch have once again turned down their invitation to raise Muniu in Vienna as their own son. At least for now, Chajce's latest letter did give Lusia some hope that perhaps when he was a little bit older, they might yet again reconsider the offer.

Lusia knows her life has never been her own true path. Her life has always been like a river on which she floats downstream, taken along the current with the will of the wind. Never a will of her own. If only her life could go according to her wishes. If only she had more control. She has had to follow the lead of her husband to live in Vienna, leaving her family back in Stanislau. She had no control over her own fertility; nature took the lead there. Even the hobby of embroidery she has chosen shows how little control she has. Yes, it's true, she chooses the designs to embroider that suit her personal taste, but then again, these are predetermined designs, the creation of someone else's mind. She must follow along the path of the pale blue lines, leaving little control or imagination on her own part.

So far this evening, Jakob has kept Lusia in the dark as to what is in the large white box he has been hiding under his left arm. Yes, she is curious about what it contains, but she dare not question him about the contents. After all these years of marriage, she knows instinctively that he has a surprise for her, and she doesn't want to spoil his fun when he sees the look on her face when she opens the box.

The waiter delivers their meal with a flourish. Eating out at this restaurant is formal, and the waiters contribute to the festive air of the occasion. The babble of the other diners around them bubbles to a low roar. Yet it is not too loud to continue their conversation. But Lusia is not in the mood for conversation. She feels a tinge of sorrow and does not want to reveal this to Jakob. She doesn't want to spoil the moment that has yet to happen.

Just after ordering dessert, Jakob pulls out the white box he has been keeping beneath the table all though the meal. He presents it to Lusia.

"Liebling, this is for you!" Jakob says as he hands the box over to Lusia. "Perhaps you have noticed that I have been carrying this large box all this time."

"That tiny box?!" shouts Lusia with a smile, so loudly that the other diners around her can hear her. "That small box, I hadn't noticed it at all!"

Jakob and Lusia giggle in unison. The first time in a long time they seem happy together after all they have gone through.

Lusia graciously takes the box and slowly opens it. She has an inkling of what it might contain but doesn't want to jinx it by wishing too hard for something impossible to attain. Filled with expectations and anticipation, she removes the lid to reveal a layer of white tissue paper covering her gift. Lifting the tissue paper, she reveals a black sort of cloak. Indeed, this is what she had been wishing for all this time. And here it is in the box on her lap, a Persianner coat!

Jakob knows that this coat is more than just a coat for warmth. To Lusia, it represents all that she's ever wanted in life. The sum of her heart's desire. A culmination of wishes and dreams all rolled up into a black wooly coat. Both stylish and practical.

Today, Lusia has received her heart's desire. There, beneath the gilt and mirrors on the walls, she has opened her box and pulled out the coat. She gets up and models it for all the other restaurant patrons to see. Like the gilt on the walls that masks the base wood beneath, the coat which now sheathes her body is glamorous on the outside, masking her pain within.

A bittersweet moment for Lusia. Her fur coat is a consolation for the family she cannot attain. Like a dream, the coat substitutes for the loss of having a family with the gain of the coat she's always longed for. Lusia has been transformed into a glamorous being like a Hollywood movie star- Jean Harlow, Bette Davis, or Joan Crawford. Lusia and her Persianner coat!

Her perfect day! Now Lusia knows that her husband truly loves her. He has presented her with the gift of a lifetime, reaffirming that she is still the beloved woman that he married.

As if material possessions can mollify a barren life.

⇒╪+╪⇐

On the walk home from the restaurant, Lusia walks on air. She has been transformed. She realizes now she is beloved in her husband's eyes. Luxuriating in her fur coat, she sweeps it up to her face to feel the softness against her skin.

Through the darkness of the street, Lusia can make out the *Jugendstil* apartment house she has just passed, this one with a repetitive design of lotus flowers just above the doorways, flowerless window boxes in every window. There is a chill in the air.

Yet, despite everything, Lusia feels empty inside. This consolation prize, a prize she's wanted for years and has finally received, cannot replace the love a child will return to its mother; the joy of watching a baby grow, its first steps, the first day of school, a note to Mama with a pastel heart.

Lusia is speechless, so touched is she by her husband's gift that she cannot find the words to tell him just how much she appreciates it. If only he knew how she felt at this moment. Bittersweet feelings flow through her. What can she say?

In an instant, Lusia realizes she must say something to break the ice.

She turns to Jakob, "Thank you for the coat. You know it's what I've always wanted. But can we afford it? I've priced such a coat at the department stores. It must have cost a fortune!"

"Don't worry about the money, *mein Liebchen;* money is not an issue at the moment. We've plenty of it stored away in the bank.

What is more important is that you delight in the coat. It is what you've truly always wanted isn't it?"

Lusia feels a twinge of sarcasm in Jakob's voice but dismisses it in this moment of happiness.

"Yes, Jakob, it's what I've always wanted. It's all the more precious because you gave it to me."

On her way home, Lusia stares at the golden designs of the sunflowers of the Karlsplatz pavilion. Lost in thought, she ponders the nature of these permanent flowers. Unlike their real-life counterparts, these flowers can never wilt. She thinks about the cycle of flowers: birth, death, rebirth in the spring when the flowers grow again. Lusia thinks about all the flowers she's embroidered; those many hours stitching petals, pistols, stems, and leaves. Just as these bits and pieces of architectural ornament combine to create flowers, Lusia's stitches, too, create floral decorations.

Sunflowers, a symbol of hope and longing. A symbol of personal growth. Can Lusia with her Persianner coat match this kind of growth? Perhaps the obtaining of a fur coat can only stunt her personal development. A consolation prize for an empty life. A fur coat as a temporary bandage to cover the emptiness.

A fur coat just will not suffice to fill that void.

CHAPTER 15
"HIP DASHIKI IN THE SUBURBS"

New Haven, Connecticut   January, 1972

*T*he *American Heritage Dictionary of the American Language* defines *dashiki* as "a brightly colored loose-fitting pull over garment (from Yoruba, a language of western Africa)."

For as long I can remember, my mother has taken me downtown to Horowitz Brothers, a department store for fabrics and notions. Four brothers run the 8,000-square-foot shop that is filled with every conceivable necessity for sewing clothing, upholstering furniture, and creating fashion accessories.

When I was little, my mother would buy fabric and patterns there to make clothing for my sister and me on her shiny black Singer sewing machine with its gold embellishments. She still uses that sewing machine she had used back when she was a teenager and refuses to give it up for more recent model. I agree with her, too. It's easy to use and still works. I wouldn't want to give it up, either.

As we drive along Chapel Street, I spot mannequins in Horowitz's window sporting some kind of short blue dresses made out of a fabric with a brightly colored print.

"Did you see what those mannequins in the window were wearing?"

"No, I'm too busy trying to turn the corner to get to the parking lot," shrugs my mother. "What was it that they were wearing?"

"They were wearing these short dresses that were bright blue with an interesting design at the neck. They were really pretty. I want one."

"We can look for them when we get into the store. But since this is a fabric store, I'm sure you can't buy the finished dresses. Obviously, you have to buy the fabric and make them yourself."

"Then I'll make it myself. It's not a big deal."

Once inside the store, my mother approaches Sadie, the clerk who works the central nerve system of Horowitz's- the cash register at the check-out. Sadie has been a fixture at Horowitz's for as long as I can remember. As far as I know, she was born behind that cash register and will die behind it.

"Good afternoon, Mrs. Spielvogel," greets Sadie from her usual station. "How are you?"

"Fine, thank you," replies my mother.

"I see you've brought your younger child today. My goodness, she's growing up."

"Yes, she's already in tenth grade! Can you believe it?"

"My, my, she's in high school? How time has flown. I remember back when she was in second grade. I must be getting old, too." Then Sadie blurts out, *"Kein ayin hora,"* I'm so old, I may retire soon…"

"Oh, don't say that, Sadie. By the way, my daughter spotted some dresses in your window…"

Sadie leans over her cash register and looks directly at my mother. "Oh, those dresses in the window, those are Dashikis, they're the traditional dress in western Africa. But they don't come ready-made as dresses. We sell the cloth by the foot. You'll have to cut out the fabric and sew them yourselves."

"Fair enough," says my mother. "I figured since this is a fabric store there was a catch and there would be some sewing involved. Where are they located?"

"Oh, they're over there." Sadie points my mother in the direction of the bolts of fabric.

"I can see them from here; let's go over." I head over towards the fabric.

My mother follows behind me as I find the right bolt of Dashiki fabric with its bright blue design surrounded by intricate designs in red and yellow outlined in black ink.

"Now I see what she was talking about," my mother shrugs. "Each dress comes on a bolt of cloth and it has to be cut out and sewn. It makes sense to me now. But as Sadie said, you'll have to be the one to cut it out and sew it yourself."

"Sure, I'm game."

"Are you sure this is something you'd want to wear?"

I look at my mother. "What do you mean?"

"We live out in the suburbs. Will there be anyone else in the suburbs wearing a Dashiki?"

"I plan to be the only one."

"Sure why not? Go ahead. We'll have to ask for a clerk to get this fabric cut."

Back at home, I haul out the antique Singer machine from the box and plug it in. I take the *Dashiki* fabric and cut along the slashed lines that outline the garment.

"What do those words that Sadie said back at Horowitz's mean?" I ask my mother.

"Which words?" asks my mother.

"Kein something something."

"Oh, *kein ayin hora.* That's a Yiddish phrase to get rid of the evil eye."

"Evil eye?" I ask as I pick up my scissors to cut the Dashiki material.

"Yes, as Etka mentioned when she came to visit us, it's believed that there are evil forces out there, or people, who wish us harm. If you say something to invoke the 'evil eye,' you're supposed to say *kein ayin hora* to set things right and dispel the 'evil eye.'"

"Does that actually work? I mean, can you really reverse a curse or an evil wish for harm by saying that statement?" I ask as I put down the scissors and begin to pin the two sides of cloth together.

"I suppose over the years that some people have actually thought it does. On the other hand, it's probably all coincidence that evil is dispelled with a phrase when maybe there was no evil there in the first place."

I shrug at this notion as I spool blue thread into the bobbin of the sewing machine. I turn the fabric inside out and sew along the slashed lines on each side, leaving the neck area open. I turn the fabric inside out, and *voila,* a dress!

I have cut out the neck area, leaving a small piece of brightly patterned cloth that I can use to make something else. Suddenly, it dawns on me that I can sew the pieces together to make a purse. Why not?

I sew the two neck pieces together after I've found an extra tassel in my mother's sewing drawer she'd bought during a previous expedition to Horowitz's. I place the tassel at the bottom of the two pieces I'm sewing together. Once I've done that, I take two long leather thongs that I sew into the top as drawstring shoulder straps. Once everything has been sewn, I turn the purse inside out so that the tassel is dangling from the bottom. *Voila!* A purse!

Now I'm ready to wear my hip Dashiki and matching purse out here in the wilds of the Connecticut suburbs!

CHAPTER 16

"FOLLOWING FASHION"

New Haven, Connecticut   January, 1972

If what I am wearing doesn't seem as though it's quite in fashion at the moment, it's because I'm ahead of my time and I'm waiting for the world to catch up.

⇥ ⇤

It's so "in" that it's "out"…

⇥ ⇤

I stare at all the dresses from the trunk which I've hung up in my closet. If I were to wear these to school, what would my classmates think? I know they aren't all the fashion rage. Why should I wear something just because someone on TV or in a magazine says I should? Why should someone dictate what everyone should be wearing all at the same time? Why should everyone look like everyone else? If it's in, you must wear it NOW!

WHY?

Because everyone else is wearing it NOW!

Since I feel like I don't fit in with my peers at school in the first place, I follow my own path when it comes to fashion. This sets me apart from them even more.

I have tried to fit in with the rest of them, really I have. Sometimes, I think I've tried too hard. Like the time when I was in sixth grade and I was color coordinated for the first (and last) time in my life. Orange was the big color that season. I went with my family to Caldor's, and I bought a pair of shiny orange vinyl shoes and a shiny orange vinyl purse with a double gold chain shoulder strap to match. I can still remember the chemical smell of the vinyl to this day. I don't think I've been color coordinated since.

And I followed my own fashion path and wore my Dashiki in the suburbs. Then there was the time when I was ten and wore white fishnet stockings to a Sukkoth service at the synagogue attached to the religious school I was attending. Taking the term 'fishnets' literally, I'd drawn fish in pencil on pieces of paper and cut them out. I placed them in the stockings and wore them to services, thinking I was being clever because I'd made my stockings to look like I'd caught fish in a net.

In 1969, I'd strung blue and turquoise glass beads I'd planned to wear to the anti-Vietnam war rally on the New Haven Green. All my classmates and I were abuzz about going to the rally. It didn't occur to me that I might not be permitted to go. My father vehemently forbade me from going. Kathy and Ellen and Judith were chatting about how they were planning to go and what they were planning to wear.

I'd strung so many strands and strands of love beads in preparation for the rally and then had nowhere to wear them. All I remember now is Kathy had told me right before the rally: "Don't forget when you go to the rally on the Green, wear massive gobs and gobs of love beads!" As though to wear strands of glass love beads could end a war!

Then there was the time when Campbell's Soup was running a promotion, If you sent in ten labels from soup cans, they'd send you a paper dress printed with Campbell's soup labels in an homage to Andy Warhol. We sent in our labels and got the dress, but in the end, I decided it was a little silly to wear a paper dress. So I simply folded the dress and left it in my drawer.

I think about all those dresses from the trunk and what to do about them. My mother had complained that they were hopelessly outdated. Yes, these are fashions from a ghost, an unknown woman from the past. But these dresses had a life before I acquired them. Someone had worn them, lived her life in them. It's not as if they came off the rack of a vintage clothing store with no known past. They come with a story to tell about the woman who had once owned them. And I want to know what her story was.

CHAPTER 17
"THE RED AND GREEN DRESS"

Hardtmuthgasse 10   Vienna, March, 1937

"*Mein Liebchen*," Jakob begins, "Everything will be fine. After all, I've deposited money in London in Barclay's Bank. Should Hitler ever invade Austria and things get too uncomfortable, we have an escape hatch. Ever since he took power in Germany in 1933, I have been making contingency plans. We can always go to England. A bank account there gives us a financial cushion."

"I hope it will all come out well in the end. I just don't know what I'd ever do if I had to leave Vienna. After all, it is our home, and I would hate to have to leave it."

"But, *mein Liebchen,* if we must leave, we must."

⟞⟜ ⟝⟞

Lusia stands beneath the Ankeruhr, as she always has at two o'clock as Karl the Great strides across the bridge. She is on her way to Frau Ingber to be fitted for a new dress. Lusia, as always is concerned she's gained weight since her last fitting and will always need to be refitted for each new dress. *Das Hildebrandslied* plays on the Glockenspiel. Lusia smiles the usual smile as she listens to the same tinkling music that always accompanies Karl the Great at the same time every day.

"*Guten Morgen,*" smiles Frau Ingber as Lusia passes through the door of her atelier. "Ready for your fitting today?"

"*Guten Morgen,*" Lusia returns the greeting. "Yes, I'm ready to be fitted for a new dress. But I'm afraid I've been eating far too much strudel lately, and my measurements may have changed since our last fitting."

"Well, let's have a measure, shall we?" Frau Ingber takes out her measuring tape. "Come over here, Lusia."

Lusia walks towards Frau Ingber, takes off her Persianner coat, and offers her torso to the mercy of the seamstress's tape. She tries very hard not giggle as the seamstress's tape tickles her waist.

"Are you finished yet?" Lusia sighs because she has tired of sucking in her waist all this time.

"Yes, Lusia, you can breathe now."

"Thank goodness. I know I shouldn't have had that second strudel last night. It was just too tempting!"

Without skipping a beat, Frau Ingber turns towards her dress-maker's dummy. With Lusia's measurements still in her head, she begins to expertly adjust the dummy to her client's proportions.

"What sort of fabric do you want for the dress?" asks Frau Ingber just as she's finished altering the dummy's shape.

Lusia takes a deep breath. "Can I see your new assortment?"

"Yes, yes, naturally, I've only recently received a new shipment of fabrics. Here they are."

Frau Ingber points to a corner table filled with bolts of cloth, some brightly colored, some somber. All with geometric patterns.

"Let me see. I don't want anything too bright," Lusia sighs. "I suppose this cloth with the red squares with little green squares is just subtle enough."

"It's beautiful cloth!" The seamstress gives her client a knowing smile. "You've made an excellent choice! Please, turn it over."

"Why should I turn it over?"

"Just turn it around and you'll see what I mean."

Lusia flips the cloth in the bolt to reveal the underside. "Why, it's woven exactly the reverse in color on the other side!"

"Have you ever seen a cloth like it?"

"No, I haven't."

"You have your choice, Lusia. Do you want the dress to be green on the outside, or the reverse, red on the outside?"

Lusia hesitates, and then quickly says without further hesitation, "Red, Frau Ingber. I want the dress to be red on the outside."

"Very well then, Lusia, I'll have your dress ready in two weeks. You can come by the atelier then. *Gruss Gott,*" smiles Frau Ingber.

As she walks along Herrengasse, Lusia reflects on the fabric Frau Ingber will be using for her new dress. What attracts her to this cloth? Is it the fact that it is unlike any other fabric she has ever seen?

As Lusia returns to Frau Ingber's atelier two weeks later to pick up her new dress, she is excited about this new garment. She pauses at the Ankeruhr on her way to the atelier as the clock chimes two o'clock. Karl the Great toddles across the bridge.

Since the lift is out of order at Frau Ingber's building, Lusia must climb the stairs to the third floor. She is so excited to see what the finished product will look like, she hardly cares. Will it turn out exactly as she had imagined it would? Was she right to go with her decision for the red side with the green squares to be the right side up? Or should she have had Frau Ingber sew it so that the green side with the red squares would be the side to show? No, she shakes her head as she huffs up these stairs, she was correct to go with the red side. Red is more her color. Red suits her better.

"*Gruss Gott,*" smiles Lusia as she comes through the door of the atelier.

"*Gruss Gott,*" returns Frau Ingber.

"Let me see the dress, where is it?"

"It's hanging up over here, Lusia, step right this way."

Frau Ingber hands the dress over to Lusia. "It will suit you just fine!" smiles the seamstress.

Lusia takes the dress of the hanger, holds it up to admire it.

"Would you like to try it on, Lusia?"

"Yes, I'm dying to see what it looks like on me!"

"Step right this way." Frau Ingber leads Lusia to a curtained area with a full-length mirror. She pulls the dress over her head and gazes at her reflection. Lusia wraps her arms around her torso and hugs herself tight. At once, she has an attraction to this dress. With every minute, she is becoming more and more attached to it. She likes the fabric. In an instant, this dress has become her favorite of all the dresses Frau Ingber has created for her. She flips the hem over to observe the reverse of the pattern.

Instinctively, she knows that this is the dress by which she will come to define herself.

CHAPTER 18
"THE RED AND GREEN DRESS"

New Haven, Connecticut   February, 1972

I f I don't feel I fit in with what little family I have, it's even worse for me at school. At Hopkins, I feel as if I've come from another planet.

I am not one of them.
I do not belong there.

As I sit on my bed alone in my room, I stare at my favorite dress from the trunk. I remain haunted by the red and green cloth.

My decision to wear the dress to school has caused some consternation with my mother. She's still afraid I'll be teased for wearing something to school that's so desperately out of fashion. My argument is that current fashion is so out of whack with reality that I should be able to wear anything. Hems of skirts go from mini to midi to maxi and it doesn't really seem to matter what anyone wears these days. One benefit of the abolishment of the plaid skirt as the school's uniform means that I can wear the red and green dress to class without anyone stopping me. The irony being that for the first time in years since the dress code was changed; I will be wearing a dress to school.

I think of all the possible comments my classmates might make.
Should I wear it, or shouldn't I?

I just hope that if I do decide to wear the dress to school that my classmates won't laugh at me. My fear is that I'll be spending the day at school dressed in something I'll regret wearing. It's up to me to take the upper hand and ignore any comments that might arise so that I can just concentrate on my class work.

Finally, I bite the bullet and decide to wear the dress once and for all. If nothing else, I can consider this an experiment on how I am perceived by my peers. Will they accept me as someone who's cool and who follows her own path wearing a hopelessly outdated dress?

Oh heck, who am I kidding? The kids at school will probably tease me!

I put on the dress and brace myself in anticipation of their reaction.

＝╪═ ═╪═

As I enter my first period classroom, French, I try very hard not to appear to be too self-conscious. I look around at what my other classmates are wearing before I try to determine whether or not my dress makes me stick out like a sore thumb.

Over there, Cheryl is wearing a light blue corduroy button-down shirt over a T-shirt with jeans. Roberta is wearing a skirt. But then, Roberta always wears a skirt to school and has been for years. Ruth is wearing a black sweater with jeans. Ellen is wearing a blue sweater with jeans. Julia is wearing a red cardigan with jeans. Liz is wearing a white blouse with blue corduroy pants. Both Katherine and Charlotte are wearing brown corduroy pants with similar blazers.

No one is wearing a vintage dress from the nineteen thirties. And still, no one is looking at me any differently than they would have on any other normal day.

Feeling self-conscious, I turn to look at Charlotte who always sits next to me. Does she even notice I'm wearing a dress from the trunk? She's too engrossed in her chemistry book to care about what I'm wearing. In my mind, I think that everyone is staring at me. Suddenly, I realized they really aren't. I sit through French class, half thinking about the lesson, and half thinking that I am wearing a hopelessly outdated dress in front of my classmates. A dress that had once belonged to a woman from long ago. A woman whom I know nothing about.

After lunch, I zoom in on Madame K and pin her down in a corner of the cafeteria. I don't even know why I've chosen her as the person I've designated to confide in. Everything I'd been holding in during French class is now exploding in my brain.

I look Madame K straight in the face. "I've never talked about this to anyone before," I blurt out, looking around to see if there is anyone else around. Fortunately, there is no one within earshot. Then I let it all out. "My father escaped from the Holocaust and he had these relatives who didn't make it out. He has a trunk with all their possessions in it. They even packed their window curtains. These curtains were a goldenrod yellow. It's a really, really bright color. But I don't think that if I were escaping the Holocaust, I would want to pack my curtains."

"Calm down, Susan," Madame K begins, "you can slow down. Now, take a deep breath." Her facial expression tells me that she is quite startled and that she wasn't expecting me to say something like this. I'm not sure she quite knows what to make of me.

"Why don't you just take a deep breath?" my French teacher offers again. "It's okay, we can discuss this, but just why are you bringing it up now?"

"Well, I've always known that my father escaped from the Holocaust, but he's never discussed it with us all that much. He's always kept silent. He's never told me about the relatives who were killed. We recently opened up the trunk with their possessions. I was also shown a family photograph taken in the thirties with a group of my relatives. My father had never shown me the photograph before and I don't know how many of the people in the picture even survived."

Madame K's facial expression suddenly turns to one of sympathy.

"So you've only recently opened up the trunk and that's why you're upset now?"

"Yes, that's right."

"You must have been shocked. Even if this is something you've always known about, I can see why this recent change has brought out this new concern."

"I was so curious to know what was in the trunk; I didn't realize how much it would upset my father. My mother did warn me about that aspect, but I didn't know just how much I would be upset by it, too. Now that we've opened it up, I'm only now beginning to learn about those who perished. I still don't know everything there is to know about them, though. I'm even wearing one of the dresses from the trunk."

"You are? Let me see!"

I take off my grey woolen jacket and proceed to twirl around to show off the dress like I'm some sort of fashion model.

"That's very pretty. It must be from, I'm guessing, the thirties…"

"Yes, I believe that this dress if from the late thirties."

"What year did they try to escape? Do you know?"

"No, I really don't"

I suddenly realize that my fashion concerns are really masking my horror over what had happened to my ancestors. As if owning my deceased relative's possessions could compensate for their loss.

"So tell me about the people in the photograph," Madame K's smile reassures me.

"Well, in the center of this photograph is this elderly man with a beard. He's my great- grandfather. He's surrounded by his five grown children, my grandfather and his three brothers and one sister. My grandmother, my father, and his sister are absent from the photo. They weren't able to make it back to Sniatyn, that's the small city where my father was born. They couldn't go because they were busy with school, and it was a long train ride out there from Vienna."

Madame K continues to comfort me. "It was a very long time ago. I'm sure you will be okay. I'm sorry that this had to happen to your family. You have nothing to fear. You're safe here in Connecticut. You're among friends here. Feel free to talk to me about this anytime you need to."

I leave the cafeteria for my afternoon classes, feeling reassured that at least one faculty member is on my side. At the same time, I still feel as though I stand out. Not because of the outdated dress that I am wearing, but because my family was affected by the Holocaust. I can't imagine that any of my other classmate's families could have had anything as horrible happen to them in their past. I feel that they can't possibly know what I'm going through at this moment. It's as though I am living in a tunnel focused on this one issue alone...an issue that happened a long time ago that is now affecting me in the present.

⊷ ⊶

Back at home, I trudge upstairs to my room. I have a moment to myself as I flip the hem of the dress over to gaze again at the reverse of the pattern. As if to look at the reverse of the cloth is to peek into my family's history from the inside out. From an aspect I have never viewed the past from before.

I trudge down the hallway to my sister's room where there is a full-length mirror so I can observe myself wearing the dress. A moment of reflection back as I see myself in a new light as never before. An altered perception now that we've opened up the trunk. I feel like an entirely different person. Wearing the dress, I can feel my personality transform.

At the same time, I am beginning to feel a kinship with this dress. Since I know nothing about the woman who had once owned it, I find myself bonding with the dress itself. As though the dress has become my companion of sorts, a substitute for the woman who had once worn it. It envelopes my body with a certain warmth. In a way it acts as a touchstone, a good luck object. What my mother had once called "hopelessly outdated," and a *schmata*, I call a timeless classic. This dress has become a part of me now. A metaphor for my life: one side represents my life; the reverse represents the woman who had once worn it.

I begin to wonder what would have happened if this woman had had the dress sewn with the reverse of the fabric showing. If the dressmaker had switched it so that the green side with red squares was on the outside and the red side on the inside, would her luck have reversed? Would her life's outcome have been different? Might she have successfully escaped the Nazis had the dress been sewn with the reverse pattern? As though to reverse her fate.

What I know is that from now on, this is the dress by which I will always define myself.

CHAPTER 19
"ANSCHLUSS"

Hardtmuthgasse 10   Vienna, March 11, 1938

Jakob stands alongside Samuel and David in the sanctuary of the Telemann Schul, a three- block walk from Beheimgasse. Their prayer books are opened to the *V'Ahavta* as Herr Bern whispers into David's ear.

"Have you heard the news?" asks Herr Bern.

"Heard what news?" responds David, unaware of this day's late-breaking events.

"Hitler's troops have invaded Austria." Herr Bern shrugs as he fumbles to adjust his prayer shawl.

"No!" gasps David in alarm.

"It's true," concurs Herr Rosenberg. "I heard it on the radio just before coming to *schul*. They're calling it the *Anschluss*, the annexation of Austria," adds Herr Krupnik, one of the more color-ful characters with whom Jakob and David have acquainted them-selves at Telemann Schul. He is the owner of a large shoe factory in Vienna.

"Liberation? Hah!" declares David rather loudly.

A "Shhhhhhhhhhhhhhh" comes from behind. The men hush their voices, but their thoughts are now racing. Quietly, they say their prayers. Their eyes on the Hebrew words printed on the page, their heads remain on that other matter.

After services, Jakob accompanies Samuel and David on their usual fifteen-minute walk home. They are also accompanied home by Herr Krupnik just as they are every Friday night before this. But, on this particular night, there is a chill in the air for them. They watch as crowds of people begin to gather on the street corners. Many men are now running through the streets cheering, happy that Hitler has now taken over Austria.

David turns to Samuel with a look of concern on his face. "What will this mean for us?"

"I don't know, Papa," Samuel replies, shrugging his shoulders.

"I was afraid this would happen," Jakob sighs. "David, I warned you it was only a matter of time before the Germans were to invade Austria. We had our many discussions. This can't be good. Hitler does not like us Jews; he does not like us at all!"

"Don't worry, Papa and Onkel Jakob," assures Samuel. "The Jews have lived in Germany under Hitler just fine since 1933. We'll be all right. We'll survive."

As Herr Krupnik walks along by their side, he says nothing. His mind is racing, mapping out his escape route to Czechoslovakia. The next morning, he will fill his fancy sports car with as many of his belongings that will fit and flee across the border.

Upon their return to the Beheimgasse apartment, David bursts through the heavy wooden door to the apartment, shaking it almost to its hinges to make the announcement to Eva, Elsa, and Lusia. As is customary, they stay home together every Friday night while David, Jakob and Samuel go to *schul*. This night is no different.

"Such news, Eva and Lusia!" shouts David as the four of them fly through the door. "We must turn on the radio!"

"*Ach so was?*" Eva furrows her brow. "Turn the radio on? It's *Shabbos…*"

David rubs his hands together as though in an expression of trying to gather warmth. "I know it is *Shabbos,* but this is an exception. We must turn on the radio! Austria is no longer to be called Austria. Hitler has invaded our country. Now it will be called *Ostmark.* It is now the eastern boundary of the Third Reich."

"*Ach so was?*" Eva raises an eyebrow. "Austria is now to be *Ostmark?*

"That is what the radio announcer said according to Herr Bern," sighs David. "He heard it on the radio just before he left for *schul.*"

Herr Krupnik follows David and Jakob into the *Kabinett* where Samuel keeps his shortwave radio. It is a huge set, about two feet long, manufactured by the Zerdick Corporation, too large to be brought out of Samuel's room. He bought the radio with the proceeds he's saved up from sweeping the sawdust off the floor of his father's lumberyard.

"*Today, I resign my post as chancellor. Hitler will be coming to Austria. Go save Austria,*" a distraught Kurt Schuschnigg, the prime minister of Austria, announces to the listening audience with a note of alarm in his voice.

"What will this mean for us?" shrugs Eva.

"This cannot be a good thing," sighs David, his face growing redder as he gets even more upset. "We've no time. We must make contingency plans."

"You don't mean make plans to escape…do you, Papa?" asks Samuel.

"When the time is right, I fear we may have to leave this country. One can never tell the future. Jakob was right all this time. I have to hand it to my brother. I know that he had warned me long ago of such a possibility. I never believed that this day would come."

"But Papa, we can't leave now. I must make *Matura*," argues Samuel. "My graduation is only three months away."

"Samuel, there are more important things at stake than your graduation!" stammers David.

CHAPTER 20
"HITLER ARRIVES IN VIENNA"

Hardtmuthgasse 10   Vienna, March 15, 1938

There is an electric tension in the air in the streets of Vienna that the members of the Spielvogel family cannot ignore. A feeling of elation runs among the throng. They can't pinpoint it, but they have an eerie foreboding about this jubilation. As though this joy is a positive thing for everyone else but not for them. Suddenly, there is word on the street, everyone is abuzz.

Hitler has now entered Vienna. The excitement builds as people shout for joy.

Riding triumphantly by motorcade, Hitler enters through the center of Vienna along the Ringstasse. The parade is festive, as though the circus were coming to town rather than an outright political takeover.

Hitler makes his speech from the balcony of the Hofburg Palace, the palace once used by the Hapsburg Dynasty as their winter palace. An ecstatic, if not partly staged crowd, welcomes him. As a powerful orator, he is one who knows how to draw in every listener no matter where they are located in the throng. Every member of this crowd is mesmerized and believes that Hitler is speaking to him or her; and to him or her alone. Even the woman dressed in a dirndl who stands in the very last row.

The Nazi sympathizers have come out of the woodwork. The Spielvogels have been aware of their existence even before the Anschluss when anyone who was a sympathizer had worn the lapel of their jacket flapped back to show the catches of their swastika clutch pins, never revealing the front of the pins with their symbol of the Nazi Party. This is how everyone knows who had been on Hitler's side all along. No one was fooling anyone. Before the Anschluss, it had been both illegal and unpopular to be a sympathizer, yet many still wore their clutch pins. Many neighbors who live in the apartment building across the street on Beheimgasse turn out now to be pro-Nazi and stand among the crowd of well-wishers. They are glad that Hitler is taking over Austria. Many have been wearing these lapel pins backwards for many months now.

Conformity in clothing has become the new style. Everyone wants to be a part of this crowd. Everyone wants to be seen with these symbols of fascism. Swastikas are everywhere, on gummed stickers attached to posts, on armbands, on the flags the crowd waves, and on all the public buildings. It is the aesthetics of conformity. This symbol of the new order that has suddenly taken over the city is now visible everywhere.

From the outside looking in, this appears to be a happy event. And to ninety-nine percent of the people of Vienna, apparently it is. But Lusia, who watches from afar, even though she does not have much of a head for politics, knows enough that this happy crowd is an ugly scene.

Row upon row of soldiers all dressed the same in heavily belted uniforms and helmets march through the city. All looking alike. The uniforms envelope their torsos of these soldiers with a feel that is different from their everyday clothing. With these new garments, these men feel powerful. Invincible. The power of cloth changes the minds of those wearing it. Turning these men into a different type of human being; men who have lost the ability to have empathy for their fellow man. As if the brown cloth of these uniforms has transformed the souls of these soldiers into marching machines. Machines that can kill another human simply for being of a certain religion. Or one who looks different from everyone else. Today, conformity is the fashion. A conformity with evil, Individuality in thought and dress is out of fashion.

Women line the streets waiting for Hitler's motorcade, all dressed in traditional dirndls, white shirts beneath colorful jumpers, full skirts, and aprons, as the men wear the traditional *lederhosen* with suspenders, all cheering for the chancellor. To the outside observer, the prints of different designs on the aprons of their dirndls present a sea of color. The difference of print is the only thing that differentiates one woman from another in this throng. These women have always worn dirndls as their daily dress, and will always wear this traditional outfit.

Among the many in this crowd is Frau Habel, a fifty-year old woman who lives across the street on Beheimgasse. She cheers as Hitler's motorcade enters Vienna along the Ringstrasse, cheering so loudly that she loses her voice. Three days later, she will still be unable to speak.

Also in the crowd is Josef Brinsky the Elder and Josef Brinsky the Younger. The same Josef the Younger who had taunted Samuel back when he was in grade school. For him, this event will stand as a turning point in his life. It means that he will be a part of the Nazi Party; that the hatred for the Jews that his father had instilled in him all his life is now validated by the fact that the Nazis, too, share this hatred. He can't lose. All his life, he has waited for a moment like this to arrive.

In a few weeks, Josef the Younger will join the SS and put on this same brown uniform as these soldiers who now march into his city. He will feel himself transform. He will feel powerful. Invincible.

He will make sure that the city rids itself of families such as the Spielvogels.

This day marks the turning point in the Spielvogels' lives, too. After this day, whether or not they are fully aware of it, their lives will never be the same. Many of the citizens of Austria believe Hitler will bring hope and prosperity to them in the midst of the Depression. While many of the Viennese may think that Hitler's presence in their city is a good idea and that their lives will be bettered because of it, to the Spielvogels, this means that it is only a matter of time before they will ultimately have to leave this city. And not of their own accord.

Now Hitler is to be considered the savior of this country and the leader of this new order. For the past nine years, the Austrians have seen hard times. These men wear uniforms meant to impress and intimidate and at the same time hold for this crowd the promise that soon they will have food in their stomachs and new clothing on their backs. These will be empty promises. The crowd has permitted Mr. Hitler to enter their city with his rosy promises of a brighter future. The crowd will find out that, indeed, Hitler's promises will prove to be false. By then, it will be too late. Far too late. For the time being, however, they have unknowingly allowed Satan to enter their city. And they are here to cheer about it.

CHAPTER 21
"NIGHT OF STREET WASHING"

Hardtmuthgasse 10   Vienna, March 16, 1938

Lusia thinks back to all those discussions between David and
Jakob that had gone on ever since Hitler had taken power in
Germany back in 1933. Like watching a tennis match, her head
would move back and forth from one brother to the other as each
heartily discussed the best place to put his money in case of a Nazi
takeover. David had taken to putting his money in Tel Aviv, while
Jakob thought it strategically best to deposit his money in a London
bank. Each brother had his own theory. Each theory sounded rea-
sonable to Lusia.

There is tension in the air in the streets of Vienna that Lusia cannot
ignore. The feeling is no longer the same as before the Anschluss.
Perhaps for the rest of the population of this city, this feeling isn't
tension, its excitement. Perhaps it all depends on where one's sym-
pathies lie. For Lusia, however, she cannot help but feel a certain
amount of apprehension.

For the time being, Lusia has decided it is best that she stay closer to home. She feels safer here. Flipping the hem of the red and green dress over and over again, she thinks about fate and the fact that it was her decision that this dress be made with the red side showing. She thinks about the new dress she had been fitted for earlier in the day. A black rayon dress with tiny red and yellow flowers.

Suddenly, Jakob enters the apartment, interrupting her thoughts. "What is it?" asks Lusia, looking up to see a look of shock on her husband's face.

"Well, if you must know, as you were out getting fitted for a new dress, your brother-in-law was being dragged through the streets to the Brinsky Gaststube where he was forced to kneel on the sidewalk and scrub the streets clean."

"What?!" shouts Lusia as if to shake herself from her self-imposed reverie.

"While David was walking in the street today along Syringgasse, on his way back from the bank, he had the misfortune of running into Josef Brinsky, the pub's owner. He came out of the drinking establishment and grabbed David by the arm. Brinsky shoved a pail of water and a brush at him and demanded that he make himself a useful citizen and get down on his hands and knees and scrub the sidewalk. Then he called David a 'Jew swine' and told him that because he was a dirty Jew, he was obligated to scrub the sidewalk clean. Well, after David finished scrubbing the sidewalk, Brinsky then forced him to wash his black car, which he had parked out front of his drinking establishment. He shoved a bucket of water and some soap and a cloth in the direction of David's face as he insisted he make his car shine. All the while, his drunken patrons came out to make derogatory comments about the Jews. Before the Anschluss, neighbors such as the Brinskys had kept their hatred in check. Now, they are legally free to unleash their hatred upon any Jew here in Vienna. No one is safe from whatever creative hostility they can think up next. All in all, it was not a pleasant afternoon for my brother."

CHAPTER 22
"HEINZ PICKLE"

New Haven, Connecticut   February, 1972

"Well, when I was your age," my mother begins, "Grammy always dictated what clothing I should wear. She wanted me to dress a certain way and wear make-up. We fought about it constantly, I never agreed on anything she wanted me to wear. She never agreed on anything I wanted to wear. When I was in college, she wanted me to wear fur coats. I detested the thought of wearing fur coats, but she made me buy them anyway. Grammy forced me to wear that damn beaver coat and buy that leopard jacket. She made a bargain with me. I agreed that I would wear the furs if she would also buy some of the carved wooden figures that the fur importer had brought back with him from Africa. I was more interested in tribal sculpture than I was in that damned leopard jacket. After all, Picasso had been inspired by African sculpture, why shouldn't I be, too? When I was in high school, we had a seamstress named Steinie who made clothing for me. Grammy figured that custom-made clothing would fit me better than anything I could buy off the rack. She made me the skirts and blazers that I wore all through college.

"Do you still have them?"

"Oh, yes, they're upstairs in the cedar closet."

My mother continues to flip the eggplant slices in the bread-crumbs. "My favorite thing from high school was the green Heinz pickle pin I'd gotten from the Heinz Pavilion at the 1939 New York World's Fair. I wore it every day on the lapel of one of Steinie's blazers. I may not have conformed to the way Grammy had wanted me to dress, but we compromised in our own way. Of course, she always wanted me to be flashier and more polished than I wanted to be. She insisted I wear lipstick and rouge. I wasn't so worried about fashion as much as I was concerned about reading books and painting."

I shrug as I watch my mother fry the eggplant slices. "Well, I'm also more concerned about books and learning than I am about fashion, too."

My mother piles the eggplant slices into a casserole dish just before she piles on the tomato sauce. "Yes, but sometimes I think that you're too under concerned about the way you dress. By the way, what happened today when you wore that dress to school? I noticed you've changed back into your jeans. You never told me what happened. Shall I say, 'I told you so?'"

"No one teased me at all about the dress. You were wrong."

"Okay, so I was wrong. Tell me what happened."

"Actually, I was pleasantly surprised by my classmates. No one made fun of me for what I was wearing. They were more mature than the kids I'd encountered back in junior high." I try to fo-cus our conversation on the superficiality of what I was wearing to school today rather than reveal anything about the shit fit I'd had in front of my French teacher.

"So they were okay?" my mother asks me as she flips down the oven door to put in the eggplant Parmesan.

"Yes, at first I felt a bit self-conscious, but then I went about my day as usual."

I cross my fingers as I say this and hope that Madame K won't call my mother up any time soon and tell her how I'd spilled my guts out at school. "Everything went fine, today. No problems at all with anyone being critical of my choice of wardrobe."

At least this part was true. No one commented about the dress, and I was the one to blurt out everything about my father's deceased relatives. I was the one to confide in Madame K about my own fears.

My mother begins to chop the lettuce for the salad. "So, they didn't care at all about what you were wearing?"

"Yes, that's right. I was pleasantly surprised by my classmates. You were so wrong! No one laughed at how badly out of style my dress was."

⇥⋅⇤

After my experiment of wearing the red and green dress to school, I feel I can now go back to wearing my jeans. I've decided not to wear any more dresses from the trunk to school anytime soon. Otherwise, I might feel compelled to spill my guts out to Madame K again. Unfortunately, my jeans are now ripping even more at the left knee. Telltale little white threads are now becoming visible through the blue of the indigo fabric.

I realize that I need to devise a strategy to repair the denim so that my stitches will stay in place and not rip apart. I sneak into the living room, back to the location where we've piled all the items from the top tray of the trunk, including the unfinished tablecloth and new packets of embroidery thread, onto the coffee table. I pull some thread out of a skein, cut off just the right length to repair the knees of my jeans and thread the needle. As I stitch, a sense of fear arises in me. I had expressed this fear to Madame K, but I was still bothered by it. I told her that I feared that I, too, may one day be the victim of the same anti-Semitism my father's generation had experienced. Madame K reassured me that everything would be okay. I was so wound up today that I had also expressed this fear to Mrs. Goldstein, one of the school's secretaries. She put it to me this way, "Of course it could always happen again. People are so full of hatred.

Unfortunately for me, Mrs. Goldstein's words were not as reassuring as the soothing words of Madame K.

CHAPTER 23
"COLORS AND THREAD"

Hardtmuthgasse 10   Vienna, March, 1938

*H*ow can I leave my house? I'm so afraid of what people might say to me in the street. Look at what happened to David. He was forced to clean Brinsky's car, then he was forced to scrub the sidewalk. I'm too afraid to walk in the streets alone now. What will they do to me? Do I look like a Jew? I don't know what a Jew should look like. Maybe I'm making myself too afraid. Maybe it's nothing. I should go out; I need to get out of my apartment. I can't live my life cooped up within these four walls forever.

I'll go visit Frau Grauen. That's what I'll do. I can start a new embroidery project. That will get me out of the house and give me something to do.

⟫⟪

"*Gruss Gott,*" sings Frau Grauen as she comes running out from the back room.

"*Gruss Gott,*" responds Lusia.

The shopkeeper maintains her façade of politeness despite the ever increasing political difficulties posed by staying in this city.

Lusia looks around at the table piled with linen shapes pre-stamped with embroidery designs. She turns to Frau Grauen. "Today, I should like to purchase a square of linen for a tablecloth. I've just ordered a brand new dining room table, and I'd like to embroider a new tablecloth for it."

"You've just ordered a new table?" gulps Frau Grauen as she crinkles her nose.

"Yes, that's right, Frau Grauen. I know what it is you're thinking."

"I see. Then, are you sure that it's a good time to buy new furniture now with all that's been going on in this city?"

"Yes," says Lusia hesitantly.

"Very well. And just how big will this new table be?"

"It's one meter square. Therefore, I shall need a square tablecloth big enough to cover it."

"Yes, Lusia, I have just the right thing." The shopkeeper moves to the table where Lusia is standing and riffles through the pile. From beneath, she pulls a linen square stamped with a design of flowers in pale blue ink. There is a border and field of flowers with leaves and stems in the center. "This cloth looks like it should be just about the right size for your new table. I believe it should do."

Lusia holds up the white linen square. A clean slate, a new project, a new beginning to offset the troubling current political situation. In her mind, she envisions how this tablecloth will look with David and Eva, Samuel and Elsa over for a Sunday dinner. If she can envision it, Lusia figures, it will come true. Yes, that's how things will happen, exactly as she envisions it. If she wills it, it will come to be.

"And the thread to go with it…what colors would you like?"

Lusia thinks about this question for a moment, as though she were solving a complex problem of calculus instead of simply buying the right threads to accomplish her project. The design is a pleasing arrangement of flowers in patches around the tablecloth.

There is nothing terribly imaginative about this design. Lusia finds it pleasing. And that is all that matters.

These colors are Lusia's salvation; they will be what will keep her sane in the midst of the madness that is swirling around her. As long as she concentrates on the colors of these threads, it will take her mind off what is going on around her. These colors will keep her spirits afloat.

Lusia follows Frau Grauen over to the wall where, from floor to ceiling, the shelves are filled with boxes of buttons, pins, notions, and embroidery threads. She thinks of the colors of the threads she'd used when she first began to embroider. They were simple blues, greens, reds, and yellows. The palette she will need for this tablecloth is far more complicated a color scheme with a more intricate design than anything she had worked on when she was a child.

"Let me see. I'd like brown and gold ochre for the stems...a dark green and a lime green for the leaves..."

"Wait...wait, Frau Spielvogel, slow down! Let me get to the threads you've mentioned already."

"But, of course, Frau Grauen."

Once the shopkeeper catches up with her requests, Lusia begins again. She holds up her hand as though to count off on her fingers. Pink, dark blue, dark red, light blue..."

"Slow down, stop!" Frau Grauen grabs as many colors as she can remember.

Lusia pauses. Once she notices that the shopkeeper has all the skeins of floss she's requested so far in hand, she continues on. "Orange, lavender, and a golden yellow for the flowers."

Again, Frau Grauen holds her breath. As she grabs at the skeins of golden yellow, Lusia begins again. "Oh, yes, I think I'd like brown and ochre for the three border rows of cross-stitched stars. That means I'll need more skeins of that same brown and ochre than what you've given me already."

"Fine, Lusia, I'll just climb back up and grab some more skeins of the brown and ochre.

Now, are you sure you have enough?"

"Yes, Frau Frauen, *Danke!*"

The two of them catch their breath. As Lusia pays for her purchase at the cash register, she notices something out of the corner of her eye she hadn't noticed all the time she'd been in the store. There, painted in white in reverse on the outside of Frau Grauen's store window is the word, *Juden,* along with a Star of David. This very much upsets Lusia and puts her mind back on the situation she had come to the store to get away from.

⊰ ⊱

Never self-conscious about walking through the streets of Vienna before the Anschluss, Lusia feels all too aware of the strangers she now passes in the same streets she's always walked along all these years. The change in the air is palpable, as though she can touch it with the tips of her fingers. At first the change hadn't bothered her; the atmosphere felt rather festive. Everyone around her had been celebrating the change, so much so that even she for a time had felt swept up in all the commotion. It never occurred to her that she shouldn't share in the celebration along with the throng. She thinks about these people she's seen in the street who've been Nazi sympathizers all along. The ones who displayed their lapels backwards showing the clutch of the pin. No one was fooling anyone. All along, everyone knew that on the other side of the lapel was an enameled swastika pin. But now after observing the white Star of David in Frau Grauen's window, she knows that this is a party to which she was never invited. Festive for everyone else. Never meant to be festive for her.

⊰ ⊱

Back at Hardtmuthgasse, Lusia pushes the memory of the white star painted on Frau Grauen's window out of her head. She takes the tablecloth out of the brown paper shopping bag, and next, takes out each skein of thread, one by one. Looking at the colors, she searches for some solace from her predicament, searching her brain for memories from her past from which she can find something to hold on to. These colors remind Lusia of the time when her mother had first taught her to embroider. As she gazes at the light shade of green thread, she is reminded of all the picnics she had at the lake with her family. How the grass had smelled, how her mother had yelled at her for getting grass stains on her new dress. The brown thread reminds her of the first time she went to her father's leather factory and saw the brown leather being cut into shapes to be made into valises. She can still hear the hissing and whirring of the machinery in her head. All these associations with colors come from happier times in her life.

Once comfortable on her couch, she kicks off her shoes and begins to embroider her tablecloth. As she begins her stitches, embroidering along the pale blue guidelines, she thinks about Muniu and how she had once wanted to bring him to Vienna. Realizing that just as much as this might not be a good time to begin a new embroidery project, it also isn't a good time to offer her nephew a new life in this city.

Maybe it wasn't such a good idea to have offered to adopt Muniu and bring him to Vienna after all. We had hoped to raise him as our own and have him educated here, but now I know for certain it's not the right time. In fact, I don't know how much longer Jakob and I will be able to stay here ourselves if things get too difficult for us.

Maybe Frau Grauen was right; it's not a good idea to start a new embroidery project. I know it's a big tablecloth. Maybe too large a project to start just now, considering what's going on here in Vienna. But I know I can do it! I've finished every other embroidery project I've ever started.

CHAPTER 24

"COLORS AND THREAD"

New Haven, Connecticut   February, 1972

After my gut-spilling session with Madame K in the cafeteria last week, I have been left with even more emptiness and no answers to soothe my soul. My thoughts turn to that half-finished tablecloth from the trunk. When I first brought it out into the daylight, I thought of how pitiful it was. Who could use a half-finished tablecloth? I felt sorry for it, trying to think up ways it could possibly be used. Perhaps it could be folded in half with the embroidered side displayed on a table.

Then the thought hits me!

Since the tablecloth had been packed with extra thread, and the outline for the pattern stamped in pale blue ink is there for me to follow, I could be the one to complete it!

I march into my mother's art studio where she is now applying pen and ink against the background of sorrowful newspaper headlines to create the outlines of the unborn children for *Matrix of the Unformed*.

I bounce my idea off her. "I want to complete the tablecloth from the trunk!"

My mother furrows her brow as she is about to dip her pen into some more black ink before drawing the face of an unborn child into a headline about an automobile accident. "You want to do what?"

I look at her half-finished painting and its images of the sorrowful children yet to be born into this world.

"Remember the tablecloth from the trunk? The one that's halfway finished?"

"Yes, what about it?'

"I've decided I'd like to finish it."

My mother puts down her ink pen and stares up at me. "You've never embroidered before, have you?"

"No, but I could always try."

"Surely you don't want to try it on that tablecloth without practicing on something else first. You'll have to learn on a sampler of some sort before you ever put a stitch into that relic of a tablecloth."

"Do you know how to embroider?"

"I've done it now and again."

"Could you teach me, please?"

"I can try. Do you think you can learn quickly?"

"I can try."

"But the cloth is ancient. It was started by someone a long time ago. Are you sure you're up to the responsibility?"

"Yes," I assure her.

With my assurance, my mother walks me over to the drawer beneath the built-in china cabinet. From the bottom, she pulls out a medium-sized needle, scissors, and an embroidery hoop. Then she goes into the living room and grabs a tiny piece of embroidery thread that was left over from the trunk.

We sit down together on the living room couch as my mother looks at me, filled with reservation. "If you're going to take on such a great undertaking you're going to have to learn the different types of embroidery stitches that are needed for the tablecloth.

But first, I'm going to show you how to embroider on a test piece of cloth."

"But I want to start right away on the big cloth. Can't I skip the training part and just begin?"

"I know that you're anxious, but trust me, it's better to learn on a test piece first. You don't want to mess up on the original."

"I know I can handle it. If I do mess up, can't I just pull out all the stitches and try again?"

"Pull out all the stitches? Of course not! You must have patience. Once you've pierced the cloth, you can't go back. The needle can leave a hole in the linen you can't cover up once it's there. Besides, you'd be wasting thread. You've got to be very careful."

"Exactly how much embroidery have you ever done before?" I know full well that my questions will annoy my mother. "Are you an expert?"

"I know enough to take a needle and thread and create a design."

"You don't have that much more experience with it than I have, do you?"

"Yes, I do. I'm trying to teach you. Either listen to me or you won't be prepared. If you don't have the patience to practice, what proof do I have that you've got the patience to complete this project"?"

"Oh, all right," I give in. "Just show me how to do the stitches."

My mother takes the needle threaded with some of the blue thread she's borrowed from the trunk. Then she holds it up in her right hand. "Watch me. This is how you embroider. You take this hoop to keep the fabric taut and place it over the location where you wish to begin. Now, I'm ready to push the needle into the cloth and create a stitch. I'm going to show you the cross-stitch first because I can tell just by looking at the tablecloth that it's one of the major stitches used over and over again in the design."

I watch as my mother continues with her demonstration. I resent her for trying to teach me, thinking I can quickly catch on without her instructions.

My mother continues. "See how I place the needle from behind so that the knot won't show? Then I pull the needle through the spot on the design where I want it to be located, see?"

"Yes, I see."

"Then you place the needle about a quarter of an inch away from where the thread has gone through the cloth. Next, pull the thread taut. From behind, you figure approximately where the thread should come through for the cross-stitch, and push the needle through. Cross the second stitch over the pre-existing stitch, see?"

"I see," I say glumly, with no emotion.

"But you're going to have to practice. I suggest you create a sampler of your own design first."

Etka's words run through my brain about how in Sniatyn, as soon as a girl turned ten, an embroidery needle was put into her hands as though it were some sort of biological rite of passage, like puberty. Etka said how she'd had little interest in embroidery. But I'm not being forced to embroider the way she had been, so I have no reason to resent it.

With my mother's demonstration, I realize that embroidery is a tradition that has been passed down over the generations from mother to daughter, much in the same way that my mother with her infinite patience is doing now. I am not judging this act as an old-fashioned practice I should not be doing because I am now living in the modern world, I am doing it out of my own free choice.

I follow my own fashion in clothing, so now I am also following my own fashion in my handicrafts. It's all part of my being an independent thinker.

Deep down in my heart, I know that my mother is right. I really do need to create a practice piece before I put a threaded needle into that ancient cloth. At once, I set about devising my own sampler using the same stitches from the trunk's tablecloth. From my mother's stock of fabric she's stored away in the bottom of the dining room cabinet, I search for just the right piece of cloth. I come upon a larger white square of cloth, larger than the one my mother had used for her demonstration, not quite linen but still a suitable piece. I bring it over to the table and place it alongside the trunk's tablecloth. Taking a thin black magic marker, I carefully follow the path of my ancestor to recreate a small portion of the ancient cloth's floral pattern.

Borrowing some more of the same blue floss my mother had used in her demonstration, I thread the needle. Little by little, stitch by stitch, I reproduce a small star burst of a flower. I refer to the Coats and Clark guide to embroidery stitches my mother had stored away in her drawer. Next, I refer to the stitches on the actual tablecloth, looking up the same stitches in the illustrations in the Coats and Clark book. I find the pages that demonstrate how to stitch the herringbone pattern for the leaves and the crisscross patterns for the star border. I continue until I've completely embroidered over my own magic marker pattern.

I've consciously left out the French knots, although I know I'll need to stitch them in order to complete the tablecloth, I take one look at the instructions in Coats and Clark and figure I will wing it to improvise and create my own knots when the time comes.

After taking several hours to finish the test panel, I now feel confident enough to begin embroidering on the vintage cloth.

I know that I am ready. Even if it is my mother's opinion that I am not.

CHAPTER 25
"DAVID'S ARREST"

Hardtmuthgasse 10   Vienna, May, 1938

"Terrible news, Lusia," shouts Jakob as he rushes in through the door of the apartment. "It's shocking, terrible!"

"What is it? Slow down; you're breathing too fast. You'll get a heart attack at the rate you're going. What's happened?"

"I received a telephone from Eva at my office. The news was so upsetting that I came home right away."

"Jakob, what is it?"

Slowly, Jakob is able to catch his breath and begin to speak. "It's David. They've taken him away."

"Who are 'they' and where have they taken him?" asks Lusia.

"The Nazis. Apparently they've arrested him. Yesterday, a plainclothes detective came to their apartment early in the morning. Samuel was about to go out on his way to school when the man knocked on the door. Without so much as a thought, Samuel opened the door. The man asked for David and Samuel. He handed Samuel a note requesting that he and his father appear at the police station yesterday morning at eleven a.m. to answer some questions."

"What sort of questions would the police want to ask David?" sighs Lusia.

"Eva did not know what the police might possibly want with him," says Jakob.

"So what happened?" asks Lusia.

"Eva says that Samuel offered to go to the police station later on in the day after school." Jakob has a look of anguish on his face. "The detective crossed his name off the list and said he didn't have to go. He told Samuel something along the lines that he would just arrest the next person down on his list to take Samuel's place. Then the detective let Samuel go to school, but David left for the police station just before eleven. Eva questioned him, asking whether or not he should go. In the end, David insisted on going. He took off his wristwatch, handed it over to Eva for safekeeping just so that it would not fall into the hands of the Nazis. He turned and walked out the door. Eva hasn't heard from him since. She's scared, Lusia. She doesn't know what they've done with her husband. She's too afraid to go to the police station to find out what's become of him."

"How awful for Eva," sighs Lusia.

"The very same thing could happen to us at any time," says Jakob. "These are not easy times for us, Lusia. I knew it wasn't a good thing when Hitler's troops marched into Vienna back in March. Hitler in his motorcade, everyone cheering. I told David a long time ago it could happen. He was afraid, too, but I knew it would not be a good thing for us if Hitler came marching into Austria. We had our discussions. But now with this, I fear it may be too late for my brother."

"What will Eva do?" asks Lusia.

"I suppose we'll have to help her out, perhaps support her, but I don't know how we can help her find out what's become of David," sighs Jakob.

"What about Samuel and Elsa?" asks Lusia.

Jakob continues. "So far, they're safe at home. Samuel went to school. When he returned home, he discovered that his father never returned home from the police station and has not been heard from since. Samuel is lucky. If that detective hadn't crossed his name off the list, he would be missing along with his father."

"Is the detective going to come back to Beheimgasse to get Samuel?" asks Lusia.

"I don't think so," affirms Jakob. "I think once he crossed his name off of his list that was that. I can't be sure about this, but that was what Eva has led me to believe."

"What will Eva do if David doesn't come home?" asks Lusia.

"There's no reason why he shouldn't come home," says Jakob. "There's no reason he should have been arrested in the first place."

"Why should he be detained? I don't understand. What he has done?" asks Lusia.

"I don't know. Eva doesn't know. She's at her wit's end," shrugs Jakob.

"I suppose we should go over to Beheimgasse to see what's going on for ourselves," offers Lusia.

Jakob adds. "At this point, I guess that all we can do for Eva is give her the comfort of our company."

CHAPTER 26

"SAMUEL'S ARREST"

New Haven, Connecticut   February, 1972

S hortly after dinner, just as I am about to begin work on my
history homework, my father comes over to me and says, "I've
never told you this before; I might as well tell you now."

Although I have a heavy load of homework this evening, reading up on the lords living in their manors with the serfs tilling
their soil during the middle ages, I can't pass up this chance to
hear about a part of my father's past he's never revealed to me
before.

"Yes, what is it?" I ask my father, not wanting to show him just
how pressed I am at the moment with multiple assignments.

"I know I have been reluctant to tell you things, but you might
as well know that I had a warrant for my arrest by the Nazis…"

"The Nazis wanted to arrest you?" I am stunned. This certainly is a subject my father usually does not discuss with me. "What
happened?"

My father begins slowly, showing very little emotion. "Well, early
one morning, shortly after the Anschluss, a plainclothes detective
came to the apartment. He wasn't expecting anyone to be at home

since it was so early in the morning. He had a letter in his hand with him that he was planning on just slipping under the door and leaving immediately, as quickly as he had arrived. He wasn't expecting to have any human contact; he was merely the messenger. The letter he was about to slip under the door was in fact an arrest warrant for my father and I. In fact, I was just about to step out the door to go to school for the day when the detective knocked. I opened the door quickly because I was standing right there, my book bag slung over my shoulder. The detective appeared startled when I opened the door."

I am taken aback. Up until this time, I had no idea that the Nazis had actually come to the door looking to arrest my father. Since my father's emotions appear to be at an even keel, I try to keep my emotions on an even keel, too. "So you surprised him rather than him surprising you?"

"Yes, I could tell that I had surprised him by the startled look on his face," my father continues, his facial expression continues to be one of eerie calm. "The plainclothes detective wasn't expecting any human contact; he was only supposed to slip the letter under the door. Once he realized my father and I were home, he began to engage us in conversation. He told us that my father and I were to appear at the local police station that morning at eleven a.m. Now that I was face to face with the detective, I began to talk to him freely. I told the detective that I was on my way to school and since I didn't want to miss my classes I could go to school in the morning and return to the police station later in the day. The detective looked me up and down and then told me that I could go to school and he would simply cross my name off his list. He told me it was just a matter of him having to fill his quota of the day and he would just contact the person whose name was next on the list. Because I was able to talk to the detective in person, I was able to talk my way out of appearing at the police station. The detective told me that my father could answer any questions on my behalf that they might have to ask me. I left for school. On the other hand, my father arrived at the police station at eleven a.m. He had no idea why he should be summoned to appear at the police station. My father had done nothing wrong, at least nothing that he knew of. He reasoned that if he did not show up, the police would think he had something to hide.

"When I returned from school later in the day, I asked my mother where my father was and if he had returned from the police station. My mother told me that he never returned home and was angry with him for insisting on showing up at the police station in the first place. Apparently, after I had left for school, my parents had had an argument over whether or not my father should appear at the police station. My mother had told him not to go, that there was no need. Since he had done nothing wrong, she believed that he must have been summoned by mistake. She didn't even want him to appear at the police station to correct whatever mistake the police must have made. My father knew he was innocent of any crime. On the other hand, he was adamant about appearing since they must have summoned him for some good reason. After all, his name did appear on the detective's list. He was afraid that if he did not show up, the police would come to the apartment house to get him. He didn't want any trouble in front of our tenants or lumberyard customers."

"Did your father ever return?" I ask, almost not wanting to hear the obvious answer.

"My father did not come home. He was gone. But I'll tell you some other time about that."

"So the Nazis never came for Omi or Elsa?"

"No, they never came to arrest my mother or my sister. At that point in time, they weren't interested in arresting females, only the males. Later on, it was a different story. It was only a matter of time before they arrested everyone in Vienna who was Jewish. But this was early on before they had come to a Final Solution, and at that point in time they were only interested in my father and I, not my mother or my sister."

"And the Nazis never came for you after that?"

"No, that was it. I avoided arrest with that one incident. In all the time my family remained in Vienna, the Nazis never came back for me. You have to remember that this was early on, before the Nazis began to transport the Jews en masse from their homes to the concentration camps. My family lived in the Seventeenth District where there were only a few Jews scattered about. It was not like the way it was in the First or Second District, where most of the Jews of Vienna lived. Later on, the Nazis brought trucks into those neighborhoods to transport the Jews. They would block each end of the street so that no one could get away. Then they would load up the trucks and transport away the Jews to the point of no return."

I look at my father with incredulity. "So what the plainclothes detective was calling a summons to appear at the local police station to answer some questions was really a guise for transportation to a concentration camp?"

"Yes. At the time, my mother could not understand why my father had been arrested. She reasoned that he had done nothing wrong. Later on, there were rumors in the neighborhood that he had been arrested for passing bad checks. The only problem was that he never had a checking account and paid for everything in cash. Since this was early on, the Nazis were very secretive of their agenda. They did not make it publicly known that their intent was to round up all the Jews of Vienna to take them to concentration camps. All that was known was that the Jews were being persecuted and discriminated against under Nazi rule."

"So had you known what the Nazis' agenda was, you would have wanted to flee, wouldn't you? You wouldn't want to stay and be taken away to a concentration camp."

"The Nazis were so secretive that when my father was arrested, we were unaware just how many other Jews were being arrested or how many Jews would be arrested in the future. We didn't understand why he should be arrested. All we knew was that he never returned home after he appeared at the police station that morning."

"How could the detective get away with fooling your father for him to fall for the trick?"

"It was the local Gestapo's way of arresting Jews at the time. They were trying to make it look like you might have done something wrong so you need to show up at the police station to answer questions. I suppose that if the Nazis had made it publicly known at the time that they were out to arrest all the Jews and transport them away, it might have caused panic. My father, being trained to obey authority, felt compelled to appear at the police station. In his mind, he had done nothing wrong and so saw nothing wrong with showing up. Since he was innocent of any crime, he thought he would just show up, answer the questions, and come home."

"It didn't occur to him that he would be arrested just for being a Jew?"

"No, because at the time, the Nazis weren't making that public. To answer your question, yes, the detective got away with tricking my father but only because he felt he was being obedient. And what choice did he have? Perhaps if he had not appeared on that day, the Nazis could have sent out a warrant for his arrest. So the only choice my father felt he had was to show up."

I am dumbfounded. I can't imagine why they would not want to arrest everyone in the family. I am amazed at my father's chutzpah. "I can't believe you talked your way out of having to appear at the police station. I don't know if I would have had the guts to talk back to the detective the way that you did. That must have taken a lot of courage."

I know I would not have been able to think on my feet like my father did. I wouldn't know how to talk back to a Nazi official just like that. I would have probably just skipped school and appeared at the police station, worried that they might come after me to arrest me for not showing up.

My father continues, "I suppose the courage came out of the air. It just came to me out of the blue to think on my feet and speak up to the detective. I can't imagine what would have happened if the detective had come when we were not at home, after I left for school, or if he just left the letter under the door. I would have followed the instructions on the letter and arrived at the police station at eleven. I would not have been able to talk the detective into crossing my name off his list. Circumstances could have been very different, and I would not be here today to tell you this story."

CHAPTER 27

"LET IT BE"

	The Herringbone Stitch
	The Light Green Thread
New Haven, Connecticut	February, 1972

"Let It Be" plays on the stereo as I sit on the living room couch. My feet are comfortably tucked beneath my body. The tablecloth is draped over my lap as I carefully examine the stitches of the tablecloth.

It's as if this lonely orphaned tablecloth needs me to complete it. It needs someone to take pity on it.

To care enough to take up stitching where my ancestor left off.

To complete this tablecloth would fill the void I feel in my own life.

The stitches fill me with a sense of purpose.

Where to begin?

Where shall I begin my stitches in the completion of the tablecloth? Do I start with the leaves? Simple stitches, really. Do I start with the connecting stitches? Even simpler stitches. Do I start with the star border? Much more complicated stitching. Do I start with the flowers? Quite intricate. If so, which ones? The larger ones?

138

The small ones? These are much simpler. Should I do the more intricate stitches first to get them out of the way? Or should I be much more logical and start with the simpler ones first to learn the ropes? And from these, go on to the more difficult ones?

Finally, after about ten minutes of careful consideration, I choose to start with a group of leaves over on one corner of the tablecloth. These leaves are created by embroidering one half in a herringbone stitch with dark green thread and the other half in a herringbone stitch in light green thread. These seem to be the easiest of all the stitches. I open a skein of the bright green floss with its two black and silver paper bands still intact. Pulling loose what I think is a sufficient length; I cut the thread and push the end through the eye of the needle. Carefully, I knot the end, but the knot seems ungainly. It's too large to be of any use, even if nobody will see it from the other side. I quickly take my scissors and cut it off.

My nerves are beginning to get the better of me. Suddenly, I'm beginning to have second thoughts.

Am I getting in over my head with this project, after all?

Using my fingers wrapped around two ends of thread, I create a new knot. I hope that this one will be just the right size. Reassured of my skills, I carefully place my mother's hoop from the china cabinet over to the spot where I need to begin to embroider. I pierce the white linen fabric with the needle for the very first time since the tablecloth had been packed away in the trunk all those years ago. Using my ancestor's luminous light green thread and her own stitches as my guide, I begin to follow the path of the pre-stamped design. Doing my best, I try to match her tight stitches of experience with my loose, immature ones.

In an instant, I realize that I don't have the same expertise. In an instant, there is no turning back. The needle is already through the cloth. I can't turn back. I can't decide that I don't want to complete this project, after all. Not after all the grief I gave my mother over wanting to dive in prematurely without even so much as learning the rudimentary embroidery stitches first.

My heart skips a beat.

Maybe my mother was right. After all, this is an ancient cloth, and I really have no business to just take a needle and thread and pierce the linen just like that without knowing what the heck I am doing. But I feel compelled to go back to the tablecloth and complete it. It makes me feel wanted, useful. It needs me to complete it, to make it whole. It needs me to right the wrongs of history, to complete what a relative had begun and could not live on to complete.

This will not bring her back.

But it will make me feel whole.

I have come to view the tablecloth as a sort of friend. Unlike a friend from school who might criticize me or not accept me for what I'm wearing or what I believe, the tablecloth is an inanimate object which does not judge.

It accepts me for what I am.

Stitching with the bright green floss, I pull the thread taut against the white linen. My mind begins to wander. I begin to put myself back in Vienna. Not the Vienna of Hitler, but from the time before, back when life was simple. Back to the city of Strauss waltzes.

I open my eyes, pick up the needle with its leafy green thread, and proceed to pierce the cloth once again. Is this piercing an act of violence or an act of creation? I decide that it takes the painful act of piercing for an act of creation to take place. I also realize that to create beauty, one must go through an act of boring repetition, but the reward at the end is worth it. There is something soothing about piercing the cloth and leaving a mark of thread that will eventually become a pattern. In this case, it will be a leaf.

How could I ever really get to know the woman who had created the first half of this tablecloth? Who was she? As if to interlink our generations through this thread would get me closer to her. No matter how hard I might try, no matter how much detail my father could ever tell me about her, how could I ever get to know her?

Let It Be repeats in my mind. But I don't want to let it be. I want my answers. I want my words of wisdom.

By opening up the trunk, one question has been answered. What had the trunk contained?

The question now remains: Just who was this "woman of the trunk" and who had her husband been? And just how had these people been related to me? I knew that the answers to this mystery were still locked up inside my father's head. It's a simple matter, isn't it, just to ask?

Do I have the courage to ask him these delicate questions?

How do I go about asking the unaskable?

If I don't get up the nerve, I know that I will never know.

CHAPTER 28

"FASHION FORWARD"

The Herringbone Stitch
The Dark Green Thread

New Haven, Connecticut

February, 1972

I can't accessorize to save my life, but my sister can carry off any ensemble. She has the imagination to take different scarves, jewelry, belts, and pull it all together. Me? I just put on any old thing. Even if I added a scarf to an outfit, it would be the wrong color or a clashing print, and I wouldn't even realize it. I just can't pull it off.

As I pull the dark green thread for the other side of the leaves, I think about my ancestor's dresses. To my mother, they're just some old stuff from the trunk. Is clothing really unwearable just because it's outdated? Isn't fashion only a matter of perception, something dictated by some fashion magazine editor or some clothing designer?

But what's the purpose of those girdles? I'm too thin to have to worry about wearing a girdle to pull in my tummy. These girdles from the trunk have some hard material sewn inside them to keep flesh in its place. Are they wires? Animal bones? I can't say for sure.

I notice the initials "LS" embroidered on the girdles in blue thread. A clue, perhaps? At the moment, however, these initials do not register in my brain.

I pull the dark green thread taut for another herringbone stitch. I don't get the concept of foundation garments. It baffles me! My mother wears a rubber girdle to pull in her stomach on special occasions. All this to look just a few pounds slimmer. Mom says the rubber of the girdle gets all hot and sweaty around her stomach. That adds to weight loss without having to exercise. Maybe if I were a middle-aged woman and overweight, I might need a foundation garment to tuck in my tummy.

Tying a knot for a second finished leaf, I wonder is it worth it to feel uncomfortable in order to look good. What does the term, "foundation garments" really mean anyway? A woman isn't a house with a foundation, is she? Those women's liberationists are burning their bras at protest rallies. They're burning girdles as well. Now I'm beginning to understand why. Personally, I prefer comfort over appearance.

I pull the thread taut for another dark green half of a leaf. I think about how, if anything goes in fashion, then why do I feel so self-conscious at school? I stitch another herringbone stitch and think how I'm self-conscious about my very existence. Why am I here? Why am I here at all? My father is alive and here despite all the odds. My self-image as a teenager is based partly on how my ancestors were treated. Growing up in New England, the tweed capital of the world, where conformity is the conformity, I feel I stand out like a sore thumb.

But as far as I'm concerned, anything goes in fashion. Or at least it should. The rules for women's fashion are now relaxed. They've become so relaxed; in fact, that sometimes it's hard to tell what is in fashion anymore. It seems as though any clothing worn is acceptable, like the song, "Everything Is Beautiful in its Own Way," every piece of clothing worn is beautiful in its own way. Even worn and tattered jeans.

Having finished some of the leaves, I still have many more to go. I am dismayed to discover that I've run out of the dark green thread, leaving half-finished leaves behind in my wake.

CHAPTER 29
"FASHION FORWARD"

Hardtmuthgasse 10   Vienna, May, 1938

With every chime of the Ankeruhr, the Nazis gain more and more momentum. As the citizens of Vienna gather in the streets to watch the passing pageantry, Lusia becomes more and more anxious. She is impressed by the sights and sounds of the marching soldiers and all the red and white striped banners with dark black swastikas in the center flying freely from all the tall buildings. Even the Votivkirche, the medieval church with its double spires that stands near the *Rathaus*, the city hall, is emblazoned with these evil banners.

The Ankeruhr continues on chiming the hours, playing joyful music in tribute to Austria's past. The area around this antique clock is the traditional Jewish quarter of Vienna. Standing at the heart of Vienna's Ring, the Judenplatz has been the center of Jewish life since the twelfth century. Now the very existence of the Jewish populace is being threatened. Beneath the street of this square lie ruins of city streets from Roman times when Vienna was called Vindobona. The outpost of Vindobona was Galicia, where present-day Sniatyn is located. Linking the two locations back to ancient times.

As she walks the narrow streets to Frau Ingber's atelier, Lusia questions her rationale for being fitted for a new dress. After all, David has been arrested by the Nazis and taken away to places unknown. The crowds in the street are beginning to intimidate her. On the surface it appears as though a celebration is going on. What holiday is this?

Like birds of prey gathering on the utility wires, the Nazis gather, poised to pounce and dart to pluck their plunder from the Jews. The government has made the theft of property of this particular religious group totally legal.

Firm in her decision to go ahead with her fitting, Lusia holds her head high as she walks toward the Renngasse. Innocently living her own life with her own fashion concerns, she balances her life between the current political climate and concerns for her personal appearance.

Lusia turns the corner, walking away from the direction of the crowds. Without the visual reminders of Nazi occupation, Lusia's thoughts return to her own figure and the girdle she is wearing. The girdle controls her figure; it tucks her tummy in so that she doesn't have to walk around consciously sucking in her stomach muscles at all times. Her undergarment has become a constant companion of sorts. Like a security blanket, it surrounds her, comforts her. It reassures her that her figure is now perfect even though it takes a little help. This sort of reassurance is something she needs in these troubling days.

Is it worth it for all this discomfort? Lusia asks herself. At the same time, she is grateful for her girdle on which she has lovingly embroidered her initials into a corner.

To the casual observer, Lusia is the image of grace, of fashion without care. As with any other woman of Vienna, she is no different in her concerns over her appearance. After all, rigid rules for appearance apply here in this city. She can't break from these rules now. She needs a new dress for spring, and she makes it her point to be fitted by Frau Ingber today. A Nazi rally can't deter her from her fashion regimen.

Finally reaching the Renngasse, Lusia takes the elevator up to the third floor.

"Good afternoon, Lusia," smiles Frau Ingber. "Ready to be fitted for a new dress?"

"Yes, Frau Ingber," Lusia sighs, not wishing to reveal what she is really thinking about are the rallies she has passed on her walk to the seamstress. She feels cocooned, safe, in Frau Ingber's neighborhood. After all, she has been coming to her atelier ever since she and Jakob were married and had moved to Vienna.

"How are things?" asks Lusia's seamstress and confidant for so many years.

"Things could be better."

"What's wrong?"

"How am I supposed to think about fashion at a time like this?"

The seamstress offers s façade of pleasantness. "My dear, having a new dress made for you can take your mind off any problem. What is it?"

"It's just that my brother-in-law has been arrested and taken away to parts unknown."

"Oh, I see. Well, who knows, maybe it's too soon to tell. Perhaps he will be released and returned sooner than you think."

"But we don't know when David will return. We don't know when David will return. We don't know why he's been arrested."

"He's Jewish, isn't he?"

"Yes, but why should he be arrested for that? He's done nothing wrong."

"He's Jewish, that's all that matters to the Nazis. Maybe he'll be coming home any day now.

Who knows? In the meantime, go about your daily life. Dress up."

"I suppose you're right. Silly to fret. Who knows what tomorrow will bring?"

"Maybe the news will be better tomorrow."

"All I know is that Helen Neckar, the daughter of one of David's tenants, has been telling everyone in the neighborhood that the Jews are our misfortune. Even though her landlords are Jewish, she still says these things. Imagine that?"

"Oh, I can well imagine. Believe me, I've heard it all," sighs the seamstress.

"I suppose that Jakob and I must leave Vienna once we feel too uncomfortable living here."

"I think that's what the Nazis are trying to do. They're trying to make us all uncomfortable so that we will all want to leave. Where do you suppose you will go?"

"We're not sure yet. Maybe England. Maybe Belgium," shrugs Lusia.

"How soon will you be leaving?"

"We don't know yet, but Jakob and I have discussed possible plans. Once we've decided where we'll be going, I suppose we'll have a better idea when we'll leave."

"I'll miss you. You've been coming to me all these years now. We've shared events in our lives. It's such a shame that we will have to part our ways." Frau Ingber forces a smile.

"I'll miss you, too."

"I suppose it's only a matter of time before I'll be packing up and leaving, too."

"Where would you go?"

"Much of my family live in Germany. But since it got too uncomfortable for them there, many went to Switzerland, some went to America. I suppose I could go to either place," affirms Frau Ingber.

"Switzerland, now there's one place we haven't considered."

"For me, Switzerland seems the safest bet. So far, they're remaining neutral."

"Sounds like a good place to go."

"Have you and your husband ever thought of going to America?" asks Frau Ingber.

"Not at all. That's so far away. On the other side of the Atlantic. We know no one there. We'd be totally lost. Better to stay closer to home somewhere in Europe. Somewhere safe from the Nazis"

"You said you were considering Belgium."

"Yes, we're seriously considering Antwerp."

"Why Antwerp?" asks the seamstress.

"Because there's a large Jewish population there. We'll be in familiar territory. There's safety in numbers."

"Do you know anyone there? Any relatives?" asks the seamstress.

"No, but my cousin has a friend there who's a diamond dealer."

"Yes, yes, it is the center for diamonds, isn't it? Well, good luck wherever you go."

Tears begin to run down Lusia's face. "I feel so uncomfortable just walking in the streets. Jews are being treated as though we're less than human."

"That's all part of it. They just want us to leave. They don't want us living among them anymore," sighs Frau Ingber.

"I've overhead people saying things like 'do they eat?' or 'they're not like us.' People in the streets stare at us Jews like we're monsters. It makes me feel so uncomfortable. And if that's their intent, they're doing a marvelous job." Lusia forces herself to smile despite her discomfort.

Back at Hardtmuthgasse, Lusia pulls the dark green thread taut for the herringbone stitch for half a leaf that goes with a large purple flower. To her, embroidery is as easy as breathing. Like second nature to her. She's been doing it for so long, each stitch comes out perfectly every time. As she trims the thread, she thinks about knots. To her, knots have never been something she's found difficult to handle. Sometimes she even thinks of them as bringers of good luck.

Wishing for luck on this knot, it should grant Jakob good luck for the safe return of his brother. With so many knots on this tablecloth, at least one of them should do the trick.

As Lusia stitches, she looks forward to the day when Jakob will walk through the door of the apartment and she will say, "Surprise me with the good news. Has David returned?" And the answer will be "yes."

Every knot a wish.

Every wish a knot.

Every prayer a stitch.

Every stitch a prayer.

CHAPTER 30

"REVEALED"

The Lazy Daisy Stitch
The Yellow Thread
February, 1972

H aving finished with the leaves, I begin to work on the large yellow flowers which require that I learn the Lazy Daisy stitch. Turning to page sixteen of Coats and Clarks' *One Hundred Embroidery Stitches*, I note that each petal of the flower is created with a loop and stitch in the center to fasten it against the cloth, creating the appearance of the petal of a flower. I take the embroidery hoop, loosen the screw, and place it over the section of flowers closest to the finished half of the tablecloth.

Sitting on the couch in the living room, my thread and needle are poised for the plunge of my first Lazy Daisy stitch. I smile at my childhood notion that the trunk was a pirate's treasure chest. All those times we played dress-up and danced around it. We'd even added icons of buried treasure with a hand-drawn skull and crossbones banner and a treasure map with an X marking the spot.

The act of piercing the cloth emboldens me.

Using the existing stitches of my ancestor as my guide, I finish my very first of the large flowers. I knot the end of the yellow thread, feeling the satisfaction of completing even this minor task, knowing that these are my first steps towards the completion of the tablecloth. I find just the right spot for the next yellow flower and gently remove the wooden hoop to relocate it to the next location.

Knotting the end of the new yellow thread, I pierce the linen to embroider the next flower. Lazy Daisy. Lazy Daisy. Knot, Another large yellow flower is finished.

And still, the mystery and clues behind the trunk and its owners remain locked tightly away in my father's head. Except for that one clue: "LS" embroidered on the girdle in blue thread.

⚔

Just who had been the trunk's owners?

As I move the embroidery hoop back to the first flower patch, my mind wanders back to the family photograph my father had shown us. Nimbly, I thread the yellow floss through the eye of the needle to begin a Lazy Daisy stitch for another large flower.

Seated on a living room couch with the tablecloth draped across my lap, I get enough nerve to ask my father.

"Who owned the trunk?" I blurt out. I hold my breath and hope against hope that my father won't get too angry at me for trying to dig deeper.

Suddenly, he appears withdrawn. He leans back in his armchair.

I continue. "It wasn't Genia from Sniatyn, the woman whom Etka had spoken about, the one in the photograph?"

"No."

"It wasn't that other woman in the photograph, the one with the two little children standing on either side of her, was it?"

"No, that woman was Chajce, and no, she isn't the one, either."

"Then who was it who owned the trunk?"

My father begins to speak very slowly. He takes a deep breath and then continues. "I've never spoken about them before. Their names were Tante Lusia and Onkel Jakob. They were my closest relatives when I was growing up in Vienna. Onkel Jakob was my father's brother. He's the man standing in the back row of the photograph, the one on the extreme left with the mustache and the striped tie. Like my father, Onkel Jakob, too, was a lumber merchant. Like Tante Genia, Lusia was a native of Stanislau, Poland. She and Onkel Jakob were married in 1924 in Stanislau and had their wedding reception at the social hall there. As with other marriages in my family, including my own parents, this one too, had been arranged through a *shidduch,* a match made through a *shadchan,* a matchmaker. After the wedding, my aunt and uncle moved into the apartment on the first floor at Beheimgasse 21. They lived there for many years before moving to a new apartment on Hardtmuthgasse in the Tenth District so that Onkel Jakob could be closer to his own lumberyard. Unfortunately, Lusia was never able to have children. They tried for many years, but to no avail. At one point in time, they had the notion to take in Muniu, Chajce's son who lived in Sniatyn. They were going to have him move to Vienna to live with them so that they could raise him and send him to school. He is the little boy wearing a white shirt who appears on the right-hand side of the photograph. He was very young and Chajce probably was hesitant to send her son so far away from home. For whatever reason, their plans fell through. Muniu was still quite young when the Nazis invaded Poland.

"If you must know, the contents of the trunk come from the apartment on Hardtmuthgasse. They lived at Hardtmuthgasse 10."

Tante Lusia!

Tante Lusia!! That's the name of the woman whose very stitches I am now using to guide me. "LS" Lusia Spielvogel!! Now I have the name to go with the tablecloth, but I don't have a face to go with that name, do I?

"She isn't in the family photograph is she?

"No, she isn't," sighs my father.

"Why not?"

"She never went to Sniatyn for the funeral of my grandmother, the occasion for which the photograph was taken. For one reason or other, she stayed behind in Vienna."

I momentarily put down the yellow thread. I had been sitting in the same position for some time and now need to stretch out my arms. I look up at my father. He appears sullen, withdrawn as usual.

There are so many more questions that I need answered. One among them: If Tante Lusia and Onkel Jakob packed the trunk in an effort to escape from Vienna, what happened to them? Were they actually able to escape, and if so, why hadn't they survived?

For now, I am satisfied with simply having a name to attach to the contents of the trunk. I must make do with the knowledge that I will never have a face to go with that name. But at least it's a start to my knowing about her.

I thread the needle with more yellow thread and begin to feel as though Lusia's spirit might possess me as I pull the thread taut. I could only wish that her spirit could help guide me with her stitches.

Lazy Daisy. Lazy Daisy. Knot. A large yellow flower.

Could the spirit of the former wearer is trapped inside the red and green dress? Someone told me that in Japan, they don't like to wear second-hand clothing because they believe that the spirit of the former wearer is trapped in the cloth. I'm not sure I believe this to be true, but I'm starting to feel a connection to Lusia in my own way.

Threading some more yellow floss through the eye of the needle for yet another large flower, and realize just how tricky embroidery is. After all, somewhere at the end of this thread, there's a needle with a really sharp point.

As I sit on the couch to embroider, I bend my knees under my body. The position creates tension on the knees of my jeans. Looking down, I notice the left knee of my new jeans is now beginning to tear even more. To preserve my pants for a little while longer, I decide to wear the red and green dress as I embroider.

I go upstairs to my room to change. As I tie the matching belt around my waist, I think about the woman who had once worn this dress. I am at such a loss, thinking I will never ever truly get to know her! I trudge back downstairs where I take my position back on the couch. I take up some of the orange thread from the trunk and proceed to stitch up the knee to bridge the ever widening gap in the denim. It occurs to me that if I have to keep stitching up my pants at this rate, they will begin to look like Frankenstein's jeans. But at least they'll still be wearable!

Just knowing Lusia's name makes me feel better. As though by knowing her name makes her a complete human. Without knowing that fact, she would have remained a missing person. Giving her a name gives her an identity.

What sort of person was Tante Lusia? Was she happy with her life? What things did she find important? Was she happy before she had to leave Vienna?

Lazy Daisy. Lazy Daisy. Knot. A large yellow flower.

I push the needle with the yellow thread into the cloth for my last flower of this color. My side of the tablecloth is beginning to look almost decent. I am proud that I have the courage to attempt to stitch as well as Tante Lusia, although I know that my stitches will never in a million years compare to hers. From the number of pieces from the trunk, I can tell that she must have spent much of her adult life embroidering.

I am beginning to find the act of embroidery relaxing, although I must admit that at first I was quite nervous. As much as I was putting up a bold front for my mother, I was truly terrified when I first pierced the cloth with the needle.

Following along the same design path stamped faintly in blue ink that Tante Lusia had once stitched, I realized these are the traces of her life she left behind in stitches. If only she could have lived on and come to America to transfer her embroidery skills to me.

I know she is still here with me, if only in spirit, to guide my stitches.

Once again, I stick my thumb with the needle!

My bravado does not allow for a thimble. It's maddening! Yet, I'm determined to persist.

Without Lusia herself present, how could I ever come to know her except through her clothing and her stitches? As though I can reach a spiritual connection through her thread, which now links my life to hers.

CHAPTER 31

"CROCODILE ROCK"

The Lazy Daisy Stitch
The Purple Thread

New Haven, Connecticut   February, 1972

E lton John sings "Crocodile Rock" on the radio as I pull the thread taut for one of the large purple flowers. My mother's four tribal elders stare down at me from the built-in shelves in the living room. They're the wooden statues she'd snagged from the furrier as a bribe to get her to agree with her mother to purchase the leopard jacket. They came in the shipment from Africa along with the furs, and since the furrier only dealt in furs, he had no use for the sculptures. The four of them have their own distinct personalities. I look up to them for answers. They stare back down at me from the shelf, their blank expressions all too blatant. Maybe they'd just rather keep it all to themselves at this moment.

Continuing the Lazy Daisy stitch with the purple thread, I think about how my sense of identity is seemingly changing. The ghosts of the previous generation are all that I have left to connect with my family. Yes, there was a break with the past, but slowly, slowly, as I embroider these large purple flowers with the Lazy Daisy stitch,

I have gone from feeling a break in the strand to a feeling of connectedness. By continuing on with the embroidery of her tablecloth, I am giving a life and a voice to Tante Lusia. A voice I know she could never have had in life.

Early on, I had been discouraged by my lopsided stitches. I felt I'd never be an accomplished enough embroiderer to finish Lusia's tablecloth. Now I'm beginning to feel more worthy and up to the challenge.

I pull the purple thread taut for another large purple flower, and I think about how my artworks are my own original conceptions. Unlike my other endeavors, the tablecloth has a pre- set design for me to follow. I normally start from scratch for all my own artwork, but I appreciated having Lusia's stitches here to guide me. I can tell that the tablecloth had come with a pre-stamped design. Here I am, following the same path Lusia had once followed.

I contemplate the Lazy Daisy stitch; even the name, "Lazy" connotes artless or art without effort. Art without thinking because someone else has thought up the original concept for you. It takes a certain amount of imagination to come up with an original design. And a certain amount of talent to complete art from a kit. It's a different sort of talent. One is cerebral, the other is good hand—eye coordination.

Despite all the time I've taken doing my own artwork and working with my hands, I was not ready to do embroidery. To be honest, after all the stitches I've stitched since I began working on Lusia's tablecloth, my abilities remain mediocre. I was so eager at first to weave Lusia's threads into my life. My rebelliousness had gotten the better of me. My refusal to have my mother teach me the stitches and have me practice some more has taken its toll on my completion of the tablecloth. My cross-stitches are lopsided. My leaves overlap. My Lazy Daisy petals are wilting. I thought I could just teach myself and just jump in and embroider. It's not as easy as it had once looked!

I look back up at the four tribal elders on the shelf. Their expressions seemingly have changed. Must be a trick of the light. Their expressions no longer blank now seem to have slight smiles as if to show approval of my endeavors.

Had it not been for the trunk as a starting point, my father could have kept Tante Lusia and Onkel Jakob's existence a complete secret. But the trunk was far too large an object to hide!

Over time, I hope to learn even more about them and about the others. The ghosts who haunt my father every day of his life must be restored to us as revered and remembered relatives.

CHAPTER 32

"SUPERSTITION"

Hardtmuthgasse 10   Vienna, June, 1938

Lusia wishes she could magically change David's current situation as simply as she changes radio stations. After one month, Eva has not heard a single word from her husband.

No one knows where he has gone.

All of Joachim's superstitious beliefs about the evil eye will not help bring David back home to his family. Or make the Nazis leave Vienna.

Lusia is at wit's end to grasp onto something of meaning. Something that will help her through the current situation.

She goes back to the couch to continue to embroider on her new tablecloth, taking the pink thread she begins to make a stitch.

Lazy Daisy. Lazy Daisy. Knot. A large pink flower.

Once again, Lusia finds solace in the stitching of her flowers.

The thought of Joachim's insistence that everyone who comes to visit his home carry a clove of garlic in their pockets to ward off the 'evil eye' makes Lusia giggle.

Lazy Daisy. Lazy Daisy. Knot. A large yellow flower.

As she embroiders another large yellow flower, this practice of carrying garlic strikes Lusia as funny all of a sudden, even though the Nazi occupation of Vienna is no laughing matter. All her life, loved ones around her have held onto this superstition. Even her grandmother back in Stanislau believed in it. At this moment, in this modern day, she can't understand how such a belief can persist. Despite all the technology that surrounds her in this city—telephones, automobiles, radios; all these things that connect people to one another at a rapid pace--people can still cling to a notion that a clove of garlic can protect a person from evil. No longer in the *shtetl*, a tightly knit community where such presumptions are widely acceptable, she still encounters such beliefs even in Vienna. Even her dressmaker Frau Ingber had once mentioned to Lusia her own personal belief in this practice.

A clove of garlic for protection! Hah!

Evil Eye! Hah!

Lusia's mood grows more serious as she thinks of the current political climate marching on just beneath her corner window.

How can a clove of garlic protect me from the Nazis? How can that protect me from all those who hate me?

Lazy Daisy. Lazy Daisy. Knot. A large yellow flower.

Lusia ponders the idea of cause and effect. According to *shtetl* superstitions, bad events were caused by those who would curse you. If Lusia had to extend this logic, the Nazis are brought about by someone's curse; The Nazis are the evil eye incarnate.

Lusia thinks of the superstitions about buttons her mother used to tell her about back in Stanislau. She'd told her that a person couldn't have a button sewn back on while wearing a shirt because then their wisdom would be sewn on and they'd never be able to get it back. And if someone passed a chimney sweep on the street, it was considered good luck, and if you quickly touched a button on your clothing, your wish will come true.

A wish will come true.

Lusia's wishes for a family were all dashed. She had relied on modern science to make a miracle. Suddenly, she thinks she should have wished on a button. Or some other such nonsense from the *shtetl*.

These superstitions are irrational. They don't make a bit of sense. It may have made sense to my grandmother and to my father-in-law, but it doesn't make sense to me now.

For Lusia, wishing on a knot is a superstition of her own making.

To hold a needle and thread in her hand is something concrete. Not the meanderings of the superstitious minds of the past that might link an irrational cause with an effect. If I spill the salt, then something bad will happen. To Lusia, embroidery is something real, something solid. No hocus pocus here. Just the immediate satisfaction of creation. Embroidery is her own way of meditation, taking her mind off the troubles in her marriage. And the troubles now in the world just below her goldenrod curtains.

Lusia gazes at her stitches and wonders to herself. A simple act of a few strategically placed stitches when put together has created a thing of beauty. A thing of peace. How can the ugliness of the Nazis go on around her? How can such ugliness have infiltrated her own family? It has been four weeks and still no word of David's whereabouts.

Do we even know if David is still alive?

Lusia pulls hard on her yellow thread in an attempt to put that thought out of her mind. As if to pull hard on the thread can remove a thought.

No, he can't be dead. He just can't?

She pushes the needle back through the linen cloth, pushing back her tears. Neither she nor Jakob have uttered the name, "David," since the time of his disappearance. Not since the day of his last known whereabouts at the school at Karajangasse 14.

Lazy Daisy. Lazy Daisy. Knot. A beautiful yellow flower.

A thing of beauty.

A thing of peace.

A feeling of connection to all the other souls like herself who seek comfort in the repetitive act of embroidery. And all those who seek solace in the thread.

The thread of her own existence.

Creating images stitched in cloth to last beyond her lifetime.

CHAPTER 33

"SUPERSTITION"

New Haven, Connecticut

S tevie Wonder sings "Superstition" on the radio as I think to myself. *What do I do for good luck?*

A rabbit's foot? A horse shoe? A four-leaf clover?'

I turn the screw of the embroidery hoop taut to begin working on the large light blue flowers. I loop the light blue thread for the Lazy Daisy stitch as my mind wanders to thoughts about a book I've read called *Superstitious, Here's Why*. It gives historical reasons why people are superstitious about standing under ladders, black cats, broken mirrors and rabbits' feet. Ever since I was in Fifth Grade, I've always had a four leaf clover charm on a keychain for good luck dangling off my purse. Every time I change my purse, I dangle my keychain off the new one. I bought my good luck charm at Jackson Marvin hardware store in New Haven. The four leaf clover charm keychains were displayed on a cardboard square, painted in various colors: green, red, blue, and white. I'd chosen the basic green model. I've never really questioned why I do this particular practice or even why people think a four leaf clover can carry good luck in the first place. But I have no doubt that I'm guarded from bad luck!

What do I expect from luck? Good grades on tests? That people will like me? That I will be protected from harm at home or when I'm traveling? That I will be successful and earn lots of money?

I hold on to this unwavering notion that whatever good luck charm I carry will bring me only good fortune. There is no disputation in my mind that the charm will bring me luck. While I bank on my lucky four leaf clover, my American grandmother swears by her collection of lucky elephants. She insists that all her elephants must have their trunks facing up. Without a doubt in her mind, if the elephant's trunk is down turned, it will not bring luck. Are they not good luck because their trunks are facing down? Or do they carry bad luck because their trunks are down? Whenever we have given her an elephant statuette for her collection and if the trunk is facing down, she will actually give it back to us. All that I do know is that my grandmother does not want to court trouble by bringing these downward-trunked pachyderms into her home. So far, we've given her elephants made of glass, alabaster onyx, rosewood, and ivory (how ironic!), and even smoky topaz. All with their trunks up, mind you.

My father had mentioned to me that his grandfather, Joachim, had insisted that he put cloves of garlic in his pocket whenever he went to visit him in Sniatyn to ward off the evil eye. Apparently, my great-grandfather was adamant about this. He believed with great certainty that garlic was a tried and true protective device against evil.

My mother told me about the trip to Israel she'd taken in the early 1950s with my father shortly after they were married. She was told by a guide that the color turquoise protects against the evil eye. In Jerusalem, there are houses that had shades facing east painted turquoise for protection. She also told me about *chamsas,* "mystic hands," and how a small turquoise stone in the center is supposed to protect against evil.

The more I try to fend off any feelings these notions are outdated, the more I'm convinced there is truth to the effectiveness of good luck charms. Who can argue with the results? The more I carry my charms, the better my luck has been. Can't just shrug that off as coincidence, can I? I'm a modern person, why should I fall back on an old-fashioned superstitious belief? No matter how hard I try, my rational mind keeps going back to the notion that I need a good luck charm to help me through my life, in school, or in social situations. I've come to realize I can't shake the notion these charms actually work. I don't want to risk it by going through life unprotected. As irrational as that might sound. Too many people around the world believe in good luck charms and have held this belief for many centuries. If the rest of mankind can hold the notion that some inanimate object hanging off a chain can change a person's fortune, so can I. Since I don't know what the future holds, I might as well stock up on all the good luck charms I can for protection.

I turn the silver screw tight against the linen at the closest flower patch to where Tante Lusia had left off. I begin the Lazy Daisy stitch for the first of the large light blue flowers. Stevie Wonder's lyrics echo in my brain as I stitch.

Lazy Daisy. Lazy Daisy. Knot. A large light blue flower.

After finishing the blue flower, I undo the silver screw of the hoop and gently move it over to the next flower patch. I push some more light blue thread through the eye of the needle and knot the end.

As I pierce the linen with the needle holding the light blue thread for the next large flower, I can only imagine what my great-grandfather, Joachim, might have thought had he lived long enough to see his descendants living in modern-day Connecticut. I'm sure that he wouldn't have approved of my American upbringing, and I suspect that my father may be all too self-conscious of this notion. Joachim would probably have had a fit if he could have seen his great- granddaughters in America wearing blue jeans. He probably never in his life left the *shtetl* and probably never saw a female wearing pants!

⊷ ⊶

Lazy Daisy. Lazy Daisy. Knot. A large light blue flower.

I gaze into the flower I've just finished and wonder about my grandmother's side of the family and wonder if they were equally as affected as my grandfather's side had been. After all, my grandmother is still alive and living in Vienna. Her sister, Mali, is still alive and living in Lyon, France, with her husband. What could possibly have happened to that side of the family if my grandmother and her sister are both still alive?

My father comes over and sits on the couch opposite where I am sitting. I look up at him to see a thoughtful look cross his face.

I take a deep breath. "Did anything bad happen on Omi's side of the family? Omi is still alive, after all."

"I suppose I should have told you about my mother's side of the family a long time ago. They were the Handels. My grandfather, Hertzel lived in Sniatyn with his wife, Perel. He was a grain merchant and sold his grain every Tuesday at the market in the center of Sniatyn. He stored the grain in giant vats in the basement of his house. You know very well about your grandmother in Vienna and you know that her sister, Mali, now lives in Lyon. But what I've never told you before was that my mother also had two brothers."

"Well, I've always thought that Omi came from a family of two sisters."

"The reality is that it was a family of four children…"

"So what happened to the brothers?"

"One of my mother's brothers was named Rachmiel. He lived in Sniatyn. His wife was named Batsche. They had two sons named Willie and Moische. Unfortunately, all of them perished."

I stare at my father in disbelief. "Do you mean to tell me that an entire family of four was wiped out and I never even knew about them?"

"Yes, unfortunately, none of them survived the Nazis."

I sit there, stunned, fully realizing that had this family lived, it's possible that they could have eventually come to America; that I could have had more cousins my own age. Last November, I was bemoaning the fact that I had no cousins nearby to come to a birthday party, and here was a family with children who could have lived on to have children of my generation. Suddenly, having a cousin at a birthday party seems like a minor thing compared to not having a whole generation of cousins not existing on this earth.

I regain my composure. "And what of her other brother?"

"My mother's other brother was named Yankele. He lived in Vienna in the Second District on Wipplingerstrasse with his wife, Hertha. He was a shoe wholesaler. I remember one Passover going with him to get a new pair of shoes. Hertha was a seamstress; she sewed women's dresses for a living."

I raise my eyebrows. "She sewed dresses? She wasn't the person who sewed the dresses form the trunk, was she?"

"No, those were sewn by someone else."

"Did Hertha and Yankele have any children?

"No, they didn't."

The light blue thread suddenly begins to bunch up as I try to pull it taut. Can I unknot it without my father noticing? I don't wish to appear inept in front of him. My mother had cautioned me from starting this project in the first place. And here I am, I've come to a knot. Finally, the thread comes untangled. I pull the thread taut. How unlucky!

Knot, what knot? I ask myself.

I begin to develop my own superstitious beliefs about knots. If they don't come out just right, I'm convinced that I'll have a bad day. If they come out perfectly, then it will be a good day.

I regain my composure and begin to embroider again. I go to change hoop positions, but the silver screw is stuck. I sit meddling with it, hoping to get it to budge. Finally, it turns. I change the location.

Lazy Daisy. Lazy Daisy. Knot. A large light blue flower.

I think about the correlation between superstitions and events and can see where someone might jump to the conclusion that if one thing happens, it will cause something else to occur. Superstition is nothing more than cause and effect. Even if the effect was totally unrelated to the cause. We have the technology to put a man on the moon, and yet we still can believe that a horseshoe can bring good luck.

Lazy Daisy. Lazy Daisy. Knot. I finish the last of the large light blue flowers and wonder just where all these superstitions come from.

CHAPTER 34
"DACHAU"

Hardtmuthgasse 10   Vienna, June, 1938

"Eva has finally received a postcard from David," a mildly relieved Jakob tells Lusia as he enters the apartment, his old fears alleviated now that his brother's whereabouts are no longer a mystery. David's location, on the other hand, is what is now problematic to Jakob.

"Where is he?" asks Lusia dressed, in her red dressing gown. It is obvious by the look on her face that she, too, is relieved.

"He's in Dachau."

Lusia gazes at her husband in dismay. "Dachau?" The expression on her face turns to one of perplexity.

Jakob's face is stone. "Yes, now at least we know where my brother is." His icy appearance intimidates Lusia.

"What sort of place is Dachau?"

"I'm not quite sure, but it's where they're taking all the Jews from David's neighborhood," says Jakob.

"All the Jews?" Lusia is even more confused than before. "When did she get this postcard?"

"Just yesterday," shrugs Jakob.

Lusia furrows her brow, confused as to the true nature of just what is really going on. "But what is this place?"

Jakob sighs. He finally takes off his jacket. "I believe it's some sort of resettlement camp."

"But I don't understand why David was arrested in the first place," says Lusia. Eva told me of rumors being spread in the neighborhood that David had been passing bad checks."

"Who would say such a thing about my brother?" asks Jakob.

"I believe Eva said she overheard the Brinskys spreading these lies," sighs Lusia. "David couldn't possibly have passed bad checks; he doesn't even have a checking account at the bank.

He always pays for everything in cash."

"The same person who had forced my brother to clean his sidewalk and wash his car in front of his Gaststube," says Jakob.

"Yes, he's the one and the same Brinsky," shrugs Lusia. "According to Eva, he's been telling everyone in the neighborhood all this time that David had been taken to Dachau."

"But how would he have known that?" asks Jakob.

"Your guess is as good as mine," sighs Lusia.

"Why should he know more than anyone, unless he was behind it in some way? And why should David have been taken to a resettlement camp anyway?" asks Jakob.

"Eva will have to find these things out," says Lusia. "She told me that she plans to write a letter to Gestapo Headquarters at the Hotel Metropol now that she knows where David had been taken."

"What will she say in her letter?" asks Jakob.

Lusia lets out a breath. "She plans to write a request that David be released immediately since there appears to be no reason why he should be detained."

Lusia just wished things could go back to the way they were before the day David was arrested. Back to the way things had always been.

Is that too much to wish for?

Lusia thinks to herself, *David's been taken away. Es tut mir leid! I've heard bad things about this place, this Dachau. I don't know if Eva knows how serious this situation is. What more can she do to get her husband home? So far as I know, she is trying everything she can-- she's writing letters; she wants to go to Gestapo Headquarters.*

All that we are left to do is pray. Pray? I suppose that's all we can do! Will it work? I don't wish for good luck, I just wish that things could go back to the way they were before.

And I pray that when the time comes, Jakob and I may make it out of Vienna safely.

CHAPTER 35
"PATH OF STARS"

Hardtmuthgasse 10   Vienna, June, 1938

Lusia just wishes things could go back to the way they were before the day David was arrested. Back to the way things had
always been.

Is that too much to wish for?

Poised to stitch the border of the ochre stars with needle about
to pierce the cloth, Lusia thinks to herself, *Before David's arrest, his
brother Leo came from Sniatyn to smuggle back his great-grandfather's gold
watch to take it out of the country lest it fall into the hands of the Nazis.
Joachim had sent Leo to Vienna only to take back the precious heirloom. He
also smuggled some kosher salamis and meats with him because Joachim
had heard through the grapevine that the Nazis were now outlawing the ko-
shering of meats. He grew concerned that his family no longer had access to
meat properly prepared according to the laws of Kashrut. It's as if Joachim's
only concern for his family was their diet and not their safety.*

She pulls the ochre thread taut. Exhales.

One stitch of the ochre leads to another a she travels along the
cross-stitched star border of the tablecloth. This border has now
become a microcosm into which she can escape. Lost in her own

path of stars, the woven cloth has become her solace. The stitches her salvation.

Lusia embarks on a return trip to Frau Grauen's thread shop. She stands before the Ankeruhr at two o'clock in the afternoon. The neighborhood shows no sign that a rally had taken place here just a day before. The echo of the *rat a tat* of the drums against the building's stone facade have left without a trace. Replaced now is the simple tune played by the clock's mechanism. Kaiser Karl the Great walks across the bridge as the clock plays *Das Hildebrandslied.* Lusia waits until the music is finished and then steps beneath the clock as she has always done. She notices even more swastikas on gummed stickers on all the walls than she had ever noticed before.

Finally, Lusia reaches for the door to Frau Grauen's shop. She has come here to escape into her world of embroidery thread. Instead, the world has just become a little more inhospitable at the sight of those swastika stickers. Lusia thinks of David and his detainment in Dachau, still wondering why he was ever taken away in the first place.

"*Gruss Gott,*" smiles Lusia as she enters the shop, setting off the bell on the door. The bell's very existence reassures her that at least some things are still the same.

"*Gruss Gott,*" returns Frau Grauen. She has a worn look on her face that shows she is less than happy to continue her business with the Star of David painted in her window. She wonders why Lusia, who has come into this shop all these years, still continues to risk her life by coming here. Now only Jews can shop here, and by walking into her store, she is marking herself as one. She wonders if Lusia is fully grasping the implication. After all, not all women these days are politically savvy. They were never raised to be so. And since Frau Grauen's customers are mostly female, she has seen a range of her customers' responses to the current political situation, from outrage to indifference.

Although she appreciates her customers' loyalty, she questions why they and for that matter, even she, remain in Vienna for a minute longer.

Frau Grauen gets up the nerve to ask, "Lusia, any word on your brother-in-law?"

"Why yes, Frau Grauen; just recently my sister-in-law, Eva, received a postcard from her husband."

"Did she now? Where is he?"

"Dachau."

The shopkeeper takes a step back. She knows that Dachau is not a good place to be. Instead, she just smiles and says, "Well, I guess your sister-in-law must be relieved to have heard from her husband after all this time."

"Yes, she is. We're all relieved." Lusia forces a smile.

Frau Grauen changes the subject. "So what is it you will need today, Lusia?"

"I came for some more ochre thread I've been using for the tablecloth's border. This tablecloth is a bigger project than I thought it ever could be."

"Yes, I've heard it all before. Not everyone has the patience for embroidery."

"Oh no, Frau Grauen, it isn't that. I've always had the patience for embroidery; I've been embroidering since I was ten. It's just that ever since the invasion of our city, I've been on edge. I feel uneasy; my hand is unsteady at times. Some of my stitches are not coming out so evenly. Sometimes my hand even shakes. You're the only one I'd tell something like this to. I'm anxious for the future."

"Don't worry, Lusia, you're not alone. We're all on edge here. No, you didn't choose a large project. I know you to be a competent embroiderer. It's no wonder your hand shakes."

"It's just that lately I've been thinking about my brother-in-law, David. My sister-in-law, Eva, has been trying every which way to get him released from Dachau. There are rumors on the street how to get a loved one out of a resettlement camp. If you know of any way, please tell me."

"I haven't heard of any ways. All the people I've known who were taken away have never come back."

"Please don't say that! Please!"

"But it's the truth."

"I know you're not trying to scare me, Frau Grauen. I know I have to face facts. That still doesn't make me feel any easier."

"What was that thread color you said you came here for?"

"Oh, yes! I'd quite forgotten. It's ochre. Ochre for the path of stars along the border."

"Right! Ochre! I'll get those skeins right away, Lusia."

"Thank you, Frau Grauen." Lusia forces a smile. She feels as though her life has come to a knot, stuck in one place. With an unknown future, she is unable to move forward.

CHAPTER 36
"THE DARK BLUE THREAD"

The Lazy Daisy Stitch
The Dark Blue Thread

New Haven, Connecticut   February, 1972

How can I connect with Tante Lusia?
Now the right knee of my jeans is starting to give way a little further. Instead of the usual orange this time, I decide to use some of Lusia's dark blue thread. Pulling just the right length of thread from a skein, I cut it. I push the thread through the eye of the needle and push the needle into the shredding knee. Stitching up the hole, I am grateful to Tante Lusia for providing me a means to repair my jeans. I don't think I would have had the integrity to make these repairs and keep my "new" jeans wearable had we not opened up the trunk to reveal the embroidery thread.

It's becoming rapidly evident just how much I need to conserve Lusia's remaining thread. It's a gamble. Just how much can I leave on the needle before there isn't enough left to make the knot? And if I ever do totally run out, where would I go to find new packages of thread of the same colors?

Carefully, I remove the dark blue thread from the black and silver papers which bundle the floss together. I pull out just the right length to begin embroidering a large dark flower.

Do they even make thread like this anymore?

Panic begins to set in!

What if I run out of thread?'

What if Tante Lusia hadn't packed enough thread in the trunk to finish this project? If I do run out and this kind of thread is no longer being manufactured, I know I would never be able to go back in time to the Vienna of the 1930s to buy more. Without the replacement thread, the tablecloth will have bald patches all over.

Looking up at the wall, my glance catches my mother's painting of me as a baby playing on the floor. It's done in subtle pastels of pinks and blues. A portrait of me in happier, innocent times. Before I began to understand more about the world I have been born into.

I pull out the remnant of dark blue thread from the eye of the needle and set it aside. If I do begin to run out, I may have to fall back on whatever tiny pieces of scrap remain. After moving the hoop to the next location, I push the thread through the eye of the needle to embroider the last of the large dark blue flowers.

What could I possibly have in common with this woman from another time period? She lived at a time in which women had little say in their lives. When women weren't as widely educated as they are today. Did Lusia ever read books? Was she friendly and outgoing? Was she shy? If I were to pass her on the street (if it were possible), would I ever be able to recognize her?

As a teenager living in America, I seek a common thread with Tante Lusia. I am following the common path Lusia set up for me before she set the embroidery aside and packed it in the trunk. Before this, I followed my own path. Now, without hesitation, I willingly follow this same pale blue garden path Lusia had once followed all those years ago.

As hard as I might try, I can never separate my family's past from my very existence. Many other members of my father's family had been killed, too. What meaning do family ties have when your family has been almost all but wiped out? All I am left with are ties with ghosts. Like the blue indigo dye of my jeans, my family's past is an integral part of me. The loss of family has become a part of me. It will always be there, absorbed within my soul. No matter how hard I tried to separate myself from it, it will always be there to haunt me.

Just for once, I would like to know what it's like to have a fully intact family. To know what it's like to enjoy family gatherings and holidays. To know what I was missing that my classmates take for granted as an integral part of their lives.

Lazy Daisy. Lazy Daisy. Knot. A large dark blue flower.

To meet with an ancestor I could never possibly meet. If I were able to make a connection would give meaning to my life. But how could I ever make this connection?

The trunk brought Lusia's dresses out from her time period into mine. From a different époque when women dressed far differently and had a very different sense of glamor. I am living in the time of women's liberation and *I Am Woman*. My generation is being taught that a woman can do anything if she puts her mind to it. A woman has the right to an education and a career. A woman has the right to be politically aware and politically active. We are taught to speak out against injustice and to question authority. A woman's sense of glamor is equally as important as capability.

Lazy Daisy. Lazy Daisy. Knot. A large dark blue flower.

From the trunk, I have unearthed uncommon shades of common colors. Sure, I've seen these colors before, but never so luminous. These blues, greens, purples, pinks, oranges, and yellows have all been transported through time from the distant past into my life. From the era of the Holocaust into the seventies. From a time period when clothing was custom made for an individual.

When women had more leisure time for hobbies. For me, the trunk is like a time capsule from which I can learn about the kinds of clothing people once wore, the sorts of handcrafts that were common at that time.

Blue is my favorite color. From nothing in common, we have something in common: the color blue. The dark blue thread from the trunk matches the color of my blue jeans. A common color. A color in common.

Lazy Daisy. Lazy Daisy. Knot. Another large dark blue flower.

Tante Lusia left behind her life's autobiography written in her stitches. Stitches tracing what she'd left behind of a life cut short. Whatever we do have in common will be found in these threads.

I know that I can spend all my time feeling sorry for myself and feeling guilty over Lusia's loss. Lately, at school, I have spent much of my time distancing myself from my classmates because I feel different from them. Voluntarily placing myself in isolation, exiling myself from them.

It is through these colors that I am connected to Lusia. As though an invisible thread holds us together. Whatever plans the Nazis had to destroy Tante Lusia and her legacy, whatever plans they had to destroy my family, the bonds were so strong, the threads so strong, that they could never break,

I tie the knot on my last dark blue flower, the last of the large flowers using the Lazy Daisy stitch. As I remove the hoop from the cloth, it seemingly gives a sigh of relief as if it is being freed from the hoop's tight grip.

CHAPTER 37
"A LETTER FROM FLORENCE"

Hardtmuthgasse 10   Vienna, June, 1938

"I have some news, Tante Lusia," shouts Samuel as he reaches the door to Jakob and Lusia's apartment. She is relieved to see his familiar face. After David's arrest, she is extra cautious about just who it is that she opens the door for.

Although it is late in the day, Samuel is still dressed in his school clothing. "I have some news. I wanted to tell you and Onkel Jakob in person."

"Well, Onkel Jakob isn't home yet," sighs Lusia, the wariness showing in her voice. "It is about your father, Samuel?"

"No, it's about an opportunity for me. I wish I had more news about my father, but alas, not today."

"Come sit down, Samuel."

Samuel goes over to the couch by the corner window. As he sits, he soaks in the apartment he's been visiting all these years as he has been growing up. Realizing this may be one of the last times he will ever come here, he tries to memorize every piece of furniture, every knick knack. As if to keep a mental photograph of this apartment in his mind's eye forever.

"So what's the news, Samuel?" Lusia asks as she hands Samuel a cup of hot chamomile tea.

"At school today, our director, Herr Kellner, came into our *Matura* class. He had an important announcement for us."

"So what was this announcement?" asks Lusia.

"A woman in Ireland had written to Herr Kellner to ask if there might be a student from the school who might be interested in going to Ireland as a means to get out of Vienna and have a safe haven. She would sponsor one student for a visa to the United Kingdom should anyone wish to take her up on her offer."

"So was there anyone in your class who wanted to go all the way to Ireland?"

"Yes, Tante Lusia."

"Who in your class was it?"

"It was me, Tante Lusia."

"You, Samuel!?"

"Yes, I was the only one in the class who was brave enough to volunteer. I was the only one who raised my hand."

"Then this would mean that you have to go to Ireland?"

"I suppose so," affirms Samuel.

"What does your mother say about this?" asks Lusia.

"I haven't told her yet," shrugs Samuel. "I believe she will say that it's fine with her. At least this gives me safe place to go."

"I suppose you're right," smiles Lusia. "It's just that it's so far, far away."

"Well, if I need a place to go, I will have one."

"I suppose it's for the best, at least you will have someplace to go as a backup."

Just now, Jakob walks through the door, unaware they have company.

"*Mein Liebchen,*" Jakob sings as he throws his sweater over his left should. He notices his nephew sitting there on the couch.

"Oh, Samuel, I hadn't noticed you there."

"Good afternoon, Onkel Jakob," Samuel smiles.

"Such news," Lusia turns to Jakob. "Samuel must tell you what has happened in his school today. Samuel, tell Onkel Jakob about the letter from that woman in Ireland."

"You see, Onkel Jakob, today at school, Herr Kellner, the school's director, read a letter to my class. It was from a woman in Belfast named Florence Hobson who was offering sponsorship for a visa to Ireland for one of the school's students."

"And," Onkel Jakob taps his foot impatiently, "what of this woman from Ireland?"

Lusia adds, "Jakob, she's sponsoring one student for a visa. A visa is required for entry into the United Kingdom."

Jakob throws his sweater over the back of the dining room chair. "Samuel, do you really plan to go to Ireland?"

"Yes, I was the one who raised my hand in class to volunteer. I was the only one."

"And why were you the one to volunteer?"

"I thought it would be a good thing. I can get out of Vienna and take refuge in the United Kingdom."

"Does your mother know about this?"

"Not yet. But I'm sure she would agree that it might be a good idea. I don't know what was going through my mind. I just raised my hand without thinking; I know it means that I must now go to Ireland. Up until now, I assumed that one day I would one day be emigrating to Palestina. As you know, I've been involved with a Zionist youth group. I always thought I'd go there to Mikvah Israel or live on a kibbutz and become a farmer."

"But that's so far from home."

"Yes, I know. But I do know that I need a place to go. I know I can't stay in Vienna forever. I'll need to leave here soon before the Gestapo come to take me away, too. This is probably the only opportunity I'll have for a safe haven."

"And what is the name of this woman who might be sponsoring you for a visa?"

Samuel shrugs; up until this point this has all seemed like a good opportunity for him. It hadn't occurred to him that the offer might not be valid or feasible. "The woman in Ireland's name is Florence Hobson, Onkel Jakob. She lives in Belfast."

"Who is this Miss Hobson?" Jakob raises his right eyebrow.

"I suppose she's a nice lady who wants to help out."

"Yes, but what do you know about her? How do you know that her offer is sincere?"

"Now, now," Lusia interrupts. "Why shouldn't Miss Hobson's offer be sincere?"

Jakob again raises his right eyebrow. "It's just that she's a stranger living far away. Why would she make such an offer to someone she doesn't even know?"

"I'm sure that that may be true; but according to Samuel, she seems sincere. Herr Kellner, the director of the school, must trust her; otherwise, why would he have read her letter to the class?"

"That's true." Jakob sits down on the couch alongside his nephew. "I suppose I'm being too suspicious. But then, these are hard times. Can't be too cautious of strangers."

"I'm sure that she must be someone Herr Kellner trusts; otherwise, I don't think he would have brought it to my class's attention. I think she must know someone from my school; otherwise, how did she get the school's address?"

"I just hope for your sake this is a true offer, Samuel," Jakob sighs.

"Yes, now as I recall, Onkel Jakob, Herr Kellner did say there was a connection to the school. Apparently, there was someone from my high school who graduated last year or the year before who is now in Belfast studying to be a doctor. Yes, that's what it was. The student, by the name of Jakob Schrager, had made the acquaintance of Miss Hobson and had mentioned that he had graduated from the Chajesrealgymnasium. She had read about the plight of the Jews in Vienna and had wanted to do something to help."

"Well, that's different," says Jakob. "Then there is a connection to your school, after all, and Miss Hobson's offer must be sincere."

Lusia gazes at her husband. "That's what Samuel's been trying to tell you all this time, Jakob. I don't see why you would doubt such an offer."

"Because, my dear, these days one can't be too careful, that's all. I'm just looking out for my nephew's well-being."

"And by looking out for his well-being," sighs Lusia, "it is probably for the best that he takes Miss Hobson up on her offer. Our everyday lives are changing, aren't they? Who knows when we will have our families reunited again?"

"Tante Lusia, I'm sure that everything will be all right."

"We'll just have to all hope for the best, Samuel," Jakob smiles optimistically.

CHAPTER 38

"A LETTER FROM FLORENCE"

The Straight Stitch
The Yellow Thread

New Haven, Connecticut

February, 1972

"**A**nticipation" sings Carly Simon on the radio.

It's time to begin stitching the small flowers. These are created using straight stitches around in a circle. A far less complicated procedure that the Lazy Daisy stitch.

I thread my needle with some yellow floss. I continue the straight stitches in a circle of thread.

Stitch. Stitch. Stitch. Knot. A small yellow flower.

My father enters the living room as I embroider. In his hand is a white envelope with British stamps with Queen Elizabeth's profile.

I look up from my embroidery. "A new letter from Florence?"

"Yes," replies my father. "This just arrived in the mail today. It's a follow-up to her letter from Christmas."

"What does she say?"

My father reads the letter aloud to me.

Dear Samuel:

Thank you for your most generous Christmas present and for the thought that goes with it. This I appreciate very much.

We keep in touch with your public affairs as you do with ours. We always listen to Alistair Cook's 'Letter from America' once a week, and he keeps up the quality exceedingly well and has now been writing it for 25 years. On Saturday, he talked of your election next year and the possible presidential candidates! He can be very facetious when he wants to be and often is.

We had a lovely Christmas. Declan and a very dear friend I've known for 50 years, and four was a nice number-not too few nor too many. I was well able to eat everything there was and am still eating away at the Christmas cake.

Our troubles go on and on and indeed it affects everyone. Declan came from a boat to Helen's Bay Station, as a taxi could be held up in a road block or check. You could be caught any time any place.

No one can see the end or solution. My next door neighbour's office windows were all blown out. People work behind boarded-up windows. It makes people very nervous.

With love and best of wishes, Florence

I look at my father. The message I get from the letter is a contradiction. Florence talks of happy holiday festivities, yet she also complains of the dangers people face in her region because of religious differences. What irony!

I reach for an unopened skein and thread the needle with more of the yellow thread.

Stitch. Stitch. Stitch. Knot. A small yellow flower.

As I complete another yellow flower, I think about Florence's recent letter. I can sense that she is a kind and sensitive soul, but reading between the lines in her letters, I can also tell how frustrated she is with the political situation currently tearing her country apart. And no matter how much of a gentle soul that she is, Florence is helpless to change those around her.

I thread the needle for the next yellow flower and think of how religious intolerance can divide people's lives. I think about the hunger strikes of the Irish revolutionaries I've heard about on the news. They believe that by starving themselves they can change people's lives.

Stitch. Stitch. Stich. Knot. A small yellow flower.

But this is not the last of the small yellow flowers. There are six more left to go, and I now come to the realization that I've just run out of the yellow thread. I am now upset but don't want to get my emotions in my way of completing the tablecloth. I know there must be a way somehow to find new embroidery thread.

CHAPTER 39

"THE TRUNK"

Hardtmuthgasse 10   Vienna, August, 1938

One hot August morning, Jakob and Lusia board a tram, bound for a store far off on the northern outskirts of the city. The pleasant conversations of the passengers around the couple mask the fact that their trip on this day holds a more serious purpose.

"Don't worry, *mein Liebchen*," affirms Jakob.

"I'm afraid," sobs Lusia, trying desperately not to cry too loudly so as not to be heard by the other passengers.

"There's nothing to be afraid of, *mein Liebchen*. It's a simple matter. All we will be doing is buying a trunk so that we can ship our belongings out of the country. This way, we will be able to keep our possessions and retrieve them at a later time."

"But I don't want to be separated from my nice things."

"It won't be for too long. It can't be for too long. Reason says that things will change in the future. This will all blow over and some-day, *mein Liebchen*, you shall be reunited with your belongings."

Upon their arrival at the store, Jakob is horrified at the sight of the *Achtung Juden* sign that has been painted in the window with white paint. Two Stars of David flank the writing, also painted in white, blocking the shop's window display.

"All we need is a trunk which will serve our needs," says Jakob. "One which will hold all the soft goods from our apartment."

"I understand, Jakob," Lusia sighs. "For the last time, I know we can't buy a trunk that is too big because it would be too big to ship out of the country. You've reminded me of that a million times already."

The store's clerk approaches. *"Gruss Gott,"* smiles Chaim, the son-in-law of the store's owners.

"Gruss Gott," returns a nervous Jakob.

"May I help you?" smiles the harried Chaim, hoping to be helpful. Ever since the *Achtung Juden* sign was painted in his storefront window, all of the store's clerks have been wary of anyone who sets foot in the store.

"We are in need of a trunk," affirms Jakob.

"Very well." The clerk forces a staged smile. "Exactly what size are you looking for?"

"Something that's not too big, but not too small, either." Jakob smiles as he begins to relax just a little.

"Well, you'll have to be more specific than that," shrugs Chaim.

"Can we see what you have in stock?" asks Lusia.

"Why, certainly. Step right this way." Chaim leads Jakob and Lusia to a rear corner of the dark store overcrowded with brick a brack, pots and pans, and other housewares piled up high on shelves.

"What about that one over there?" asks the clerk, pointing to the trunk that is the most accessible to where they are standing.

"Which one?" asks Lusia.

"That one over here, the white canvas one with the brass handles," says the clerk.

"That's too small for our purposes," shrugs Jakob.

"What about that one over there?" asks Chaim.

"The black one? No, that's too big. I don't think it would be humanly possible to lift that one off the ground, let alone send it away on a train."

"What about that one?"

Jakob looks in the general direction where Chaim was pointing. "Which one?"

"The one over here of grey canvas with wooden spines reinforced with metal." The clerk points to the grey trunk located a little bit higher on the shelf, just out of reach.

"Ah, yes, that one," smiles Jakob. "It looks like it's just the right size to suit our needs."

"Very well," says Chaim. "If you take one handle, I'll grab the other and we'll bring it up to the front."

Once the trunk has been paid for, Jakob stands out on the curb and hails a taxi. With the assistance of the driver, Jakob forces the trunk into the trunk of the cab. As it's too big to fit entirely, Jakob and Lusia ride with the oversized luggage sticking out of the back of the cab all the way to Hardtmuthgasse.

Lusia laughs. "Look, Jakob! Look how big this trunk is! She climbs into the empty trunk as it sits on their apartment floor. "What shall we do? Send me ahead instead of the linens!"

"No, *Liebchen,*" says Jakob. "That would not be too comfortable for you. You must travel first class…only the best for my wife!

"Oh, Jakob, what is to become of us? We must leave everything behind that we can't fit in the trunk. All that we've worked so hard on for all these years…"

"But we'll be alive," sighs Jakob. "And that is all that matters."

"We'll come back to Vienna one day when it's all over, won't we?"

"Yes, if that is your wish, we'll come back. It's only a matter of time before this madness will end. For now, we Jews are not wanted here, and the only thing for us to do is to leave."

"It isn't fair. I don't want to leave my life behind! Lusia holds up her current project. "I haven't even had time to finish the table-cloth I've been embroidering."

"You'll just have to pack that along with your other projects. Don't worry; there will be plenty of time to finish your needle-work when this whole mess is over. We have to come to terms with the fact that the people who have seized power in Austria hate us Jews."

"But Jakob, what shall we pack? What do we take with us, and what do we leave behind?"

"I'll leave that up to you. One thing I can tell you, you must not pack anything that might get broken. No dishes, no *tchotchkes*. We must leave all those things in the apartment. And shoes! Shoes, those would only weigh the trunk down all the more. We can't possibly pack everything we own. We'll need to hold onto some of our clothing. After all, we'll still need something to wear once we've left Vienna."

"I'm going to miss my dinnerware set, my nice china tea cups."

"We don't want any surprises at the other end. If we pack anything that's breakable, we'll find it broken into a million pieces when we unpack."

Lusia looks around. Her eyes fall on the yellow curtains hanging in the corner windows. She had originally chosen such a bright color to cheer up her home.

"You're not thinking of taking those curtains, are you? Jakob asks as he spots Lusia staring in the direction of the goldenrod curtains. "Who knows if they will ever fit our future windows. What use will they be to us?"

"We'll take them," Lusia sighs.

"But why, *Liebchen?*"

"We'll take them and see. You never know, maybe they'll fit in windows at our new place of residence."

"Yes, but it's only extra weight we'll have to pack."

"I'd prefer to take them with us even if we can never use them ever again. I'd rather we keep them than have them fall into the hands of the Nazis."

"All right, then," shrugs Jakob. "If that is your wish."

Jakob pulls the dining room chair over to the window. He climbs the chair and pulls down the goldenrod curtains. Gently, he hands them over to Lusia, who in turn, takes each panel and lovingly folds them up.

Lusia now glances at the embroideries adorning all the tables around the apartment. She goes over to the round table to fold the circular tablecloth, the one she'd worked so patiently on at all those doctor's waiting rooms. She recalls her thoughts and hopes of one day having a family of her own. Now, that circular table-cloth only symbolizes the emptiness she feels and the hours spent to no avail. Glancing at all the other embroideries she created, she remembers her vow to herself as a child never to repeat the same design as she watched her father's factory workers patiently stitching the same stitch on the leather over and over again. Stitch for stitch, she remembers all the feeling she has had as she embroidered. Her moods, her moments all returning to her in an instant.

Suddenly, she feels emotionally drained at the thought of being separated from all her dresses. She takes a step back and realizes that it is just possible that she must save her life by being separated from her possessions.

But what memories each dress brings!

The floral dress she'd worn to the opera, the polka-dot dress she wore to the Yiddish Theater on Sundays, her favorite, the red and green dress, the one she's worn to host Jakob's brother and his family for Sunday night dinners when she'd served her famous egg and potato dish, *Balybuchenek*.

Together, Jakob and Lusia move about their apartment, continuing to collect all the items to go into the trunk.

"Let's pack the linens first along with the *Federdecke*," Lusia shouts to Jakob from the other side of the apartment. "They're the heaviest; they should go on the bottom."

After that layer, Lusia packs her pink *gotkas*, those long underpants, mid-thigh in length. She packs the girdles she'd embroidered with her initials "LS" in blue thread. Next comes Jakob's clothing, his sweaters and striped silk shirts, all with "JS" lovingly embroidered on them. His detachable collars have all been tied separately in a neat bundle.

Next comes Lusia's dressed and hand-knit sweaters. Then come the silver *Shabbos* candlesticks, the silver spoons, and the silver salt and pepper shakers.

Lusia reluctantly folds the Persianner coat, the attainment of all she's ever wanted in life. Not wishing to take it with her to Antwerp, she must now give it up to the trunk. She gingerly places it inside the oversized coffer.

Jakob then sets the long flat tray onto the top of all the folded clothing and linens. Lusia slowly and lovingly folds her smaller embroidered pieces. Among these pieces, she places the silk matzo cover.

Shall I pack the unfinished tablecloth? I was holding on to the notion that I might be able to stay in Vienna long enough to finish it. I might as well go ahead and pack it away. After all, what use will it be without the table I was making it for?

Lusia slowly and lovingly folds her half embroidered tablecloth and hands it over to Jakob along with the extra thread needed to finish the project. She adds some other embroidered pieces on top of the tablecloth.

Together, they stand at each side of the trunk as they shut the lid tight.

Jakob and Lusia look around at the now nearly bare apartment. For the moment, whatever problems the two of them had gone through together to try to have a family have now melted away. At this moment, none of those trials and tribulations matter. Now all that concerns them is that they can escape together safely.

They hug one another tightly, apprehensive of the future. Each aware that it is possible that they may never see one another or Vienna ever again.

Certainly, they know they will never see David once more.

⊰⊱

Samuel helps his uncle carry the trunk to the cab as they head towards the Westbahnhof. All poor Lusia can do is stare out the cab's window on the ride to the train station as the architecture of Vienna passes before her eyes.

Once at the station, Jakob and Samuel do their best to carry the heavy trunk by its handles. Samuel at one end, Jakob at the other, they lug the chest over to the shipping window.

"Gruss Gott," Jakob says to the shipping clerk who stands behind the brass grid that shields his face from the customers.

"Gruss Gott," returns the middle-aged clerk, a swastika armband on his sleeve which Jakob discerns from behind the brass screen. "Where will you be shipping this trunk?"

"To London," shrugs Jakob, trying hard not to look too conspicuous. "I'm sending the trunk to London, in care of my nephew." Jakob pats Samuel on the back in a gesture of camaraderie. Trying to keep up appearances, despite this trying situation. "He is to travel to England shortly to continue his studies. I should like to be kept in long-term storage once it arrives there."

"You will have to put the trunk in long-term storage after it arrives there," objects the clerk. "You can't do that from here."

"Very well, then, my nephew will gladly make those arrangements once he arrives in London, won't you?" Jakob nods to Samuel, who in turn nods back to his uncle.

"And what are the contents of the trunk?" asks the shipping clerk.

"Clothing, personal effects, linens, dresses, that sort of thing. I have an inventory of all the contents right here." Jakob forces a smile in order to avert any suspicions as he hands the list over to the clerk.

"Very well. If you would just fill out these papers for customs, please."

Jakob looks over the empty spaces he is to fill out on the forms. *Address?* Should he give his true address or make one up? Should the trunk not reach London for some reason and need to be returned, he would not be there to receive it. Would the Nazis assume the trunk is being sent by a Jew trying to flee and come back to his address to arrest him? He'd be long gone by the time the Gestapo would come looking for him. He settles for his actual address of Hardtmuthgasse 10.

Jakob hands the finished paperwork over to the clerk who briefly looks it over. The clerk's face shows no tell-tale expression of suspicion.

"One moment please," says the clerk. "I must get my assistant to come help me lift this heavy trunk."

The five-minute wait seems endless. Finally, a young clerk accompanies the middle-age clerk back to the counter. Together, the two men load the trunk onto a large cart, which they pull away into the back room out of sight.

Lusia begins to look as though she wants to scream. But she dares not. Her entire life is packed away in that trunk. And now it is slowly slipping away.

As though through the eye of a needle.

CHAPTER 40

"THE TRUNK"

New Haven, Connecticut

I am growing confident that my embroidery is on its way to matching Tante Lusia's stitch for stitch.

I pierce the white linen with the needle to begin a straight stitch for the first of the small purple flowers. As I embroider, I recall the dream I'd had when I was in Kindergarten after I'd pulled the green cloth away from what I'd thought was a table to discover that it was a trunk underneath. In my dream, I pulled up the lid to discover that the trunk was filled to the brim with gold doubloons, strands of pearls, and faceted gemstones. So glittery.

When I awoke the next morning, I recalled the dream. I looked around me. The treasure was gone. I couldn't understand why. Because I was so young, I was convinced that I could merely close my eyes and go back into my dream, grab the treasure, and run out of the dream with the treasure still in my hands into my waking state.

Lost in my recollection of that dream, I put down the embroidery hoop, leaving the small purple flower I am working on temporarily unfinished. Having seen the Disney version of Peter Pan when I was five, I'd assumed the trunk must have belonged to Captain Hook. At the time, it seemed like the natural conclusion. I realize that by opening it, though, I've made my dream a reality. Only the treasure I've uncovered isn't gold doubloons, it's an unfinished tablecloth. The treasures are Tante Lusia's bright colors brought out from her world and into mine. As if when we opened up the trunk was a waking dream. As I remain awake, the trunk's contents remain with me.

I pick up the hoop again and continue to embroider another small purple flower. Stitching the long straight stitches in a circle, I close my eyes and imagine what Tante Lusia's life must have been like in the last days before she fled Vienna.

I think about Tante Lusia and the quantity of items she'd packed away in anticipation of a new life outside of Vienna. Her entire life had been packed up into the trunk. All her dresses. All her dreams. All her hopes for the future.

I am now living in the world of what would have been Tante Lusia's future had she lived. The War from Lusia's time has ended. And yet, now in one location or another, the world is still at war. I think about what they are called the "Troubles" in Ireland. Florence writes to us about it in her letters. Things there seem to be getting worse and worse. Again, people hate others just because of their religion. In Belfast, there are families who have to pass through the next block where people of another faith live just to get to school or work or the grocery store. They can't live their lives in peace without being attacked for what they believe; for worshipping the way their ancestors had. This scenario sounds all too familiar to me. I would have thought that after the Holocaust, the world should have learned.

Will the world ever know peace?

Straight stitch. Straight stitch. Straight stitch. Knot. A small purple flower.

I am so caught up with my own thoughts that I have not noticed that I'd completely run out of the purple thread. In an instant, I am dashed as I realize I will be unable to finish the rest of the purple flowers.

CHAPTER 41
"A TWIST IN THE THREAD"

Hardtmuthgasse 10   Vienna, August, 1938

Lusia looks over her emptied apartment.
So unfamiliar.
So lifeless.
So bare.
Where once her life had been in full bloom.

Not the same warm, welcoming space where she had spent so many years of her life. Having left word with Eva that they were leaving Vienna, Lusia has finished packing her valise with just enough of her clothing left to begin her exile in Antwerp.

This is where she had lived her life with expectations of a future filled with happiness. Straight jacketed to the notion that Jakob might one day accept his life as it was and would stop blaming her. Lusia stares at the corner where she had once stood in anticipation of telling Jakob the news from Herr Doktor Porges. Her ghost appears as a shivering, skinny woman not in control of her own situation. The ghost's white outline stands against the bare walls of the emptied apartment.

Jakob's *"For what do I live?"* echoes off the back wall back into Lusia's head. She looks to the ghost of herself outlined against the wall in the hopes that Jakob's often-repeated phrase, *"For what do I live?"* will stay behind in this apartment with this specter of herself. She leaves in the hopes the phrase will not follow her to Antwerp.

"I'm all packed, Lusia," Jakob sighs. "That's all I can take in my valise. The rest of the things will just have to remain here in the apartment for whoever is next to move in."

"It's too bad we can't take everything-- my shoes, the dishes..." Lusia shrugs.

Jakob gazes at his wife in disbelief. "You knew we couldn't have taken everything."

"Such a pity. If we were moving under peaceful circumstances, we'd be able to transport everything we own with no problem."

"I suppose we're lucky to take whatever we're able, *mein Liebchen*. We'll make up for it at the other end. I know we will."

Late that warm June evening, as darkness is falling, Jakob sticks his head out the front door of the apartment house. Looking both ways, he makes sure that the streets are empty. Once the coast is clear, he motions by waving his arms to Lusia, who stands back in the hallway to follow him out the door.

Carrying only one suitcase apiece, Jakob and Lusia tip-toe softly out the front door. Flagging down a lone cab, they make their way to the Westbahnhof. From there, they will catch the overnight train to Belgium.

"Come, *Liebchen,* I'll take your valise. You may go up the steps first." Jakob grabs Lusia's luggage as he motions to her to climb the stairs to the second-class compartment.

Once safely on the train, Jakob sits back in his seat, breathing a heavy sigh of relief. As the train leaves the station, he watches out the window as the city he had once called home now grows smaller and smaller in the distance. Once the city is no longer in view, his thoughts turn to the humiliation his brother has suffered washing the streets and of his arrest and deportation to Dachau.

Lusia sits back in her seat. She takes off her sweater in an effort to try to make herself more comfortable. Agitated, she repositions her body many times over before becoming more relaxed. For the first time since she had been informed by her doctor that she could never have children, Lusia feels a tinge of relief.

Who would want to put a child through all this?

In the moonlit darkness of night, Lusia observes the landscape of hatred as the train passes from town to town with signs posted at every station advocating the glory of the Third Reich. Trees and villages pass so quickly that it makes Lusia's head spin. The train makes it through Germany. Jakob and Lusia have shown their passports at the crossing without incident.

Lusia resents having to leave her home with its warmth and familiarity as a trade-off to life in exile. Although she knows that this is what she must do to stay alive, she still resents having to leave her old life behind. Yes, she is grateful just to be alive and be with her husband, knowing that no matter where they end up, he will be there with her.

As the trees and the miles fly by, Lusia's thoughts now turn to those dresses packed away in her trunk.

I'm on to a new life now, anyway. We'll be starting anew. All our old problems are behind us now. Jakob now accepts the fact that I cannot bear him a child. We'll be living in a new city with a new set of friends. I'll get a new set of clothes once we've settled down. Everything will be fine!

The train carrying Jakob and Lusia crosses safely and without incident across the frontier into Belgium. By all outward appearances, the terrain looks the same. But they know there is a difference. A major difference. They are out of Nazi territory! The sight of the border sign is reassuring to the two of them.

They are free!

CHAPTER 42

"A TWIST IN THE THREAD"

The Straight Stitch
The Light Blue Thread

New Haven, Connecticut   March, 1972

"American Pie" plays on the radio as I stare at the small flowers I've been embroidering. The patches of the orange flowers are starting to take on a life of their own. With the exception of the bald patches where the missing purple and yellow thread were supposed to go, what once had been designs stamped in pale blue ink are now becoming garden beds alive with color.

I thread the needle with the light blue thread.

Straight stitch. Straight stitch. Knot. A light blue flower.

I stitch a second small light blue flower.

With every stitch, I know I'm always one stitch closer to the completion of the tablecloth. I move the hoop over to the next flower patch and begin the straight stitch for the third small light blue flower.

I switch hoop locations to the next flower patch.

Straight stitch. Straight stitch. Knot.

I complete the fourth of the small light blue flowers.

As I embroider, it occurs to me that my father never told me the circumstances of where the trunk had been sent and where Tante Lusia and Onkel Jakob had gone when they fled Vienna.

⚔⚔

I take the first opportunity I can to ask my father as he sits on the couch in the corner of the den sipping his coffee. "Where did Tante Lusia and Onkel Jakob send the trunk?" I hope I'm not bothering him too much with the question.

In between sips of coffee, my father calmly replies, "They sent it to London."

"London? Is that where they escaped to?"

"No."

"Then why was it sent to London?"

"Because there was a point in time when they thought they would eventually make their way there. They knew that I was going to go to Ireland through Florence's sponsorship, and they had hoped one day to meet up with me in the United Kingdom. And if it turned out that they didn't get to London, at least they knew that I would be living close enough to be able to look after the trunk."

I put down my needle filled with the light blue thread and look up at my father. "Well, then, where did Lusia and Jakob go?"

"At first there was some discussion that they would go to London, but then they got a bit discouraged when they saw how hard it was for me to obtain a visa from the British government even with the sponsorship of Florence. Since they had no sponsorship, it would have been impossible for them to obtain visas on their own. It was then they decided that they should go to Antwerp instead."

"Antwerp?" I interrupt as my father's voice begins to trail off.

"Yes."

"But why there?"

"Because it's a major center for diamond dealers; they knew there was a large Jewish community there."

As I embroider, I begin to wonder if Lusia and Jakob had made their way to Antwerp and what happened to them after they got there. At this moment, I don't want to further upset my father by asking any more probing questions. I know that when my father lost his aunt and uncle, a part of him must have died with them. I'm sure he has never been the same person since. At this same moment, I realize I have run out of the light blue thread.

CHAPTER 43
"ARRIVAL AT ANTWERP"

Kreeftstraat 27   Antwerp, June, 1938

Shortly after their arrival in their new city, Jakob and Lusia walk beneath the arched tunnel of the elevated train tracks to make their way to their new neighborhood. They carry with them their heavy valises packed with all their remaining worldly possessions for their new life in this unfamiliar city. Once on the other side of the tunnel, they walk the long, wide boulevard to what is to be their new location. Finally, they arrive at the Dageraadplaats with St. Norbertus Church located in the center. Around the square, they see quaint outdoor cafes. Lusia is impressed with the fact that this is a lively neighborhood, with mothers watching their children at play on the swings. One woman shouts to her son to be careful not to fall off. No sooner does she shout her warning than he falls backwards onto his head.

At the far end of the square, Jakob and Lusia take a left over to Kreeftstraat. The three-storied red brick house at Kreeftstraat 27 is sandwiched between the two pale white stone buildings. The first floor has two high arched-topped windows. There are three windows across the second floor, while the third story is a garret with a black roof and two windows peeking through. Above the windows on the first floor of their new apartment house, yellow and blue bricks playfully create rick-rack patterns. Above the second-story windows, the blue and yellow bricks are set at angles in recessed half-circles.

"This is to be our new home," Jakob smiles as he unlatches the heavy white front door with a key provided by the new landlord. The referral for the apartment had come through a network of Jakob's acquaintances in the Jewish community back in Vienna. Lusia looks up at the tall, narrow windows. "Which one is to be our new apartment?"

"That one over there, on the right." Jakob points out the window with the empty flower boxes.

Once upstairs in the new apartment, Jakob and Lusia let out sighs of relief. Having made it out of Vienna in one piece, they have finally arrived at their new place of residence.

"We must unpack our things, Jakob," says Lusia with a tired tone to her voice.

"Yes, *mein Liebchen,*" smiles Jakob. He too is tired, but he knows they must settle into their new home. Not a simple task for a middle-aged man.

"We have to start our lives all over again."

"It will only be hard if you look at it that way."

Lusia looks around at her new apartment. Yes, it is much smaller than the one she has left behind in Vienna. Yes, it needs furnishings. But she also knows that she is safe here. She goes over to the window and looks up at the sky and reassures herself that she can make a new start as long as she and Jakob are in this together.

"Our new neighborhood seems to be quite pleasant," beams Lusia. "There's everything we'll need here, a grocery, neighborhood restaurants."

"Aren't you hungry, Lusia, I know I am," says Jakob.

"Where shall we go to eat?"

"Those restaurants that we passed on our way here on the Dageraadplaats all looked good. I'll leave the choice up to you."

"I'm starving. Let's go."

"We can always unpack when we come back. We're in no rush now. We're here to stay."

"I think I am going to like it here," smiles Lusia.

"Tomorrow, we shall send Eva a letter with our new address and news of our safe arrival."

CHAPTER 44

"LUCKY"

The Straight Stitch
The Dark Red Thread

New Haven, Connecticut   March, 1972

As I embroider the small dark red flowers, I make a mistake with the stitching. I'm rapidly running out of the dark red thread and I don't want to waste it. I can't just pull out the stitches and try again.

What should I do?

The flower is coming out lopsided. I can't help it. My stitches aren't anywhere near as perfect as Lusia's.

Maybe I'm not anywhere near as perfect as Tante Lusia either.

I'm doing my best, but I'm afraid of running out of the thread. I can't afford to make any more mistakes!

Should I consider myself lucky? Should I set aside the feelings that I'm different from my classmates and reach some common ground? I know that it is the fact that the members of my family were killed in the Holocaust is what makes me different. That's a fact that will never change.

I imagine my classmates leading charmed lives with everything handed to them; no struggles. Are they being made to feel guilty that they are here on earth when the last generation of their family was wiped off the face of it?

What joy am I allowed to feel?

I am not allowed to smile, not allowed to laugh in deference to these ghosts of whom we do not speak. I resent my classmates for their ability to laugh and smile; to feel joy, while my father admonishes me not to laugh. Especially now that we have opened up the trunk; the contents are constant reminders that Tante Lusia and Onkel Jakob are not *here*.

At school, I feel as though I'm in a room with a one-way mirror looking in on my classmates. I'm behind the glass not being one of them, not belonging. I'm looking in on their lives, not being able to fully participate. As though there is a glass wall that separates me and them.

I leave the lopsided flower alone and move the hoop over to another field of flowers. I begin to embroider the next dark red flower. It is rapidly becoming evident that this flower will be lopsided, too. I have to bite the bullet and just leave it as it is. I can't waste anymore thread because I don't have the luxury of an unlimited source. As if to make the same mistake twice is to make the first one okay. As if two wrongs make a right.

It is now evident that I have indeed run out of the dark red thread. Many more small flowers need to be embroidered to fill in those gaps. I can possibly fill in with another color, but it still won't look the same as Lusia's half.

CHAPTER 45
"ESCAPE INTO STITCHES"

The Straight Stitch
The Pink Thread

New Haven, Connecticut   March, 1972

The small pink flowers are next in line to be embroidered. Breaking open the two black and silver wrappers from an un-opened skein, I pull out a length of thread.

My mother has chided me on being behind on a history term paper on the Renaissance. It's due next week, but I'm so caught up in my embroidery and my father's recounting of his family's past that I'm hard-pressed to concentrate on schoolwork.

Because my father had written to Florence a few months back telling her that I was interested in archaeology, she's just sent me a book, *Treasures of the Armada*, by Robert Stenuit. It's about nautical archaeology and reclaiming sunken treasure off the coast of Southern France. We didn't find any gold doubloons in the trunk. The Armada treasure, it turns out, is where the real doubloons are actually located. The book is filled with full-color photographs of real sunken treasure-gold rings, gold ducats, doubloons, lapis lazuli cameos surrounded by pearls, gold chains, and rings with inscriptions like, "I have nothing more to give."

On the frontispiece is a quote from Freud: "Happiness is a childhood dream fulfilled in adulthood." Florence has sent me this book because my father had expressed to her my interest in archaeology, although I'm sure she is unaware about the dream I'd had back in Kindergarten.

As I stitch the straight stiches for a pink flower, I think of Florence and observe what a delicate color pink is. Not bold like the red or the deep, dark blue. Aiming my gaze directly at the needle, I think about Florence as I push the point through the pale blue ink outline stamped on the surface of the cloth. Had it not been for Florence's help, my father would never have survived, and I would not be here to complete Tante Lusia's tablecloth.

In a way, Florence has become the replacement for the aunt that I had lost. Had Tante Lusia lived, I'm sure that she would have sent me letters and presents through the years and watched me grow up from afar the way Florence is doing now. Florence takes an interest in what interests me and sends me gifts accordingly. The way an aunt might do.

My hoop slips down from my lap. I reach down to grab it as my father sits down on the living room couch opposite me. "You stayed in Vienna long after your father was arrested; weren't you afraid that the Nazis would attempt to arrest you again?" I boldly ask.

"I suppose we knew it was a matter of time before we could all be rounded up, but we were so caught up in our daily lives that we didn't have time to think several steps ahead. As it turned out, after my family left Vienna, the Gestapo closed off the ends of the streets in those neighborhoods, such as the Second District, where there was a higher population of Jews. Once the ends of the streets were sealed, the Gestapo then went into the apartment houses and rounded up all the Jews. Before we left Vienna, however, we had no idea what the Gestapo had up its sleeves for the future of the Jewish population."

"Wasn't it a matter of time before the Nazis returned to your home to arrest you and the rest of the family?"

"We had no way of knowing just when the Gestapo would be coming to our door. We weren't privy to a timetable that might warn us if our arrests would be imminent. After all, the way the Nazis operated was to keep their agenda a secret."

"So what did you do?"

"Our lives went on as usual; we bided our time until we knew we could safely leave the city. Given the situation, that was all that we could do."

I am slowly escaping into the stitches, escaping from the horrors of Lusia's death, escaping from my heavy load of schoolwork. I meditate on the stitches as I wish for a better world.

Straight stitch. Straight stitch around the bend. The last of the small pink flowers is finished.

CHAPTER 46

"FRENCH KNOTS"

New Haven, Connecticut

The French Knot
The Brown Thread
March, 1972

I 've finished embroidering as much of the flower patches as I can. Having run out of all the brightly colored thread, I am unable to embroider any more flowers. It's time for me to begin on the French Knots, the stitch used as the centers for all the small flowers. French Knots are knots that are created to be seen from the front of the cloth, unlike the usual knots that are always meant to be hidden from view. Tante Lusia had used pale green, brown, orange, and yellow for her centers. I decide to begin with the brown thread first.

On a whim, I decide to invent my own way to create the knots, rebelling against the preset notion of how the knots should be created according to the Coats and Clark book. Okay, maybe I don't have the patience to sit down and absorb the instructions. As a result, I am devising my own method for the French Knots much in the way I had created my own macramé knots.

Each time I knot the thread, I cut off the excess, and push the needle through the middle of the flower. I have to pull the knot just so, or else it will fall forward and droop. French knots are a tricky business.

I tie another brown knot. Having only halfway mastered the French Knot, mine are not nearly as elegant as Tante Lusia's. I am being rebellious by not following the Coats and Clark book. And I'm taking the risk that by not following the exact directions, my knots won't be as perfect as a result, and they won't come out exactly as Lusia's had. Again, I pierce the linen with the needle.

To me, the French Knots I am creating are beginning to look like tiny belly buttons. After my tenth knot, however, I am amazed at how similar my knots are when compared to Tante Lusia's.

I thread the needle and push it through the cloth. Another brown knot. This one doesn't look quite right. After a moment's hesitation, I decide it best to take it out and try again.

After I try one more French Knot which doesn't go quite the way I intended it to, I grab the tablecloth and decide to go over to the dining room where my father is sipping his coffee.

"So how did you get to Ireland?" I dive bomb the question on my father.

My father puts down his coffee cup and looks up at me, stunned. He has to take a moment to reflect on what it is that I've just asked him. "Well, I had to negotiate with the British Consulate for the visa. They gave me a hard time and told me that they had to first verify Florence's sponsorship. I couldn't leave Vienna without the proper paperwork for entry into the United Kingdom. All in all, it took a year before the visa came through."

"You mean to tell me that you stayed a whole extra year in Vienna? Wasn't it dangerous to stay?"

"That was the risk I took. I had no other choice."

Knotting another brown French Knot, I aim to master the technique. I pierce the cloth with the brown thread as my father continues.

"In high school, I was thinking of becoming a farmer and moving to a training farm called Mikvah Israel. I had been also toying with the idea of going with my family to Palestina. At that time, the British were in control of Palestina and had placed a quota on how many Jews they were allowing in. My only option left now was to take Florence up on her offer for Ireland. I understood why the British Consulate needed to double check with Florence as to the sincerity of her sponsorship. It was nerve wracking because the consulate was taking so long. One year after I first received sponsorship from Florence, I got word that my visa for Ireland had finally come through."

I have now finished all the brown French Knots that serve as the center of the large flowers. Although I still don't believe I can consider myself a master of the art of the French Knot.

CHAPTER 47

"PASSOVER"

New Haven, Connecticut   March 29, 1972

"I t's time to start cooking for our Seder." My mother speaks cheerfully about our annual festival of hours of cooking and cooking and grease sputtering. We are getting a late start. My mother lunges after me with a spatula. "You need to help me out in the kitchen."

"Why do I have to help out?" I whine, wincing at the thought of one more year of pulverizing apples for *charoset* using that primitive food chopper my mother uses every Passover. The contraption has a red metal knob at the top. At the bottom is a spring with metal blades which, when plunged into the glass cylinder, chops the apples and walnuts. Each year, I injure the palm of my hand as I push down with all my strength over and over until all of the apples and nuts are crushed.

"It's about time we get you into the kitchen and get you to do some cooking," insists my mother.

"I do so do my share of the cooking," I protest. "Every year, I make the *charoset*. Why can't my sister be here to make the *charoset*?"

"She's away at college. And you know it's your job, it's always been your job. Even if she were here, it would still be your job."

"Oh, all right," I give in, "give me the apples to chop."

I join my mother in the kitchen as she is peeling the carrots.

"I'm going to chop some parsley and celery for the soup," my mother says as she brandishes a sharp knife in my direction. "You can help me when you finish the *charoset.*"

"Okay," I say as I pick up the top of the contraption with the red wooden ball on it.

"And let's not forget the parsley for the Seder plate," my mother reminds me. "Remember last year. We forgot to set out the parsley."

"Whose fault was that?" I shrug.

"Oh, yes," my mother adds, "let's not forget to make the hard-boiled eggs. Every year we forget to eat them. They always sit there on the table in a bowl long after we've eaten our meal. Yet we've got to make them all the same. It's the tradition."

Just as the sun is setting, the three of us sit down for our Seder. The palm of my hand is still throbbing from the chopping of the apples. There is an extra setting at the table symbolically left for Elijah.

At the last minute, my mother decides to use the matzo cover from the trunk on our Seder table. This will be the first time it has been used since it was packed away all those many years before. A proud heirloom which under normal circumstances might not be an issue for concern. Why is this night different from all other nights? My mother is oblivious about what memories this heirloom might trigger.

No small reminder for my father. There is an unusual edge in the air on this night. Unbeknownst to me, this month, March is the anniversary of the Anschluss. It was exactly thirty- four years ago this month that Hitler had marched into Austria. I am unaware of the significance of this, but my father cannot escape the association.

As we recline on our cushioned seats in anticipation of our family's holiday meal, the candles are lit and everything is in its place. Suddenly, my father's mood precipitously changes. There is now a tension in the air we can all feel, as though the opening of the trunk has become a Pandora's Box.

As the youngest child and the only child here, I have the task of reciting the 'Four Questions.' Hesitantly, I begin to chant in Hebrew, *"Mah nishtahnah, ha- laylah hah- zeh mi-kol ha-leylot?'* Why is this night different from all other nights?"

Suddenly, seemingly without provocation, my father who has been staring at Tante Lusia's matzo cover all this time breaks down in tears. He sobs and keeps sobbing until I momentarily stop my recitation.

Little by little, my father gets up enough strength to speak. "I miss my family," he sobs. "I wish they could be here with me instead of them being in Vienna. I miss them so very much. I miss the others…who…" With this, my father's voice trails off, unable to speak another word.

My mother and I become frightened. We've never seen him crying like this before. We've placed pillows on our chairs to relax and recline. Instead, we are unable to relax and sit bolt upright in our seats.

In between false starts and stops and sips of wine, the three of us continue on with our Seder. Finally, we finish the reading of the Haggadah. It is very late, indeed.

My father begins, "It was Sunday, April 9, 1939. Tante Hertha and my mother accompanied me to the Westbahnhof. They came to see me off on my final journey out of Austria. I was leaving with the reassurance that the rest of my family had the credentials for safe entry into Palestina."

"I brought along with me two valises which held all that I had owned in the world at the time: my clothing, the *Lederhosen* I'd worn climbing mountains on my summer vacations, my Contax camera. My *tefillin* remained packed in the blue velvet pouch. I brought along ten Deutsches Reichmarks, the modest sum of money that the Nazis were permitting me to take out of the country. I also took my *Maturazeugnis,* that is, my high school diploma from the Chajesrealgymnasium, which would provide me with the necessary proof I was qualified to enter a university.

"'I've prepared a little something for your journey,' my mother tearfully told me, as though I was about to embark on a trip to the mountains or a visit to my grandparents. 'I've packed some extra sandwiches and some fruit for you.' She forced herself to smile, and then she kissed me on the cheek. She whispered in my ear, '*Gehe mit Gott,*'...'Go with God.'

"'Is there really such a thing as God?' I asked her in return. My mother offered me no response.

"I climbed the steps of the third-class car as my mother blew kisses to me. As the train pulled away from the station, my mother waived her white handkerchief so that I might be able to still see her in the distance. I couldn't bear the separation, but I knew that this was my one and only chance for survival. Even though it meant that I might never see my family again.

"I took a seat in the third-class compartment. The bare wooden benches were very uncomfortable. After all, this was no frills travel. Just then, a young man of 'pure German blood' sat down in the seat opposite me. He looked to be about my age, and he carried a knapsack with a cloth-covered aluminum water bottle hanging at its side.

"After a little while, I grew hungry. I peeked inside the bag of food my mother had packed for me. I knew I would have to ration out the food she prepared to make it last through my journey.

"The Aryan youth began to exchange pleasantries with me. '*Guten Abend,*' he smiled.

"'*Guten Abend,*' I returned with my best poker face, trying my best not to reveal that I was Jew escaping from the Third Reich.

"'*Heil Hitler,*' said the youth in a most sincere manner.

"'*Heil Hitler,*' I repeated having no other choice but to respond in kind. At the time, it was illegal for a Jew to utter that phrase, I knew I had to repeat it specifically so that this young man would not suspect that I was a Jew.

"'My name is Peter,' said the youth. 'What's yours?'

"'My name is Emil.' I returned, knowing full well not to tell this young man my real name, not after my childhood experience with Josef Brinsky who had bullied me for having the name of Samuel. And that was long before the Nazi era.

"'I'm nineteen,' the Aryan boy told me. 'How old are you?'

"'I'm nineteen, too,' I replied.

"'I'm on my way back home to Cologne. I was just vising my grandmother in Vienna. Where are you going?'

"'I'm on my way to Belgium. I'm visiting my aunt and uncle.' I didn't want to reveal that I was escaping from the Nazis. But it was the truth; I was going to visit my aunt and uncle in Antwerp.

"'Do you live in Vienna?' asked Peter.

"'Yes, that's where home is.'

"'Do you like living there?'

"'It's a pleasant city…there are museums and the theater.'

"'Sometimes I think I would prefer to live in Vienna instead of Cologne.'

"'I see,' I smiled. The conversation was waxing too pleasant for my comfort. I knew I had to speak with my guard up, trying very hard not to reveal my true identity…trying even harder not to reveal my religion.'

"'Do you have any hobbies?' Peter asked me.

"'Yes, I like to play chess,' I replied.

"'Chess, ah, now there's a game I've never liked to play. Me, I like active sports. For me, skiing and hiking are much better. I'm an outdoors person.'

"'I also like to hike. Every year, I go with my family to a resort in Austria called Reichenau. Reichenau an der Rax. Do you know of it? It's very famous in Austria.'

"'Yes, yes, of course I've heard of it. I've never been there, though. We have so many mountains in Germany. I would not like to say they are any more or any less beautiful than those of Austria!'

"'*Naturlich.*'

"'*Aber Naturlich!* Since Austria had now become part of Germany, the rivalry over what is more beautiful or which foods from which country taste better are no longer issues.'

"'*Aber Naturlich!*'

"'*Naturlich!*' echoed Peter.

"The conversation between Peter and I continued until it was time for him to get off at the station in Cologne

"Just as the train was slowing into the station, the young man turned to me. 'My full name is Peter Franz Schmidt. I live on Heinsbergstrasse. Look me up whenever you're in Cologne.'

"My full name is Emil Spielvogel. Stop by my house for a visit whenever you're in Vienna. I live at Beheimgasse 21.'

"'Beheimgasse 21,' repeated Peter. 'I'll do that. *Auf Wiedersehen,* Emil.'

"'*Auf Wiedersehen,* Peter.'

"Once off the train and on the platform, Peter turned to wave at me. He was smiling broadly. The train gave a loud whistle as it headed away from the station. I was now on my way towards the Belgian border.

"I breathed a sigh of heavy relief. I was happy I had passed so convincingly as an Aryan through the entire conversation. And I hoped such success would continue. But, the truth was what was stamped in red ink on the pages of my passport. I was now a citizen of the Reich, although a second-class one at that. I was required to turn in my Austrian passport for a German one, and my new passport was stamped with a huge red letter 'J' for Jew down the center of it.

"After Peter got off the train, I continued on towards the Belgian border at Aachen. It was there that I hit a snafu. Suddenly, I looked up and there was a stormtrooper in full black uniform staring me in the face.

"'Passport!' yelled the stormtrooper in a loud voice. I obligingly gave him my passport, but, as soon as he spotted that big red "J," I knew I was in trouble.

"'*Kommen Sie mit mir, bitte,*' commanded the stormtrooper. 'Are those your valises?' he pointed to my two suitcases on the overhead rack.

"'Yes, they are," I replied.

"'You must take them with you, *bitte.*'

"I wasn't sure what he meant when he said 'take them with you,' but I complied. I got up to take down my luggage, when suddenly the train lurched to a halt for the stop at Aachen. Just then, one of the suitcases fell from the rack, accidentally hitting the stormtrooper square on the shoulder. I could tell by the expression on his face that he had become quite angry with me.

"'*Entschuldigung Sie mich bitte,*' I said, hoping to soften the accidental blow by apologizing profusely."

At this point of his reminiscence, my father begins to sob openly. Tears stream down his cheeks. I sit there frozen, unable to take another bite of whatever food remained on my plate. I had never seen my father like this before. Now I know why he has never opened up to us about this before the trunk was opened.

Regaining his composure, my father slowly begins to speak again. But I can't get myself to eat another bite.

"The stormtrooper dragged me off the train," he continues, with tears streaming down his face. "I took my two valises along with me. The stormtrooper ordered me to strip my clothing off and bend over. I had no other choice but to comply. Because I was a Jew, he suspected me of smuggling diamonds in my bodily cavities. There I stood, naked in front of him. It wasn't that I was self-conscious; my only concern was that the train would be taking off without me, leaving me there stranded on the platform. I grabbed my clothing and quickly dressed myself. I had no time to lose. All the while, I kept my eye on the train, making sure it wasn't leaving the station just yet. As I kept trying to make my way back to the train, the stormtrooper kept trying to make sure I wouldn't escape.

"Suddenly, out of the corner of my eye, I saw that the train was starting to move slowly out of the station, so I made a mad dash, grabbing my two valises as I went. As luck would have it, I just barely made it up onto the steps of the train with my suspenders still down. The stormtrooper tried to catch up with me. Just as I was getting a good enough grip on the bannister of the train's stairs, the stormtrooper tried to reach out and grab me. I turned to push him away to save myself. The train began to speed up. I managed to break free. As the train moved faster, I could tell that the stormtrooper had fallen to the ground below. I was still gripping tightly onto the handles of my valises as I climbed back onto the train. At that point, I didn't know what happened to the stormtrooper. I don't know if he was injured when he fell. I don't know if he was killed in the fall. I don't know. The train took off out of the station, so I was never able to look back to see.

"Once we crossed the border into Belgium, I knew I was free. I stuck my head the open window and spat back in the direction of Germany."

All my life until this point, I had been sheltered by my father's silence. Hearing the tale of his escape knocks the wind out of me. I am distraught even more now than when I had that shit fit at school and blurted everything out to Madame K.

CHAPTER 48
"A VISIT TO ANTWERP"

Kreeftstraat 27   Antwerp, April, 1939

The train that had only hours before held Samuel in terror, now calmly approaches the station at Antwerp. He is a bit ragged and shaken from his experience on the train, but he has survived.

Samuel is still bewildered by the time the taxi driver drops him off at Kreeftstraat 27, where his aunt and uncle are now living. He is clutching his two valises very, very tightly. Onkel Jakob comes down the stairs to meet his nephew at the front door. Jakob looks at Samuel with tears in his eyes, happy to see him once again.

"Samuel, you've made it out of Austria safely! Come upstairs. Tante Lusia is waiting to see you!"

Samuel does not wish to upset his uncle by telling him of his ordeal with the stormtrooper on the train, so he just smiles back at him. He follows him up the steep, narrow stairs. As he enters the modest apartment, he looks around at his aunt and uncle's new surroundings. Here they are, familiar relatives now living in an unfamiliar setting.

Jakob takes Samuel's valises and places them down onto a new rug that Lusia has only recently picked out. He winks at Samuel and says, "The Tante is becoming used to the idea of staying here. She is furnishing the apartment a little at a time. Our lives are slowly getting back to normal."

"Samuel, Samuel, let's have a look at you!" Lusia's eyes light up when she sees her nephew again for the first time in so many months. "How well you look…how tall and handsome! I was just thinking the other day how I used to cook *Balybuchenek* for your family for Sunday dinners. Do you remember, Samuel?"

"Yes, I remember."

Samuel looks around the apartment for the first time, searching for the familiar furnishings, but realizes that everything he has grown accustomed to had been packed away in the trunk and sent ahead to London. Or left behind in the apartment on Hardtmuthgasse.

"It's a good thing Miss Hobson's given you sponsorship, after all," smiles Jakob. "Otherwise where else could you have gone?"

"I don't know…"

"We've been very lucky here. We've been able to stay here without a problem. Belgium did require us to obtain visas, as you were required by the British government. But it hasn't been that easy for everyone, I assure you. Not everyone has been so welcoming of us Jews."

"I've become all too aware of that." Not wanting to worry his aunt and uncle, Samuel continues to keep his traumatic train trip to himself.

"Lusia, why don't you fix Samuel a hot cup of chamomile tea?"

"Yes, Jakob," Lusia dutifully responds as she goes over to her small kitchen, much smaller than the one she'd left behind in Vienna. Her new appliances still seemingly strange to her, she cheerfully boils the water in a shiny stainless steel kettle just big enough for two cups of tea.

"Are you excited about going to Ireland, Samuel?" Lusia smiles as she hands Samuel his tea. She is trying her best to be cheerful despite being detached from her former life.

"I'm just happy I have a place to go, even though I'll be far away from my family."

"What plans do you have to continue your studies?" Onkel Jakob asks.

"Once I settle in Ireland, I plan to apply to a university. I have my Certificate of Matura with me. I should like to go to Queen's University in Belfast. I hear they have a good program in engineering there."

"So, you will be studying engineering, after all. Remember that compass set I gave you when you were in high school? You can put it to use now! I'm so pleased to hear that you want to continue in that direction. Which branch of engineering do you plan to study then?"

"Civil…"

"Civil engineering! Why, Samuel, that's wonderful!"

Samuel puts his hot cup of tea down on the table. "How do you find life here in Antwerp, Onkel Jakob?"

"It's been pleasant…we can't complain. The neighborhood suits us fine. There is such a large Jewish community here, we feel as though we're among family."

"Do you ever plan to go on to London, Onkel Jakob?"

"We plan to stay here for the time being. One day, when the time is right and should circumstances warrant it, perhaps we shall move on to London. We can pick up our trunk once we arrive there. We'll let you know whenever we get to England. Oh, and by the way, you will be stopping in London on your way to Ireland, won't you?"

"Yes, as a matter of fact, that's where I'll be taking the train to my boat connection to Ireland."

"Very good then, Oh, yes, and Samuel? Once you do get to London, won't you please keep a lookout for our trunk? Make sure that it has arrived safely. And remember what the clerk at the Westbahnhof said; you must put it into long-term storage. Don't forget!"

"I won't forget, Onkel Jakob."

"And make sure that when it gets stored that it gets stored in a secured spot."

"I promise I'll do that."

"Do write us as soon as you land in Ireland with your new address. Promise you'll write"

"I promise."

"Thank you, Samuel, One more thing. Once you do get to Ireland and are accepted into a university, I would like to send you some money for your first semester's tuition. Let me know how much it will be, and I will wire you the money from my account in London at Barclay's Bank. Whatever amount you will need for the first semester. A little something to get you started on your education."

"Thank you very much, Onkel Jakob! That's a very generous offer!"

CHAPTER 49
"INSTANT KARMA"

The Straight Stitch
The Dark Blue Thread

New Haven, Connecticut   April, 1972

After a long day at school, my first day back after my father's Passover revelations, I go back to the living room to continue with my embroidery. I flip on the radio as John Lennon sings "Instant Karma." I pick up my hoop.

I hadn't felt like facing my classmates after hearing about my father's trauma. My father had just blurted out his experience from start to finish, interrupting our Seder. My mother and I had no other choice but to listen to him, sitting around the table in silence as we had.

Hearing of my father's escape for the very first time in my life, I now know how much he had held inside him all these years. Until that night. Until his thoughts were bursting at the seams after waiting all those years for him to let loose. Triggered by the matzo cover from the trunk displayed on our holiday table.

I really don't know how I was able to face my classmates earlier today.

I listen to the lyrics of "Instant Karma" as I pull the dark blue thread taut for a small flower. Despite running out of certain colors, the flower patches are still coming along. Bright garden patches. Brighter than they'd ever been before.

John Lennon's voice reverberates in my head. Singing something about joining the human race...

I think back on today's proceedings at school. I was in the library this afternoon when I flashed back to the Seder and my father's emotional spilling of his escape from the Nazis. Up until last night, no one in the family, not even my mother, knew what had happened when my father escaped out of Austria. None of us had ever known that he almost hadn't made it out alive. My mother's decision to use Tante Lusia's matzo cover on our Seder table triggered my father's buried memories. All through my classes, I was still in shock from the night before and didn't know how to hold that jolt inside me.

Suddenly, with Alan, Katherine, and Ann in close proximity, I blurted out my father's revelations to the three of them. At that moment, it felt as though I were living outside my body. I haven't been the same person I was the day before Passover began. And this afternoon, I was numb. And am still numb. As though ice runs through my veins. I could barely communicate to my classmates my father's story of his escape. I was at such a loss for words. All that I was able to convey to the three of them was more of an emotion, a feeling, than a recounting of what my father had told to us. I was in no mind to be concerned about what others thought about me that moment.

And there I was, in the library, in front of Alan, Katherine, and Ann, spilling my guts out from my frontal lobe without thinking of the rules of politeness. I told them about my father and the young Aryan man he had befriended on the train. And I told them all about the stormtrooper who had pulled my dad off the train and tried to search him just because of the red 'J' that had been stamped on his passport. And I was passing my father's trauma over to my classmates.

At that moment I didn't care how my classmates would react to me. I just blurted everything out, injecting my trauma into their tweedy lives. Would the three of them scorn me now? Even before this episode, I thought I had so very little in common with them. I wouldn't blame them if they wanted to shun me forever after this.

But they are willing to listen to listen to me.

They are willing to accept me.

> They don't treat me like I'm an outcast after all.
> Or that I don't belong among them.
> They listen to me with sympathy.
> I am one of them.
> I am a part of the human race.

Suddenly I feel as though I have misjudged my classmates. I had jumped to the conclusion that they would treat me like an outcast if they knew about my family's history. But they were there to comfort me. They were willing to accept me and make me feel as though I am one of them. We were all wearing blue jeans. They aren't really different from me. We have more in common than I'd thought.

What I didn't confide in Alan, Katherine and Ann was that my father revealed that it is possible that he might have killed the stormtrooper who had pulled him off the train. My father had pushed the Nazi away as the train was gaining speed as it was leaving the station.

What was the stormtrooper's fate?

We will never know,

Should I hope that the worst had befallen the stormtrooper?

As I pull the dark blue thread taut for another stitch for a small dark blue flower, I begin to wonder: should I prefer to believe that the stormtrooper's life ended in that fall that he took when the train took off from the station? What does that say about me and my humanity if I wished him dead at hands of my father?

I tie the knot for a completed flower as I realize that my solitary task of finishing Lusia's tablecloth is a solitary task I am doing at home; I do not talk about it at school. It's not something I need to talk about. The subject has never come up anyway. Sure, I've shared a bit about Tante Lusia and her dresses, but not about the embroidery. What is there for me to tell them about my project? Why would anyone be interested, anyway? Just another crazy art project Susan's working on.

I listen carefully to John Lennon's lyrics on the radio.

Join the human race?

Do I fit in?'

Could I ever fit in?

Pulling the dark blue thread taut, I think about school and how I feel I am crashing someone else's party. A party to which I wasn't invited.

How can I ever feel as though I fit in?

Get myself together and join the human race? Maybe I do have more in common with them than I had once thought.

After all, we are all from the same generation, sharing the same values and beliefs as my peers.

CHAPTER 50
"A LIFE WITHOUT FINERY"

Kreeftstraat 27   April, 1939

A letter arrives at Kreeftstraat 27. It is from Samuel, telling Lusia and Jakob that he has arrived safely in Ireland. He tells them how he had first arrived at Victoria Station in London, after which he had gone over to the docks and checked on the trunk. Lusia is pleased to hear that Samuel is taking good care of her trunk and that he had transferred it into long-term storage. She is reassured that her possessions are now being safely stored in London with the Acme Transport and Storage Company. And that the trunk will remain safely in storage until she sends word to Samuel to retrieve it for her.

Most of all, Lusia is happy to hear that Samuel has made it safely to Ireland where he is now staying with Miss Hobson.

The letter lifts Lusia's spirits.

Should Lusia ever want Samuel to send her some of her dresses while she remains in Antwerp, she knows that he will cooperate and forward the dresses to her. As silly as she knows it must sound, Lusia is still concerned with her appearance even while in exile. Out of her usual element, Lusia knows she is the same person even without the same wardrobe by which she had once defined herself. She misses her red and green dress that she treasures.

How shall Lusia define herself now?

An Austrian living in exile in Antwerp?

Or as a woman with a new life living in a new city?

Is this new city so different? There are many similarities. Antwerp has a lively nightlife. There is also a large Jewish community here, too, it's true. Like Vienna, Antwerp is an historic city filled with many monuments.

It would make sense that Lusia make a new life for herself here. Although she is slowly adjusting to life in Belgium, she still misses her life back in Vienna. She thinks of Frau Grauen and wonders what has become of her. Has she fled Vienna safely yet? For all the years she had gone to Frau Grauen's shop, she was what made Lusia feel connected to her life in Vienna. She misses her friendship. Now, Lusia feels like a loose strand, disconnected from her former life.

CHAPTER 51
"WRITTEN IN STITCHES"

Kreeftstraat 27   Antwerp, September, 1939

Her autobiography written in stitches; Lusia's personal style of neatly stitching stitches has always revealed how fussy she is about everything. Everything must be neat and in its place. In the past, every stitch must be just so, no more no less than the amount of thread that it takes to do each stitch.

In this, her new city, Lusia has found a new thread shop; it's not the same as Frau Grauen's in terms of warmth of the proprietor and the volume of items available to purchase, but a suitable substitute, nevertheless. She knows she must make do the best she can.

In Antwerp, however, her new stitches reflect her unease. A bit nervous about her future, her new stitches have become slightly lopsided. Not her usual proper stitches at all. Recently, her hands have started to shake as she embroiders while thinking of all those relatives in Poland, pondering their fate after Hitler's invasion.

The newspaper headlines tell the whole story. Poland had been invaded on September 1. Lusia can only think the worst about the fate of her family and of Jakob's. The letters from Sniatyn have stopped coming. Only news of deportation or death would have brought the situation to the firm reality Lusia dreads.

Lusia stares at the headline of the newspaper that has broken the news of the invasion. "Will our families be safe? Will they have to leave Poland the way we had to leave Austria?"

Jakob shrugs his shoulders. "It's probably only a matter of time before they will all have to leave Poland."

"But where would they go?"

"To Belgium. To Switzerland. Our families are resourceful; I'm sure they will find a way." Lusia continues to embroider her new project. Suddenly, as she looks down, she realizes that she must be more upset over the situation in Poland than she had first thought. She can't believe her eyes as she stares in disbelief at the flower she's just embroidered on her new tablecloth.

Can this be? My stitches have always been exact. Just so. What is happening to me?

For the first time in her life, Lusia feels the urge to rip out her stitches. Just rip them out and start all over again.

What a waste of stitches. But if I must, I must!

Painstakingly, she cuts the thread of the flower, careful not to cut the linen cloth. Then she pulls as hard as she can, ripping out each stitch. One at a time.

I'm slipping. I hope the stitches I embroider next won't be lopsided, too.

Optimistic, Lusia threads the needle all over again and begins to re-embroider the same stitches she's just done. All over again. This time, however, she pays attention, careful to make sure that everything is in order.

Straight stitch. Straight stitch. Knot. A perfectly symmetrical blue flower.

Lusia gives a sigh of relief, reassured that her talents have been restored. Suddenly, her hands stop shaking. She continues to embroider with no ill effect.

Lusia has always been exact in the rest of her life, too. In cooking the ingredients must be just so, In her relationship with her husband, everything must be just so. No more, no less.

Everything in balance.

How much longer can things stay out of balance?

CHAPTER 52
"WRITTEN IN STITCHES"

The French Knot
The Ochre Thread

New Haven, Connecticut   March, 1972

At first, I had taken up the completion of the tablecloth as a challenge, looking for improvement in my embroidery skills with every stitch. I knew that the first stitch from the start would not be perfect, but I hoped that the last stitches might be flawless.

Wishful thinking!

Pulling out some more ochre thread from the skein, I thread the needle for the French Knots. I move the hoop over to the next patch of flowers and tighten the screw. I take a deep breath in order to get up enough courage to ask my father some more piquant questions.

As I tie another ochre French knot, I turn to my father, who is sitting at the dining room table. "What happened after you escaped from Vienna on the train?"

"I arrived in Antwerp where I visited my aunt and uncle at their new apartment at Kreeftstraat 27. They were glad to see me after being separated for so many months. I hadn't lied to Peter about that, after all, I really was visiting my aunt and uncle."

I am stunned to hear that after my father's escape, he had caught up with his aunt and uncle in Antwerp. He was actually able to see them again after they had left Vienna! This is astonishing news to me. I ask myself, *if Tante Lusia and Onkel Jakob had been able to escape from Vienna and settle in Antwerp, then why were they killed?* At the moment, I do not have the courage to ask such a question of my father.

"After my visit," my father continues, "I got on a train bound for London, which was my first stop in the United Kingdom before heading to Belfast. My uncle had made me promise that I would check up on the trunk once I arrived in England."

I put down my hoop and look up at my father. "What happened when you arrived in London?"

"I arrived at Victoria Station, I stood there in awe, overwhelmed by the sheer size of the building. I was all alone and probably appeared to be a little lost to anyone who might have been watching me. Suddenly out of the blue, I was approached by a stranger. 'Are you Jewish?' the man asked me in English with an English accent. He appeared to me to be every bit as bewildered as I must have appeared to him.

"'Yes,' I replied, thinking now that I had arrived safely in England, it must be safe for me to reveal my religion to anyone I might happen to meet.

"'Have you got a place to stay?' the stranger inquired.

"'No,' I responded in English with my heavy Viennese accent. "I had planned to sleep in the railroad station overnight. I need to make a boat connection to Ireland.'

"'Come with me then,' said the man as he handed me a card which read 'German Jewish Aid Committee.' There is a Jews' Temporary Shelter for refugees in the East End.'

"'Very well,' I replied, trying my best to stammer out the words in English. I thought to myself, 'So that's what I am; I'm a refugee.' I figured there must be more people like me in London who had fled for this man to come to me from out of nowhere and ask me if I'm Jewish and in need of a place to say.

"It was there at the Jews' Temporary Shelter that the full face of Hitler's War Against the Jews took complete awareness in my mind. I watched as orphaned Jewish children ran about wildly in shabby clothing, having escaped from Germany and Austria with only what they had been wearing on their backs."

"Did you notice the man from the shelter approaching anyone else while you were at Victoria Station?" I ask.

"I hadn't seen him do so at that moment. I imagine he walked over to just about anyone who may have looked like a Jewish refugee in need of shelter."

"Weren't you expecting to meet up with other refugees once you got to London? It sounds as though you were surprised to see that there were others in the same predicament as you. Surely, you didn't think you were the only one who had to flee."

"Honestly, none of us in Vienna realized what was happening outside of our neighborhood. Even Tante Hertha and Onkel Yankele stayed behind, with no clear-cut plans to escape. It wasn't until I'd arrived in London that the enormity of the situation hit me.

"When my father had been arrested and taken away to Dachau, at first, I thought it was because of some old neighborhood vendetta against him. We thought that maybe he had been arrested because the Brinskys had had it in for him. But then, when I arrived in London, I met up with Jews from all walks of life who had escaped from Germany and Austria. They were old, young, poor, middle class. At the time, Hitler had yet to invade all those other countries. You can imagine how many, many more refugees would be streaming into Victoria Station in the years to come after I'd escaped. And if they had made it to London, they were lucky. As it turned out; I left at the beginning, before the situation had gotten worse. Had I waited six months to a year more, I know I would never have been able to get out of Austria alive."

"And wasn't Victoria Station where the trunk was to arrive?"

"It did arrive in London, but not at Victoria Station. It started out its journey from the train station to Vienna, but at the French border, it had to be switched onto a boat to cross the English Channel to make its way to the London dock. It had to first make it out of Vienna and pass the inspection of customs agents who were possibly less than honest. I'm afraid not all the silver objects my aunt and uncle had packed made it across the border. I rather suspect a Nazi customs official must have helped himself to some of the smaller, more valuable items, such as Tante Lusia's watch, the silver spoons, and those tall silver candlesticks."

"Nothing was off limits to the Nazi, was it? They didn't think twice about taking things from others, did they?"

"No. The boundaries between right and wrong became blurred. Laws were passed in the Reich's favor. A Jew's possessions now belonged to the Reich."

"Did you check up on the trunk after you arrived in London as you had promised?"

"Yes, I kept my promise. I had to make my way over to the dock warehouse in London where the trunk had been put in short-term storage. I made sure that the trunk had arrived there safely, and then I had it transferred to long-term storage with Acme Transport, a moving and storage agency. I filled out the necessary papers, including an inventory of the trunk's entire contents. Not having any local address to put down, I gave them the Jew's Temporary Shelter's address as my own."

"What would have happened to the trunk if you had not transferred it?"

"I don't know; perhaps they would have discarded it as unclaimed freight, or possibly destroyed."

"They'd have discarded it just like that?"

"Yes."

"But why?"

"They would certainly have been within their rights. After all, it's business. They were charging us rent for the storage, and if they didn't get their money, they certainly had the right to do with the trunk as they wished. I suppose that they were also within their rights to sell the contents to break even on the missed rental fee. As soon as I arrived in Ireland, I forwarded my new address to Acme Transport. I kept receiving bills for storage charges. As it was, we were lucky they were patient with us. All that correspondence took a long time before my uncle remitted payment from Belgium to the storage agent."

"And that is where the trunk remained once you left England for Ireland?"

"Yes, that's where I left it for an indefinite amount of time while I was staying in Ireland."

"What happened after you left the Jew's Temporary Shelter?"

"Before I made my boat connection to Ireland, I spent my last two nights in London at a place called Rowton House. It was what they called a hotel for the 'down and out.' When I arrived there, I was confronted by the faces of poverty-stricken Londoners. I looked at them, and those tattered folk looked back at me with equally bewildered glances, as though I were an animal on display at the zoo. The next day, I arrived in Belfast at Florence's place."

Just as my father says this, I knot the last of the ochre French Knots in the center of the red flowers.

CHAPTER 53
"A LETTER FROM JAKOB"

Antwerp 1940

Dear Samuel:

    As you know, I called the shippers, and I gave him the order to ship the trunk to Miss Hobson. I received the enclosed correspondence. Miss Hobson is probably going to be surprised if the shipper asks her for money. Therefore, send by mail the money for the shipping and inform Miss Hobson that the matter with the shipper had been arranged. I would like to write to Miss Hobson myself, but my English is not good enough. In your card of January 11, 1940, you write concerning the trunk, that in the meantime, it might be destroyed if it were to stay in London and would be secure with Miss Hobson. I don't understand what you mean by the word "destroyed."

    Now I would like to convey to you the following: That I gave the order to the shipper to send to Miss Hobson apart from the current expenses 2.12 pounds we have omitted because we were in a hurry. We omitted adding mothballs. It is therefore the possibility not excluded that the clothing has been exposed to moths. Besides there is packed bedding matters already not used for three weeks and they could be damaged. It is now already more than a year that the clothes have been packed and there is a question of whether or not the storage of the shipper is dry. The insurance company didn't want to offer any insurance; therefore, it is necessary to examine the contents to see that everything is still there. Anyway, the matter should be attended to.

The red garment which the aunt wants to have is green on the underside. I mention this to you because there is also a red dressing gown which she does not want. Perhaps I'll sit down and write to her a letter. I hope you understand what I tried to convey to you. I'm giving you an exact inventory of the items packed in the trunk.

Amongst other things there are two girdles-one rose-colored and one blue I would like to ask you, dear Samuel, you should send the rose-colored one; she needs it urgently. There is also an old garment which she would like to have.

Take proper time, a short vacation, so that everything is ordered properly. What was the conference with your boss? You didn't tell us about it.

We have no news from Sniatyn. If you have mastered English, I would advise you to learn French. What do you expect from your profession? You probably will be busy on Saturdays. Has your builder also work? How many hours do you work daily?

Greetings from your Uncle

CHAPTER 54

"REVERSIBLE FABRIC"

The French Knot
The Light Green Thread

New Haven, Connecticut

March, 1972

I sit there, stunned, as my father finishes reading a letter Onkel Jakob wrote in 1940 while he was still living in Antwerp. *The red garment which the aunt wants to have is green on the underside.* I am in shock! As much as I have fallen in love with the red and green dress, it's difficult for me to absorb the fact that Tante Lusia had loved it, too. And had loved it so much that she wanted my father to retrieve the dress from the trunk and send it back to her in Antwerp.

As I pull the light green thread taut for a French knot in the center of a light blue flower, I feel guilty that I now have the dress. By all rights, Lusia should have been reunited with her favorite dress. I shouldn't be the one to have it in my possession at the moment. I wonder why my father never returned it to her. I wouldn't even want to ask why.

Now I feel as though I've stolen Lusia's treasure from her.

I feel terrible.

I'd give it back to her...

...if only I could.

If only I could give it back to her!

I pull the light green thread taut, the last of what I have on hand of that color, and proceed to tie the knot. I've no more of this color, and so many more of the hovering leaves to embroider. I've run out of the light green thread, and I'm running out of luck with all of my thread supply. Better luck next time--next time, I'll have more thread on hand.

The thing is there is no next time.

CHAPTER 55
"INVASION"

Kreeftstraat 27   Antwerp, May 18, 1940

The neighborhood around the Dageraadplaats is all abuzz with the news. As the bells chime the hour in the tower of St. Norbertus Church, the square is a cacophony of the sounds of a shocked neighborhood. Antwerp has fallen into the hands of the Nazis.

On the one hand, there are also signs of life going on as normal. The black chalkboard at *Die Schraalen Troost* details today's specials. The table umbrellas have all been set up. The flowers in the restaurant's flower boxes have all been watered.

Then there are signs of changes. Desperate changes. On this day, May 18, 1949, the Nazis have taken their foothold in Antwerp. Since their neighborhood is far from the downtown area of the new Nazi stomping ground, Jakob and Lusia have at least a cushion of safety before the radius of the Gestapo's influence seeps into the area in and around Kreeftstraat.

Suddenly, the same feeling Lusia had had on the day of the Anschluss returns. She does not like this feeling of fear in the pit of her stomach. She does not like the sight of these strangers' faces whose physiognomies show such anguish and helplessness over the news they have just received by way of these newspaper headlines.

Inside, Lusia is crying out for help. Help from where? Where does this help come from? Who is out there to help Jakob and Lusia now? Everyone else around them is in the same predicament. Who will help them?

This time, there is no luck to protect them. The luck has gone to protect others. Called away to other countries far afield. Too many people need help and there isn't enough luck to go around.

Underneath a table shaded by an umbrella at *Die Schraalen Troost,* Jakob and Lusia watch as one person after another passes by clutching a newspaper. A warm May breeze floats through the air as Lusia's jaw drops when she sees the headlines in giant letters.

Tears come to Jakob's eyes.

"What's to become of us now?" Lusia sighs.

"Let's not panic, *Liebchen,*" says Jakob as he turns his head away from the next person who passes by with a newspaper in hand. As if to ignore it would make it go away.

"At least Samuel is safe in Ireland," smiles Lusia, trying to brighten the situation.

"Yes," smiles Jakob, "at least he is safe. Our relatives in Sniatyn were not as lucky."

Lusia looks down at the table. For a moment's glance, it appears as though she is staring at the menu. Upon further inspection, however, Jakob spots a tear as it drops on the menu page.

"*Liebchen,* there is nothing we could have done for our family members in Sniatyn or Stanislau. You need to remember that."

"Yes, but I still have not heard word from my parents. Must I think the worst?"

"All we know is that our relatives from Sniatyn have been relocated to Kolomea and are still standing strong. We've no time to dwell on such bad thoughts. Let's just sit here and enjoy our meal."

"Enjoy our meal?!" Lusia's voice almost comes to a shout. "What about what has just happened here in Antwerp?"

"Well, there's nothing we can do for ourselves, either. We should just enjoy our meal. After that we'll decide whether or not to stay in here in Antwerp."

"We should have moved on to London when the trunk was sent there. I'd be with back with my dresses by now. And we'd be free from the Nazis…"

"Mein Liebchen, we can't dwell on these things. It's far too late for 'what if this or what if that.' The Nazis are on our heels. Even if we wanted to go to London tomorrow, we would never be able to. We are not as fortunate as Samuel. We have no Miss Hobson to sponsor us for a visa. Without a visa, we would not be allowed to enter the United Kingdom. We are forced now to deal with this present problem, and we must handle it in the best way possible."

As she eats her lunch, Lusia thinks about the new apartment. Just the month before, she had finally considered herself settled in. She thinks of all the hours she has spent decorating and making a new life for herself. She thinks of the geraniums in her window boxes that are now starting to bloom. The fragile petals she has brought into the world are now at her mercy. In her mind, she must stay for their sake to tend to them.

Lusia thinks of the new tablecloth she has begun to work on after moving to Antwerp. Of the stitches that have been unsteady of late. Of how her hands had begun to shake as she tried to embroider again after escaping from Vienna. She had come to define herself as a new person with a new embroidery project in a new city. She forced herself to make a change. To make a new life for herself. Must she give it up all over again so soon?

CHAPTER 56

"FIRENZE"

The Straight Stitch
The Brown Thread

New Haven, Connecticut
April, 1972

The other knee of my "new" jeans has now shredded through. The material is so disintegrated and so beyond repair that I cannot stitch it back together with thread alone. The gap between the two sides of the material is way too wide. The only solution is to cut out another piece from the Indian bedspread and patch that knee.

This time, I cut a circle from an inconspicuous corner of the bedspread covering the couch and return to my spot on the other couch. I place the swatch of material over the knee, and using a whipstitch and the blue thread, proceed to stitch up the knee patch around in a circle. I knot the end and cut the excess thread. Now that I have finished my latest repair, I put my jeans back on. Good as new! (Almost!)

It's time to start on embroidering the lines that connect the flower patches with one another. These are composed of parallel stitches in the brown and ochre threads. Which one should I start with first? I decide to begin with the brown thread.

I grab the tablecloth and the skein of thread and run into the dining room where my father sits at the table. I take my seat at the table opposite my father. Threading the brown thread through the eye of the needle, I ask, "What happened once you got to Ireland? Did you meet Florence right away?"

My father looks at me and begins to speak. "It was a long cab ride from the train station in downtown Belfast out to the country-side in Carnalea, County Down. There, green rolling hills sit in a peaceful landscape, unlike the cityscape of Vienna with the hatred of the Nazis I had left behind. As a stark contrast to the bloodshed which unfortunately is going on today in Belfast.

"Florence was there to greet me when I arrived at her cottage in Carnalea. At the time, she was a woman in her late fifties, with greying hair pinned back. We shook hands. I realized this must be a universal sign of friendly communication. I was just thankful that I had finally arrived at my destination all in one piece. I communicated with Florence the best I could in my broken English. Being a sympathetic person, she was very patient with me and my language skills, Or rather, lack of my English skills.

"My first day with Florence was spent as she showed me around her cottage, which she called *Firenze,* Italian for Florence. Since she was an architect by training, she had designed all three cottages on her land. She lived in one of the cottages and rented out the other two. Florence had also designed the landscape garden as well. I looked at her stately white stucco L-shaped cottage with its wooden trellises around the windows neatly kept up. I admired her front door, which had a pained glass window with black and white tile arching over the entrance.

"I continued to try to communicate half in German, half in broken English. She asked if there was any way for me to contact the rest of my family to let them know that I had arrived safely, but at the time they were in transit on their way to Israel.

"While I was escaping to Ireland, what remained of my family fled to Palestina. I was unable to join them because I was over eighteen. Since Palestina was under the rule of the British, they regulated who was able to immigrate into the country. Families required what was called a Capitalist Certificate that proved they had enough money to immigrate. The British Consulate would not allow males over eighteen to join their families unless they had enough money of their own to qualify for a Capitalist Certificate. It was a lucky thing that Florence offered me sponsorship for a visa. I don't know where else I could have gone.

"Florence explained that she came from a well-established Quaker family. She had two brothers. Her brother Bulmer was once dubbed, 'the most dangerous man in Ireland.' Even though he was a Protestant, he became a revolutionary and was involved in the Irish Rebellion of 1914. Her other brother, Harold, was a quantity surveyor who lived in England. And Ann Bulmer Hobson, Florence's elderly mother, still lived nearby.

"I looked around at the peaceful cottages and gardens that Florence had designed. I still missed my family, but I knew that my mother would be happy that I had come to a place of such beauty. Florence insisted I rest up after my long journey.

"Isolated in her garden, I could tell that Florence had only an inkling of the Nazi's torture of the Jews. The little she knew was from what was being reported in the newspapers. Neither of us knew at that moment just how bad it was going to get.

"Here we were, complete strangers. At that moment, we had no way of knowing that we'd remain lifelong friends that we are today. I spent the first few days with Florence, resting and recuperating from the ordeal of my escape. Florence was very kind to me and made me feel right at home. I missed my family and was feeling the pangs of separation. But at least I knew that I was safe with Florence. At that moment, however, I had no idea if and when I would ever see my family again. But thanks to Florence, I was able to survive and remain in constant contact with my family during and after the War.

"Florence's cottage was cozy. She was listening to a Paul Robeson recording on her gramophone. The atmosphere of her place was far different from that of the Vienna I had left behind. It was peaceful and calm out there in the rural countryside. I was glad to be far from the fascist pomp of the Nazis and their swastika-infested décor.

"Florence believed in acts of kindness, and by taking me in, I suppose, she was putting this principle to work. It was Florence's desire that once I settled into life in Ireland, I should then be placed with people my own age. She also insisted I study English so that I could go on to college in Ireland. After staying with her for a few weeks, I transferred to a place called Millisle Farm, a refugee camp for the Kindertransport children. Those were the children from Austria and Germany who had been separated from their parents and sent away to England and Ireland in order to survive. Many of them never saw their parents again.

"About a day or two after I arrived at Florence's, I met her mother, Ann Bulmer Hobson. By then, Ann was an elderly woman, though still active and lively. Even at that late age, she still had the energy to explore the ruins and cairns of Ireland. She smiled and told me how glad she was that I had made it to Belfast in one piece. She was concerned because of all the atrocities in Germany and Austria she'd read about in the newspapers."

I listen to my father's tale of Florence and her mother without interrupting him with questions. I can sense from him that he is more comfortable talking about this chapter of his life than about what had happened immediately before that. As I continue to stitch the connecting threads, my father continues, "Florence explained about her own family connections. I was amazed that she could trace her family's past so many generations, all the way back to the time of William the Conqueror."

As I continue to stitch the connecting lines with the brown thread, I think about how Florence had once started out as a complete stranger from another part of the world. As I embroider a straight brown stitch, I realize that Florence has indeed become a member of our extended family. Although she lives a world away, Florence is like a close relative, still concerned for our family's well-being.

CHAPTER 57

"MY DEAR SAMUEL"

October 23, 1940
Recebedou Camp
Perpignon, France

Dear Samuel,
I received your card of the 20 of August in which you informed me that you received my postcard from Saint Cyprien. Now young fellow, I already wrote you two postcards one after the other in which I explained my bad situation. The only card since May was enjoyable. Most of all, as you deduced from my card, I am now in an internment camp.
How are you? Are you healthy? What do you do the whole day? How are you taken care of?
I am all right. I wish you the same. Food is excellent. Otherwise did you write to the grandfather who loves you so much? How often did you receive a sign of life from grandfather? Instead, you often write and grandfather never writes.
You sent me some international stamps. Is it not in your self-interest at least to write every week?

It is my duty to write to Tante every week at Wipstrasse 4. Further, you write briefly the trunk has arrived safely. I am happy. Have the linens been aired out? And have the things been re-packed with mothballs?

I mentioned to the Tante that I wrote to you and I don't feel very well. I grieve that I can't help myself more.

Try to make contacts, meet people.

I hope that you will receive this letter and write to me in detail. Unfortunately, I didn't hear from Papa and Grandpapa, although I write them often. Dear Samuel, write to me often whether or not you hear from me. It would help me if you send me French francs or groceries, butter, condensed milk; something that will stay preserved.

Dear Samuel, I am giving you my address in the hospital:
Spitale St. Louise
Perpignon
Pyrénées Orientales
France
I end my letter with best wishes and kisses. I would be very happy to receive a letter from you.

Your uncle, Jakob

CHAPTER 58

"INTACT CLOTH"

New Haven, Connecticut   April, 1972

I hold the letter from Onkel Jakob dated October 23, 1940, in my hand. Even though it is in German, my father has translated every word.

In the letter, Onkel Jakob tells my father that he's in a camp called Recebedou. He was arrested in Antwerp and sent there, separated from Tante Lusia. My father had to explain to me that even though he was in this camp, he was still able to write letters because of his status as a prisoner of war and not as a concentration camp inmate.

What upsets me most is that even though Onkel Jakob had escaped from Vienna, the Nazis were still able to catch up with him. Despite the fact that he is in this camp, he's still concerned about the trunk and its well-being. He even writes that he is happy the trunk has arrived safely in Ireland and still wants my father to air out the linens and re-pack them with mothballs! Through his concerns that his possessions were being cared for, Jakob had something to take his mind away from his situation. It allowed him to envision a day when he might be reunited with his trunk and its contents.

All these many years later, the objects in the trunk remain intact in mint condition. Intact as though they had been recently packed. The dresses almost look as if they could have been sewn yesterday. They've withstood the test of time. No moth holes. No mildew. Unfortunately, Tante Luisa and Onkel Jakob did not live on to appreciate this fact.

Maybe my mother was right; the clothing is certainly outdated to today's modern way of living. But I find meaning in Tante Lusia's dresses. A meaning I would never have appreciated had we not opened up the trunk.

But how much do I value this knowledge that I have gained compared to the profound sadness which my father feels now that we've opened up the trunk? His melancholy shows on his face. As much as my mother has tried to shelter us all, I have exposed myself to these profound sorrows.

It has taken its toll on me and how I interact with my classmates. I had to face Alan, Katherine, and Ann on my first day back at school after my outburst in the library. It was rough on me. When I saw them for the first time after the incident, I waited for them to smile at me first, to reassure me that everything was okay. I reverted back to my cautious self- back to my shyness despite their welcoming gestures the last time I'd seen them.

Then there's that feeling again, that feeling that I want to allow myself to smile.

CHAPTER 59
"PARALLEL LINES"

New Haven, Connecticut   April, 1972

Now only the pale blue marks left on Lusia's tablecloth for which I have remaining thread are the ochre connecting lines. Fortunately, I have one skein of that color left.

To me, these stitches have begun to symbolize my connections to Lusia, my connection to Florence, my connection all those who were lost. Those who have no one to remember them.

Pulling the ochre thread taut, I look at the tablecloth and all the empty patches that remain. So many more embroidery stitches are needed to be done in order to complete this project. To me, the empty spaces have begun to represent those missing in my life. To fill in these spaces, would, in a way. restore Lusia to my life. As if to make her tablecloth whole would be to complete what she had left incomplete in her life.

I look up at the four tribal elders as if to ask where I can go for replacement embroidery thread, thread that might match up with Lusia's. Far be it for them to have that answer.

I continue to stitch along the pale blue path of the connecting threads that run parallel to the brown connecting threads. As though my life is running parallel to Lusia's.

Suddenly, as I look up, the tribal elders catch my eye again. The four of them are so somber, so serious, as though if they were human, they would never have laughed in their lives.

No matter how hard I try, I feel as though I do not measure up with my classmates because of what had happened to my family in the past.

I'm insecure about my very existence. Why am I here when there were others who didn't survive to have families? By a quirk of history and split-second timing on my father's part, I might not be here. But when I think about the tablecloth and how, without its existence, I would never have known about Tante Lusia's existence, I become thankful. Thankful for having the tablecloth to connect me with Tante Lusia. Thankful I am able to use my fingers to embroider. Thankful that I can complete what Lusia was unable to do in her lifetime.

So yes, I can think of these simple lines that connect one flower patch to the next as lines that connect me to Lusia.

CHAPTER 60
"PATH OF STARS"

The Cross-Stitch Star
The Brown Thread

New Haven, Connecticut   April, 1972

The borders of the tablecloth consist of triple rows of cross-stitched stars; one row of ochre sandwiched in the center between two rows of brown. Four simple stitches crisscrossing one another to create each-eight pointed abstract star.

As I begin by threading the brown thread, I think of how Tante Lusia had to give up her material possessions and send them ahead to London to save her own life.

Would I ever be able to do the same if I were in that situation? Do I have it in me?

Although I have to complete only one half of this border, it still remains a daunting task. As I push the needle with the brown thread into the cloth, I think how stars can have such a powerful symbolism. And such danger associated with them. After all, hadn't many of my ancestors died because of the yellow stars stitched to their clothing?

My mind returns to the task at hand, stitching the abstract stars.

I am following along Lusia's path of stars, as though I were stitching a blessing, seeking something spiritual in this unbroken thread from a previous generation.

I turn to my father who happens to be in the living room as I sit on the couch and stitch.

"So how did the trunk come to America?" I ask my father as I pull the brown thread taut.

"That's actually a long story. Before the trunk came to America, it was first sent in my care to Ireland, as I have told you before. Let me backtrack. I had left the trunk in long-term storage with Acme Transport in London before I had left for Ireland. That's where it stayed for two years. One day when I was a student at Queen's University in Belfast, I was listening to the radio when an announcer for the BBC told his listeners that there was what they were calling a *Blitzkrieg*, or 'lightning war,' being fought over the skies over London. The announcer said that all civilians were to evacuate the city and take cover in air raid shelters.

"It was then that I realized that Onkel Jakob's trunk wasn't safe in a city being bombarded day and night by bombs and mortar shells. At any moment, a German bomb could prove to be the end of the trunk."

As I am close to finishing the first row of cross-stitched stars, I think of how the trunk has always been such an integral part of my life. I'd never realized that at one point in time, there had been the real possibility that it could have been destroyed during the War.

I look up from my stars and gaze at my father. "Were Onkel Jakob and Tante Lusia still living in Antwerp at this time?" I try very hard not to create a knot as I pull the brown thread taut.

"Yes, they were. Since my aunt and uncle had given me the task of being the trunk's caretaker, I made sure that it would come to no harm."

"What could you do, though? You were in Ireland, and the trunk was still in England."

"I wasted no time. I wrote to Acme Transport immediately and requested that the trunk be sent to Belfast. Florence granted me permission to store it in her garage. Not knowing which direction the War would take, I kept my fingers crossed that the trunk would remain safe with her.

"There was much correspondence between Acme Transport and myself in order to get the trunk shipped to Ireland. At first, Acme had written that my uncle owed them back rent on the storage fees. But my uncle did not agree. When Acme Transport was finally willing to release the trunk to me, I had to arrange with Florence for her to be at home when it was to be delivered. But then Florence was not going to be at her house at Carnalea. So I had to write back to Acme, instructing them to time the shipment just right so that Florence would be at home when the trunk arrived. Finally, after all that letter writing, the trunk finally ended up in Florence's garage in Carnalea. Once it arrived, my uncle then wrote a letter to me saying how concerned he was for the safety of the trunk. He was worried what would happen to the trunk should the garage catch fire. I had to write back, reassuring him that Florence had an insurance policy which would cover any damage that might occur."

"So the trunk stayed in Florence's garage and was left unopened?"

"Well, once the trunk arrived in Ireland, my uncle wrote to me requesting that I open it up, air out the linen, and place mothballs inside so that the woolens would not be eaten by moths."

"Did you do any of that?"

"I suppose I might have. But the weight of all that clothing and bedding on top was crushing down on the other things packed beneath. Florence and I both feared that it was only a matter of time before the items might be rendered unusable. As you know, Onkel Jakob had written to me to forward specific items to him."

"But why didn't you return his things to him?"

"I don't know. I suppose that I was too wrapped up in my studies. I simply didn't have the time. I would have had to rummage through the trunk to find the right articles he was requesting, and then I would have had to find just the right-sized carton, pack it up, and bring it to the post office. All these steps take time."

Now I feel guilty. I'm the one who has that dress and all of Tante Lusia's other things for that matter. I'm the one who has the red and green dress now and I love it, but I think it's a shame that my father couldn't send it back to her. After all, she was the dress's rightful owner. I know that if he had returned it to her, I wouldn't have it today.

I put down the hoop and look down at the tablecloth. Lusia and I shared the love of the same dress. I feel sorry for Lusia because she had been separated from her possessions all those years before. And by accident, and a quirk of history, I have inherited them.

I am now on the twelfth brown star on the second row, far from the end of the line. While each star in its own right consists of only four intersecting stitches to create eight points, each one stitch has to be created just so in order to be equal in size. If not, the star will look lopsided. My pride is at stake. I insist that all my stars appear equal to show off my prowess as a needle worker. Unfortunately, my talents fall short of this goal. I inspect the line of stars I've just created. In fact, each and every one is lopsided.

CHAPTER 61

"THE FUTURE IS A QUESTION MARK"

July 30, 1942

Dear Samuel,

I received your card of the 10 of July, and I conclude from that that you successfully passed your exams. I congratulate you and wish you much luck.

Apparently, you didn't receive my last letter, so I hurry to send you the following news from the Red Cross as well as Berl Mechel. I have notes although they are only dated from the 12 of June where they tell me that our relatives are in Kolomea Shubertgasse 8-apparently all of them are in good shape. The individual members of the family are mentioned by name. I am sending this news to you, Papa, and to Tante immediately. Hopefully, they are all well.

So I conclude that the post connection for the civilian population is functioning. Further, I conclude that you are receiving my correspondence. Therefore, you can send me papers with the same address. It is a real accident that the postscript from Berl which

I forwarded to Tante has arrived. Yes, from you, as well as from Papa-the cards arrive here after six months.

People from Belgium have arrived here at the camp. Also are arriving are people from Holland. Apparently they are picking up men between 16 and 45, and they are being made to do work. There are also Quaker volunteers here at the camp. Perhaps you should write to Miss Hobson to see if she has acquaintances in France and Portugal. I can't use cash because internees don't get to go into the city. The camp is six kilometers from Toulouse.

The Tante seems to be all right. On account of the war industry, people earn money even if things are getting very expensive. They can still exist. How things will be in the future is a question mark. Onkel Yankele is in Lublin. Do you know what happened with my bank book? If you let me know of the address. I have no news of Tante Mali. They are either in Poland or Switzerland.

I changed my mind, and I am enclosing some news from the Red Cross. You don't know how thankful you should be for Miss Hobson, and it is good that you received my letters.

Greetings to you and best greetings to your Miss Hobson.

Your uncle, Jakob

CHAPTER 62
"IN YOUR OWN BACKYARD"

The Cross-Stitch Star
The Brown Thread

New Haven, Connecticut

April, 1972

I'm on my second row of brown border stars. Lusia's tablecloth is beginning to look more and more complete every day. Except for those bald patches here and there where I've run out of the various thread colors.

My recent stitches are finally becoming more even. Not lopsided like my first ever star. That was a disaster. Because I've been running out of Tante Lusia's thread at an alarming rate, I'm too afraid of wasting any more of it. I don't want to rip these stitches out and start all over again. I'll just leave them as is.

Every time I finish with a knot or a stitch, I sit there and glare at it. All I see are the imperfections. The lopsided stitches. All my mistakes glower back at me as though magnified a thousand times. Taking every lopsided stitch to heart, I remember every mistake I've ever made, even if I am the only one to notice these flaws.

Madame K gets up in front of the classroom and begins our class for the day. We are reading *Le Petit Prince*. The subject of the Rose and the importance of the Little Prince's relationship with her come up in our class discussion.

After class and our lively discussion about the Rose, Madame K comes up to me. "Are you doing okay today, Susan?"

"I'm okay," I smile.

"I was thinking of you the other day. You always seem to be seeking something, wanting to travel to Europe, travel the world. But maybe what you are seeking isn't out there in the world somewhere; maybe it's in your own backyard. Maybe it's at home. I know how much you are trying to find your own happiness, and I know that you're struggling with what happened in your family's past. I know that you want to travel to other countries, to search for what is meaningful to you. I want to tell you that you will find what you are looking for; you will find happiness in your own backyard. You're a talented artist. I still have that drawing that you did for me back in September. You do remember the drawing, don't you?"

"Yes…"

"It was a drawing based on a short-story we'd read in French about a boy who took a boat and floated downstream. I feel as though you are like that boy in the boat. You are floating downstream, seeking your life's goal."

"Yes, but…"

"I know you're on a journey of personal discovery. And I know you will find in yourself your own happiness. You're a good artist. Just stay with your talents. You're like that boy in the boat floating downstream, just letting yourself get taken along for the ride. You have the ability to change your course. Appreciate the talents that you have. I certainly do. Your strength comes from within yourself. Stay with your art. Don't run away from it."

"I suppose that I am discovering things about myself from the things inside the trunk. Every day now, my father has been opening up to us about his aunt and uncle. It's sad to think that they had almost made it out. I don't think that I will ever get over the fact that they had escaped from Vienna only to have the Nazis catch up with them in Antwerp."

"You shouldn't have the burden of that kind of worry. There was nothing that anyone could have done to save your father's aunt and uncle. Or anyone else in his family who perished. We're all filled with 'what ifs.' But in the end, there are some things you can't control; some things your father's aunt and uncle could not have foreseen."

"I understand just how upsetting this is for my father." I add, "He was in constant touch with his uncle at the time he was arrested and deported and still could do nothing to help him, making him feel all the more helpless. I suspect that this is why he has kept silent about them all these years."

"I'm sure it must have been awful for your father. This is an event in history that happened before you were born. What happened to your father's family and to all those millions of people is a tragedy. Yes, it's upsetting. Take life one day at a time. You have the right to be happy. You have the right to smile."

When I get home from school, I continue to embroider the row of brown stars and think of what Madame K has just told me. Her words seep into my brain. After a moment of reflection, I realize what has been 'in my own backyard' all along. It has been the trunk--it's been here all my life as a quiet guardian. Waiting silently to be opened up by the next generation. Giving me meaning, giving my life a new sense of purpose: to learn about my family's past and to complete a project left off in the last generation. The tablecloth had been waiting all these years unfinished until we opened up the trunk, finally getting its chance to be completed. Yes, the trunk has been "in my own backyard" all along!

I see myself in a new light as I've never seen myself before. A new perception of the world. From seeing the world as a place of cruelty to one of renewal and regeneration. Madame K has given me a sense of self-acceptance by making me feel as though I were accepted into the school's community; I feel as though I could accept myself. As I continue to embroider the row of brown stars, I think about Madame K's words, as though she has given me permission to laugh and smile. As though I need an adult to grant me permission to laugh and feel happiness. But I do!

I pull the brown thread taut after finishing a cross-stitch. I've always found it hard to be optimistic about the world given how pessimistic my father has always been. I think how different his life would have been if Hitler had never invaded Austria. He would have been able to stay with his family. How different things could have been if he had continued to live in the same city as his aunt and uncle. He would have been spared all that sense of guilt and loss.

After the second cross-stich, I think of guilt and loss. Loss and guilt.

After the third cross-stich, I think of how my mother all this time had tried to convince me not to question my father. Not to permit me to learn about the fate of Onkel Jakob and Tante Lusia. Not because she didn't want me to know, but because she was afraid of how it would upset my father. I can't get over just how much she tried to block me from knowing about my family's history and learning about the relatives who had been killed. I know she meant well and that she was trying to protect my father from feeling his pain. I can't blame her for that.

At the fourth and final cross-stitch, creating another brown star, I realize that Madame K is right; I have to convince myself to be happy.

For me, the tablecloth has become a healing in the completing. After this last star, I am stuck. I realize I've now run out of the brown thread. And I need to embroider ten more stars to finish up this row.

CHAPTER 63
"A LETTER FROM FLORENCE"

Carnalea, County Down
1947

My Dear Samuel,
Your letter to Mother arrived today-but Mother was buried on the 9. She died in a nursing home in Bangor and never recovered from the broken thigh. Nothing can be done at that age- "Too old and too frail" was the response of the surgeon. It was good of you to write so promptly. Now let me congratulate you on all your success which is no mean achievement.
About the trunk, I should think that you should sell the contents or give them away to those in Europe needing clothing. Friends Service Council are begging all the time for things to cover the naked and I think you should do this in thankfulness that you are not one of these. You are on your feet and I think that the best possible use for the thing should be to give or sell.
The things are already almost ten years in the trunk and must deteriorate in that time and you chances, Bulmer says, of getting them either to Palestine or America are practically nil. Customs will prevent and the things will not be worth anything if held up for two

or three years longer. They would just be worthless to any one. Now that is my considered advice to you as to the best course to adopt. Coupons are scarce here-so clothing is valuable.

With love and best wishes, Florence

CHAPTER 64

"COVER THE NAKED"

New Haven, Connecticut   April, 1972

I gaze at my father's face, trying to read his mind after he has read to me the letter that Florence sent to him in 1947.

"She wanted me to give her permission to disperse the trunk's contents to the poor of Europe. After the War, clothing was scarce." My father's voice sounds very small.

I begin to feel a twinge of guilt over the refugees from the War who must have had a hard time getting clothing. How many lives could have been helped by Jakob and Lusia's clothing? Florence had tried hard to convince my father to let go of the items in the trunk. She felt that after a few years they would have been worthless to anyone.

I think about what might have happened had my father taken Florence's advice, envisioning women all over Europe wearing Lusia's dresses going about their post-War lives. What alternate worlds would these dresses have experienced being worn by strangers scattered about in different cities?

I gaze at my father's face. "Why didn't you give her permission to donate the clothing to the needy?"

"I don't know. I suppose I felt sentimental about my aunt and uncle's belongings. I guess I was just too attached to them to give their things away."

"If you had given the contents away, I wouldn't have them now."

"That's true, you wouldn't. Florence meant well. She wrote the letter before you were born, not knowing that in the future I would have children who would be interested in the clothing."

I begin to think about what past events in Lusia's life might have been imprinted in the cloth. What was woven into the memory of the weave? If only the cloth could tell me about its past. The dresses are permeated with Lusia's personality; her soul is in these dresses. How could these dresses have been given away? Even if it had been for a worthy cause?

Had my father followed through on Florence's advice, the trunk would never have come to America. I would never have known about its existence to begin to ask my father all those questions. I would not be making a connection with Lusia at this very moment. I would never have discovered the tablecloth or even had the notion to complete it. To think that Florence wrote to my father back in 1947, telling him that after too long a time, the things in the trunk would be worthless to anyone!

With clothing so scarce, no one at the time was worried about whether or not it was "in style." Clothing isn't just fashion; it's a necessity of life to protect you or to keep you warm. I think about the current fashions and all the fuss over whether or not skirts should be mini, midi, or maxi. It's no longer about wearing clothing for protection against the elements; it's about making a statement.

Florence told my father to distribute the clothing to the poor "to cover the naked," and "to do this in thankfulness that you are not one of these." Yet he persisted in holding on to the possessions of his aunt and uncle. Holding on to memories he was hesitant to share with his new family in America.

Why?

I think about Tante Lusia and the quantity of items she'd packed away in anticipation of a new life outside Vienna. A new life that was never to be.

CHAPTER 65
"THE TRUNK'S SOLO JOURNEY TO AMERICA"

New Haven, Connecticut   1947

Having been left in Florence's garage in Carnalea for eight years, the trunk had waited patiently until the time was right when Samuel would write Florence from America to send for it.

Jakob's concerns over the conditions of his belongings being crushed, being attacked by moths, were all for nothing. Samuel never had the time to send his aunt and uncle those things they had written him to return. Those items that perhaps he had once upon a time promised to return to his aunt and uncle now remained folded in perfect folds in the trunk nestled safely in Florence's garage in County Down. Jakob and Lusia are now long gone. They never lived to see their trunk again.

Now that he is a graduate student at Yale, Samuel has written to Florence to forward the trunk to America.

Florence's response to Samuel's request has been less than sympathetic towards his tenacious notion that he is a caretaker of the trunk in perpetuity whether or not his aunt and uncle have survived to retrieve their belongings. Florence is of the opinion that the trunk's contents should be donated to the poor and doesn't think that the clothing will survive the trek to America. Nor do Florence and Bulmer believe that U.S. Customs will permit the trunk to enter the country.

Despite her objections, Samuel stands his ground and sends word to Florence to remit the trunk.

Finally, the trunk makes its long journey to America by way of Cunard Lines. In 1947, it arrives at the New York Harbor, past the Statue of Liberty the same way any human immigrant would have. Like a human immigrant, the trunk will have a new life in America.

Although the trunk does not know it, it will give a gift to a new generation in America. That will be the gift of a sense of belonging. One day its contents will belong to Samuel's children, the children Onkel Jakob and Tante Lusia were never able to live on to meet.

One day, the perfect folds Tante Lusia made when she packed her trunk will be unfolded by the next generation. A new generation which will live on to try to sort it all out and try to make sense of the unexplainable.

CHAPTER 66

"KNOTS"

The Cross-Stitch Star
The Ochre Thread

New Haven, Connecticut

May, 1972

There's an elegance to knots I'd never noticed before I began completing Lusia's tablecloth. Now I have a new-found appreciation for the simple twisting and knotting of thread.

I begin to think of how necessary knots are to embroidery. Knots hold everything together; they hold everything in place. Knots can be as beautiful and as elegant as the French Knots Tante Luisa had created for the center of the large flowers. My knots, the ones that are never to be seen unless someone turns the cloth over, are totally awkward. All I know is that my own French Knots that are meant to be seen are not as elegant as Tante Lusia's. All in all, I have yet to master the art of beautiful knotting.

I am now starting on the ochre stars for the border. The ochre stars are sandwiched between the rows of brown stars.

Piercing the cloth, I realize that my father's experiences before my birth had been much more traumatic than he'd ever let on to anyone, even to my mother. I realize that my father's silence was like hiding unsightly knots from public view. Knots, with the exception of French Knots, are not meant to be seen. They are always artfully hidden on the back of the embroidery cloth. My father's frightening personal experience is like a knot that he has kept from view all this time.

My father must have felt that there is a shame in being a victim. But what happens when what is supposed to be suppressed from public view now becomes exposed? I suppose that if my father had had his way, and we had never bugged him, he would have been satisfied to keep the trunk closed tight, its contents never ever brought out to the light of modern day.

Here I am, having seen items from the trunk, Tante Lusia's undergarments to be specific. These were always meant to be hidden, never meant to be seen by others. Her girdles are like the other side of the cloth that's never supposed to be seen, that's supposed to be kept hidden. As much as my father was sensitive about Lusia's girdles seeing the light of day, I, on the other hand, have a sense of detachment about these garments. After all, she was someone I've never met, never knew she had ever existed. The girdles are the personal, intimate undergarments of a beloved aunt who had watched him as he grew up. I feel nothing toward them one way or another.

I try to imagine a lifestyle so constricting that I have to wear such a confining thing as a girdle. Lusia must have been so used to the feel of this constricting undergarment that she still felt the need to wear it even while she was living in exile. I try to imagine how much time she must have spent every day dressing up. She must have had an attachment to these girdles. After all, these were the only garments packed away in the trunk on which she had proudly embroidered her initials. And she was so attached to these girdles that even while she was in exile she wanted them returned to her in Antwerp.

Did wearing her girdle boost her self-esteem? Did it make her feel better about herself? Was it to keep herself attractive to her husband? Or was it to keep up appearance with the other women of Vienna? Measuring the girdle, I can tell that she had a 29-inch waist. She must have spent her days taking great care not to eat too much so that she could maintain her figure and her 29-inch waist. Looking at the girdle, itself, I find it to be a feat of engineering. It is sewn with such care that it will tuck the tummy in at all the right strategic places with stays made of wire or bone and stretches of elastic in all the right places to mold her figure. An inanimate object – only for her to know how she keeps her girlish figure! Suffering underneath to appear stylish on the outside.

As much as my father's intentions were to always keep these items under wraps, he also seemingly intended for us to never know about Tante Lusia and Onkel Jakob. On the one hand, I am grateful to have this knowledge. On the other hand, it is such painful knowledge that I can understand why my father would want to keep such information shut tightly inside of him. Once the trunk was opened, I was even further pressed to seek out the knowledge about its owner. After my father's Passover Seder bombshell, I realize that I can never go back to being the same person I was before the trunk was opened. If I were ever to bring this up to my mother, I know she'd say, "But you wanted to know."

I pull the ochre thread taut for another star for the border. As I think about the odds the trunk went through to survive and make it to America, I am lost in thought, hardly realizing I've run out of the ochre thread. I still need so much more of it to complete the star border.

CHAPTER 67
"LOOSE THREADS"

New Haven, Connecticut   May, 1972

O ne day it was bound to happen. I'd completed as much of the tablecloth as I could until I simply ran out of eight colors of thread! Tante Lusia hadn't packed enough thread in the trunk to complete the tablecloth, after all.

As though to run out of the thread is to sever my last symbolic connection to Tante Lusia.

What am I to do?

Funny how each stitch individually is insignificant, yet when taken altogether, creates an image of beauty.

One stitch here or there doesn't really matter in the overall scheme of things. But many stitches missing will fail to create in the eye the image of a flower garden.

Like a family, each stitch interlocks with the other. To have missing stitches is like having missing members of a family.

My only option left is to ask my mother to take me to Horowitz Brothers in the hopes I will be able to find a modern match for the vintage embroidery thread.

I run to the den where I find my mother reading an art magazine.

"I guess she must have miscalculated," I blurt out.

My mother looks up from an article of Rembrandt. "What did you say?"

"I guess she must have miscalculated," I repeat.

"Who is *she?*"

"Tante Lusia. She must have underestimated just how much thread it would take to complete her tablecloth. There are bald spots in all the flower patches. I've completely used up all the light green, dark green, light blue, brown, yellow, ochre, deep red and purple threads. I can't complete the tablecloth without them."

I hold up the incomplete cloth to demonstrate my point. "You see these gaps? I thought that a half-way finished tablecloth looked bad, but a tablecloth with bald patches doesn't look good, either!"

"All right," my mother gives in. "We'll go to Horowitz's Wednesday afternoon after school."

"I just hope they still make the same kind of thread. Tante Lusia's thread is so beautiful. I've never seen anything like it. The colors are dazzling; the thread has an almost luminous quality."

"If they don't have the same thing, you'll have to make do with what they've got at the store. You know that. I'm pretty sure that they wouldn't still be manufacturing the same thread that was sold in pre-War Vienna."

⋘ ⋙

My mother and I enter Horowitz Brothers from the rear parking lot entrance, passing by the upholstery and curtain departments. Passing a table offering a variety of colorful pillows, we make our way toward the middle of the store where table after table displays fabrics of every variety, texture, color, and print.

Along a back wall are shelves filled from floor to ceiling with bolts of ribbon of every imaginable color and design. Towards the center is the notions section, with every conceivable variety of button, snap, and hook. The next section is the pattern department with pattern books displayed on the tops of the cabinets that hold the individual patterns.

"Where is your embroidery department?" My mother turns to ask Sadie, "You know, I come in here all the time and I know where everything else is. But this is the first time we've actually come in here for embroidery thread."

Sadie smiles at my mother. "Yes, Mrs. Spielvogel, if you go between those bolts of blue and purple velvet over there, you'll get to our embroidery department. There should be someone there to help you." Then she points us in the right direction.

"Thank you," my mother smiles as she heads off towards the velvet. I follow her.

After some more wandering around, we find a forest of purple and blue velvet, arriving at the embroidery department.

"Can I help you?" asks an elderly clerk with a measuring tape wrapped around her neck.

I can't help but notice the wooden hoops of varying sizes lining the wall, making it more than a little obvious just which department this is.

"Yes," says my mother, not observing the hoops, "we're looking for embroidery thread."

"You've come to the right place," smiles the clerk. "Our thread selection is what you see behind me." The clerk points to a display shelf situated against the wall with the floss displayed in a variety of hues. "Were you looking for any colors in particular?"

From her brown leather handbag, my mother produces seven bitty strands of each of the colors I need. As she does so, I inspect the thread, filled with all the hopes and expectations they would be the same exact colors and texture as the threads from the trunk. My stitches had shown a marked improvement since I had begun the project. As a result, I have grown as fussy about the neatness of my own stitches as I do about an exact match to the thread. As I draw closer, my eye focuses on the twist of the thread. In clearer view, I realize that this thread of modern manufacture is in no way a match to that which Tante Lusia had purchased back in Vienna.

I want to burst into tears!

My mother continues negotiating with the store clerk over matching colors just as I am making the grim discovery. I don't want to say anything; not only is the texture of the thread not the same, but by comparison, the new colors are dull and pale. This new variety lacks that luminous quality of the vintage floss.

"Why don't we buy a few skeins of each color," my mother tells the clerk. "That should be enough for my daughter to finish her project."

I know I can protest, but I have no other choice but to agree with my mother and go ahead with this purchase and finish the tablecloth with this thread of lesser quality.

What alternative do I have?

CHAPTER 68
"JAKOB'S FATE"

France
May 6, 1945

Dear S. Spielvogel,
I received your letter and inform you that your Uncle Jakob was deported in 1942 from Recebedou to the 'Cannibal Land.' He was deported to Villa Chandora.

He didn't have the opportunity to write. Because he was deported, he couldn't send any "sign of life."

Greetings, Itzhak Handel

CHAPTER 69

"ONE KNOT ENDS"

New Haven, Connecticut   May, 1972

I'd always assumed that Tante Lusia and Onkel Jakob must have perished in the Holocaust because they never came back to reclaim their trunk. But I never knew their exact fate. And maybe I don't want to. On the other hand, if I don't ask my father now, I will never know. I hold my breath and finally get up enough nerve to ask him the questions I have not yet had the courage all this time to ask. Not wanting to upset my father any more than I have to, I won't ask him just yet about the fate of all his many other relatives or his father, David. All I do know is that he was arrested and transported to Dachau. But I don't know all the details. I'll just have to keep this question for the right moment in the future.

I go over to my father as he sits in the corner couch in the den reading a newspaper.

"What happened to Jakob and Lusia" I know that they fled to Antwerp to escape from the Nazis, so how is it that they were killed?'

Because this question is too important to me, I do not want to be distracted by my embroidery with the new thread from Horowitz's. I want to devote my full attention to this.

My father begins to speak very quietly. I can tell by the expression on his face that this is clearly not something he is comfortable talking about. "To answer your question, I first have to go back in time. Long before my aunt and uncle escaped from Vienna, they were interested in raising a family. As it turns out, Lusia was unable to have a child. They had at one time considered 'adopting' Jakob's sister's son, Muniu, who was living in Sniatyn. Jakob wanted to take Muniu in and raise and educate him as his own."

"What happened to Muniu?" I ask, not really wanting to know the answer.

"In the end, it wouldn't have mattered; Muniu would have been killed no matter what. As it turned out, his mother, Chajce and her husband, Baruch, tried to flee from Sniatyn with their three children sometime shortly after the Nazis occupied Poland. Baruch and Chajce had hired a cart and horse and driver to drive them away to safety. The driver betrayed them and turned them in to the Nazis to collect a reward. As the cart was slowing down, Chajce pushed her oldest daughter, sixteen-year-old Elsa, out of the cart. She told her daughter to run, that it would be her only chance at survival. Of all of them, she was the one who had any hope to live on. Elsa ran away from her family to a house where they took her in as a servant. When the Nazis came to the house, she took a broom and began sweeping. The Nazis asked the family if there were any Jews living in their home and questioned everyone who lived there. When they pointed to Elsa, she began sweeping as though it had always been her job. The father of the family told the Nazis, 'Oh, she's just our servant. She's always worked for us, she's not a Jew.' The Nazis believed the family's story and left Elsa alone.

"The rest of Elsa's family went on to be transported to Auschwitz. Chajce, Baruch, and their two young children, Muniu and Brance, who was named for her grandmother and who was born after the photograph was taken, all perished. They were not as lucky as my cousin, Elsa. She lived on and married someone named Roman when she was still living in Poland. As I've told you, today they live in Vienna with their son Georg and their daughter Hanna. As you know, I am still in touch with them."

"And what happened to Leo and Genia and Bronus, the little boy from the photograph who was sitting on your grandfather's lap? Did Bronus end up in Auschwitz, too?"

"Actually, Bronus was never sent to a concentration camp. Story has it that Leo and Genia tried to save his life by placing him on a boat bound for Palestina. As with the children of the Kindertransport, they were sending him away in the hope their son's life would be saved even though their own lives might not be spared. Leo and Genia took their chances staying behind in Sniatyn."

"So did the little boy ever make it to Palestina?"

"Alas, no."

"What happened?"

"I believe the ship carrying Bronus was called the *Struma*. A group of Romanian Jews chartered the boat to sail from the Black Sea to Palestina. Because of the high fees involved, they had to gather together as many people as they could be able to afford to charter the small ship. As the *Struma* set sail, the ship's engine broke down. Finally, it reached port at Istanbul. Since Palestina was under British authority, British officials refused to allow the passengers to transport overland to their destination because they didn't have the proper visas. Instead, the boat was anchored at the port for seventy days while diplomats argued back and forth. The passengers lived in highly uncomfortable conditions with little food except for some fruits and water provided to them by the members of the local Jewish community. At the end of the seventy days, the Turkish government ordered the disabled boat to be carted out to sea. For whatever reasons he had, the lieutenant of a Russian submarine fired a torpedo at the *Struma*, sinking it instantly. With the exception of some survivors, everyone else on board, including little Bronus, were killed."

"The ship was blown up? Why?" I am astonished. "After Leo and Genia had given their only son a chance to survive, he ended up being murdered anyway?"

"Unfortunately, yes."

"But didn't the Russians know that the boat was carrying Jewish refugees…families…and children on board?"

"It was wartime. Errors and mistaken identities happen."

I am at a loss for words. "How awful for Leo and Genia," I stutter, trying to get the words out. "They must have thought that their only son arrived safely in Palestina."

"I imagine, for a time, they lived on with that notion…"

As I stare across the room, my gaze happens on one of my mother's paintings. I imagine what it must have been like for Bronus as he was placed on the train as he was being separated from his parents. What went through his mind not knowing if he would ever see his mother again? I close my eyes and put myself in Genia's shoes. What must have been going through her head as she put her only son on that train bound for the port in Romania? Lusia may not have had a son, but she had the material possessions, only to have to give these up in the end. Genia may not have had the material possessions or the home she had always wanted, but she had a son. And she ultimately had to give him up to save him, only to have him lose his life in the end.

"Then what become of Bronus' mother and father if they stayed behind in Sniatyn?"

My father lets out a sigh. "Apparently, they tried to escape together by train. Unfortunately, the Gestapo caught up with them at the station in Zalutia. It was there that they became separated. Apparently, Genia was selected for transportation to Auschwitz, while Leo was selected by an SS officer to be his valet. At that point, Genia and Leo must have assumed that Bronus had safely landed in Palestina. They had no way of knowing, of communicating with anyone, whether or not he had arrived safely.

"At the very same time, Onkel Simon, who lived in Zalutia with his wife, Feige, and their ten- year-old-daughter, Elsa, was attempting to escape with them to Switzerland. Feige had been a sickly woman all her life. As the Nazis marched towards her home, she didn't have enough strength to flee. All I do know is that Tante Feige and Elsa were somehow separated from Onkel Simon."

"What became of them?"

"Like Leo, Simon, too, was selected by another SS officer to be his personal valet. He survived the War in this way. His wife and daughter were not so lucky. They were sent to Auschwitz, where I can only think that the ailing Feige must have been marked for the gas chamber upon arrival."

"If Simon has survived as a servant, did Leo also survive this way?"

"Well, you know, it's funny the way things worked out. Onkel Leo must have ingratiated himself with the SS officer who had captured him, but then something must have gone wrong. He may have made it to the end of the War, but he was not as lucky as his brother, Simon."

"What happened to Leo?"

"He was killed somehow…"

"How? Was he shot?"

"Your guess is as good as mine…whatever way it was…he met his end."

"And what of Onkel Simon?"

"It's funny how things work out, Onkel Simon lived on. At first, he made his way from Poland to Palestina. After the War, he returned to Vienna, to Beheimgasse 21, reclaiming the building and the lumber business.

"To get back to your question about Tante Lusia and Onkel Jakob, the Nazis invaded Belgium in May 1940. Antwerp capitulated to the Nazis on May 18. Shortly thereafter, Jakob was arrested from the apartment on Kreeftstraat and transported to a camp in Southern France called Recebedou. He stayed there for about a year and a half. As you know, he continued to send me letters from the camp. I have read you some of them."

"Yes, I remember them. I still don't understand how he was able to send you letters. I've always been under the impression that concentration camp inmates were cut off from the rest of the world."

"They were cut off from the rest of the world as the War progressed, that is true, but this was earlier. And remember, Jakob was in an internment camp in France, not a concentration camp in Germany. Also, he was classified as a Prisoner of War, so that made a difference."

"I see. But how did you know what happened to Jakob? If he was dead, he would have stopped his correspondence with you."

"Yes, that's true. As it turned out, my mother had a cousin by the name of Itzhak Handel who lived in France who had also kept in touch with Onkel Jakob. On May 6, 1945, Itzhak sent me a postcard to let me know of Jakob's fate. In the postcard he wrote that he was taken away to the 'Cannibal Land.'"

"So I assume he must have been taken from the internment camp to a concentration camp and subsequently killed there?"

"That is the assumption, yes. In fact, while I was still at Millisle Farm, I had written a letter on August 28, 1945, to the Red Cross located in Paris to confirm Onkel Jakob's fate. The letter I received stated that Jakob Spielvogel, born November 11, 1893, in Sniatyn was deported from Recebedou on August 10, 1942. The letter goes on to say that since that time, the Red Cross has received no news about him. They go on to say that he was deported from Recebedou to Auschwitz."

"So it is confirmed that Onkel Jakob must have died in Auschwitz?"

"Yes, that was the 'Cannibal Land' my mother's cousin was referring to."

"And where was Tante Lusia? Was she also arrested and deported?"

"She was arrested but not at the same time as Onkel Jakob. I suppose at that time, the Nazis were only arresting the men, perhaps for slave labor. Lusia remained behind in Antwerp, but she moved around from one location to another after Jakob's arrest. In his letters written from Recebedou, my uncle updated me on Tante Lusia's changes of address. The first address she relocated to after Jakob's arrest was Wippstrasse 4. Then she moved to Brialmontlei 24. From there, she moved out of Antwerp and stayed with a family named Wandermeer who lived in Kradmecheln in the Province of Limburg. Onkel Jakob was my only link to her and where she was living. Once he had been deported and stopped his correspondences, I lost all trace of her. Not even with the help of the Red Cross could I trace her steps and track her down."

Before we had opened up the trunk, I had always known that whoever had owned it had been long dead. But after spending all these months embroidering on the very same cloth that Tante Lusia had, hearing about her fate now is all the more devastating to me. Before this, she had been an abstract figure in my imagination. But now that we have shared the same needlework project, even though I have no photograph of her, she is all the more real to me now. In my imagination, she is now a flesh and blood figure. Making her loss to me all more profound.

My father continues. "After Onkel Jakob's arrest, I lost my ability to keep up with her whereabouts. On the other hand, Itzhak Handel was able to remain in touch with her somehow. He wrote me that the Nazis had finally caught up with her. According to another letter from my mother's cousin, Nazi officers had apparently captured Tante Lusia and used her to satisfy their sexual desires. But then again, that was just a rumor.

"The trail goes cold after Onkel Jakob's correspondence stopped. I turned to the Red Cross to help me search for her. I gave them her birth date and her maiden name. Tante Lusia was born on April 12, 1904. Her maiden name was Fischler. At the time, she would have been thirty-eight years old. The Red Cross was unable to furnish me with any further information. In the end, I can only assume that like her husband, she, too, was sent east to the 'Cannibal Land.'"

CHAPTER 70
"A NEW KNOT BEGINS"

New Haven, Connecticut May, 1972

E very stitch has a voice. Every stitch gives testimony that Lusia once existed on this earth.

Funny how each stitch is a small, insignificant mark of thread. Individually taken, the mark has no meaning. Yet, when taken as a whole, each insignificant mark contributes to the entire pattern. It becomes a blooming garden.

So the trunk of grey canvas with wooden spines and metal brackets did not hold a pirate's treasure so glittery it blinded the eye.

No gold doubloons.

No rubies.

No pearls.

Yet, for me, it holds a far greater treasure.

By opening up the trunk, Tante Lusia's possessions were brought out from the past into my world. Fulfilling my childhood dream of the trunk, the treasure has broken through the barrier from dream into reality. Only now I know that the real treasure is bringing Lusia's colors into my world.

All that remains to finish the tablecloth are the missing stitches that need to be embroidered with the modern thread.

After that, I will be done.

Done!

I reflect back on the lesson of the reversible dress and how I've managed to reverse all that I've ever known about my family. I needn't worry anymore whether or not the red and green dress is hopelessly outdated. To me, it's become my own style. By a quirk of history, the dress is in my possession. My father never heeded Onkel Jakob's request for its return. I feel guilty and happy at the very same time. Guilty because Lusia was never reunited with her beloved dress; happy because I am the one who can enjoy it now. For better or worse, the dress is a part of my family's story. I am a part of that story. And it's a part of me.

I think about Florence and her kindness. A kindness that continues to this day.

I think about Madame K's words to me about finding happiness in my own backyard. She showed me how, through the knowledge I've learned from the trunk, I will appreciate myself for who I am. From now on, I will no longer look to a classmate the next desk over and wonder if his or her life is better than mine. Through Madame K's words I know I can appreciate the talents that I have. She has freed me to accept myself for the individual that I am. Reassuring me that it is alright to follow my own path.

I think of the kindness extended to me when Alan, Katherine and Ann comforted me in the library. By their being there for me, they made me feel a part of the human race. They made me feel like I belonged. I'm not the unwelcome stranger I thought I was.

I thread the needle with the new light green thread from Horowitz's. I knot the end before piercing the white linen tablecloth.

As I embroider the light green French Knots, I think about how, after discovering Lusia's dresses, I have become comfortable in my own sense of style. Lusia's dresses have taught me a sense of elegance in myself that I might want to explore changing my wardrobe. Dresses aren't so bad after all. Actually, they can be quite comfortable.

I thread the needle with the dark green thread for the other half of the leaves as I think about the trunk and how it had beaten the odds to survive the War. For me, it has taken on a life of its own and lives on in Lusia's stead. The trunk had travelled around Europe on its solitary journey from Vienna to London. Surviving the Blitz, it had made its way to Ireland before finally journeying on to America, where it stayed locked up for all those years.

Silent.

Keeping it secrets all to itself.

I know that had the trunk not made it to America, had my father listened to Florence's suggestion to disperse the clothing to the poor, I would never know of its existence and would never have been prompted to ask all those questions.

Straight stitch. Straight stitch. Knot.

Finally, all the leaves are complete.

I thread the needle with the light blue thread. As I stitch the small light blue flowers, I think about how my father spoke up to the plainclothes detective and talked his way out of going to the police station, which in turn would have meant deportation to Dachau. I know I would never have been as bold. I think about how my father had to flee with his life on the train out of Austria, on his way to visit Onkel Jakob and Tante Lusia for what was to be to be that one last time. Had he not made the split-second decision to run back onto the train and cross the border into Belgium, he would not be here now. And I would never have been born.

I think, too, about my father whose survivor's guilt was so strong that he had to keep his secrets locked within him for so many, many years.

Straight stitch. Straight stitch. A final small light blue flower.

As I thread the needle with the yellow thread for the remaining French Knots, my thoughts turn to my grandfather. All that I know about him is that he was arrested and taken away to Dachau. I feel I've bugged my father enough about Tante Lusia and Onkel Jakob to ask my father any further questions about my grandfather's fate. I'll leave him alone for now. Perhaps someday in the future, I will get up the nerve to ask my father if he ever heard from my grandfather again. I'm sure that the probability is slim.

My thoughts turn to Florence as I thread the needle with the deep red thread for the remaining small red flowers. By saving my father's life, she had also saved mine. If it had not been for her, I would never have been born to complete Tante Lusia's tablecloth.

A prayer come alive, Florence became my father's safety net, offering him a safe haven when plans to accompany his family to Palestina fell through. Now, because of her, my faith in humanity has been restored. After all these years, Florence remains in touch with us, watching my sister and I grow up from afar, sending us books and presents every year. How can we ever repay her for her kindness?

Straight stitch. Straight stitch. A final small, deep red flower.

I take a skein of thread for the remaining small purple flowers, the thread of newer manufacture, not as beautiful, not as luminous, but still, it will have to do. I thread the purple thread though the eye of the needle. As I stitch my final flowers, my thoughts turn finally to Tante Lusia and how, because of Hitler, I would never have the chance to ever meet her. I think of how she had tried for so many years to conceive a child. How she had been poked and prodded by doctor after doctor in every attempt to have a baby. She would never have a daughter of her own to pass down her embroidery skills. I think of Onkel Jakob's harsh words towards her and how he felt his life was meaningless because his wife could not provide him with children. Whatever children they might have had would, no doubt have been killed in the Holocaust. As it turned out, the child Lusia had wanted to adopt as her own, Muniu, ended up in Auschwitz.

As I stitch the ochre stars for the border, I think about the letter from Onkel Jakob requesting my father return specific items from the trunk. Lusia has worried about her appearance even while in exile, wanting her dresses and girdles returned to her. For whatever reason, my father was unable to return those items of clothing to his aunt. Instead, I am now in possession of them. Now, I have Lusia's dresses, including her favorite red and green dress hanging in my closet, and I will always leave them hanging in my closet; they will always be here for her.

As I stitch the border of stars, I have made the decision that rather than mourn the loss of Tante Lusia, I should celebrate her life and make sure that she is not forgotten. Because to forget her existence would be for her to have died twice.

I hope that wherever Lusia's spirit is now, that she is free. Free from the pain and tyranny she experienced in her life.

Hitler could take Tante Lusia's life away from her, but her stitches remain as a permanent mark in the cloth.

I had to make do with the stitches Lusia had left behind as my guide. As though her spirit was there to guide me. It is through her belongings, her dresses, her linens that I can make a connection with my family's past. Completing Lusia's tablecloth has given me a sense of purpose. Despite her permanent absence, my accidental heirlooms connect me with her.

I tie my final knot for the final brown star.

Tante Lusia's tablecloth is finished at last! To me, she will always live on in the stitches she'd left behind. This unbroken thread of embroidery intertwines Lusia's world to mine.

My own stitches are mere juvenile attempts in contrast to her experienced ones. Tante Lusia had taught me how to embroider after all! If she hadn't left behind her stitches for me to follow, I would never have been able to learn for myself. Seeing her half-finished tablecloth inspired me to complete what she'd left behind. I took it as challenge and rose to the occasion. Over so many hours and so many stitches, the tablecloth is now complete. By following Lusia's path, I have found my own way.

My stitches are not as tight.

Not as elegant.

But, after thirty-three years, the tablecloth, an endeavor from different generations, is now a completed whole.

Now I feel as though I am a part of the strand of my family.

I feel a sense of belonging.

Tante Lusia and I are forever connected by a single, spiritual thread.

AUTHOR'S NOTE

The Central Data Base of Shoah Victim's names at Yad Vashem reports the following:

"Jakob Spielvogel was born in Sniatyn, Poland in 1893. During the war he was deported with Transport 19 from Drancy, Camp, France to Auschwitz Birkenau Camp on 14/08/1942. Jakob was murdered in the Shoah. This information is based on a List of murdered Jews from Austria found in Namentliche Erfassung der Oesterreichischen Holocaustopfer, Dokumentationsacrchiv des oesterreichischen Widerstandes (Documentation Centre for Austrian Resistance), Wien."

"Ljussa Spielvogel was born in 1903. During the war was deported with Transport VII from Malines, Caserne Dossin, Camp, Belgium to Auschwitz Birkenau Camp on 01/09/1942. Ljussa was murdered in the Shoah. This information is based on a List of murdered Jews from Austria found in Namentliche Erfassung der oester-reichischen Widerstandes (Documentation Centre for Austrian Resistance), Wien."

BOOK ONE:
SEEKING A COMMON THREAD

QUESTIONS FOR READERS AND BOOK CLUBS

1) Would you have worn the clothing found in the trunk? Would you feel differently if the clothing had belonged to someone you had known or would you feel differently if the clothing had belonged to someone you had never met?

2) Does your family have any traditions that have been passed down through the generations despite a tragedy?

3) Have you ever inherited or encountered an heirloom that prompted you to ask questions about the ancestor who had once owned it?

4) One of the themes of *Seeking a Common Thread* is that if children don't ask parents about their past, they will never know about their family. Has your family ever been a part of an historic event that they don't talk about?

5) As a child, Susan dreamt that the trunk was a pirate's treasure chest. When Susan's family finally does open the trunk up, she discovers what was really inside. Before reading about what had been packed away in the trunk, what did you think was possibly inside?

6) At the end of the book, Susan still does not know what happened to her grandfather. She does not have the courage to ask her father. If you were in that situation, would you have the courage to ask your parent?

7) When Susan discovers the half completed embroidered tablecloth in the trunk, at first she sees no value in it. If you were in a similar situation, would you want to take the time and effort to finish such a project?

   Why?

   Why not?

8) When Florence Hobson sends a letter to Samuel's school, he is the only student to raise his hand to take up the offer for sponsorship for a visa to enter Ireland as a refugee. He had to wait one year before the British government approved the visa. If you had been in Samuel's situation, would you have had the courage to raise your hand? On the one hand, it would mean someplace to go to be free; on the other hand, you would have to leave your family behind.

9) Lusia discovers that she cannot bear children, despite all the money she had spent on modern fertility treatments. Do you think that it was better that Lusia and Jakob never had children because it would have been highly likely that the child would have perished in the Holocaust? Or do you think that it would have been better if Lusia had been able to have a child and celebrate the joys of motherhood even if it were only for a short period of time risking having to flee with the child or lose the child to the Nazis?

10) Do you have any personal good luck rituals? Good luck charms? Do you have any good luck objects or rituals handed down to you by your family? Do you have any superstitions that were handed down in your family?

THE TRILOGY IN
HISTORICAL CONTEXT

AUTHOR'S NOTE: My father and his family lived in Austria, the first country to be invaded by the Nazis. Since this was early on in the Holocaust, it was what my father referred to as an "experiment" before the Final Solution was set into place. My family was able to get away with things that would not have been possible later on. They remained in Vienna for thirteen months after the Anschluss.

Florence Hobson's gesture of extending sponsorship for just one student (my father) demonstrates the power of one person in the time of crisis to reach out and lend a hand to a perfect stranger to save a life.

Florence and my father began as strangers and ended up bonding a lasting and lifelong friendship. My father remained in constant contact with Florence until 1978 when the correspondence stopped. (Florence would have been 97 at the time).

SOURCES:
Personal testimony from Samuel Spielvogel, Elsa Spielvogel Singer, Dr. Dalia Singer, Dr. Silvia Singer, Etka Felsenstein and Hanna Morgenstern. The author acknowledges her mother, Rosalind Spielvogel, as the source of the chapter, "Snooping Around."

TIMELINE:

1660: Hopkins Grammar School is founded in New Haven, Connecticut, (the author's high school). The school later shortens its name to Hopkins School. The school is dedicated to "the breeding up of hopeful youths."

1881: Florence Hobson is born in Belfast, Ireland.

1883: Bulmer Hobson (Florence's brother) is born in Belfast, Ireland.

January 13, 1890: David Spielvogel (Susan's grandfather) is born in Sniatyn (in the Galicia region, then part of the Austro-Hungarian Empire)

November 12, 1893: Jakob Spielvogel (David's brother) is born in Sniatyn.

October 15, 1897: Eva Spielvogel (nee Handel) (Susan's grandmother) is born in Sniatyn.

1897: The Zionist Movement is born. Theodor Herzl, an Austrian journalist and writer encourages Jews to create a "Judenstaat" or Jewish State in what is then Palestine. The desire for the establishment of a Jewish state is a direct response to the rising anti-Semitism in Europe with a wish to create a homeland for the Jewish people.

April 12, 1904: Lusia Spielvogel (nee Fischler) is born in Stanislau, Poland. (According to records at Yad Vashem, Lusia's birth year is recorded as 1903)

1916-1922: Irish War of Independence begins Easter Week 1916. Also called the Sinn Fein Rebellion for self-rule in Ireland. Bulmer Hobson is the Vice President of Sinn Fein from 1907 to 1910. Sinn Fein is the Irish term for "we ourselves."

Although he is a Protestant, and raised a Quaker, a religion sworn to peace, Bulmer believes that Northern Ireland should be its own country. Bulmer is called "The Most Dangerous Man in Ireland" by Major Ivon Price before the Royal Commission inquiries into the cause of the 1916 uprising.

1918: World War I ends. The border changes after the War and Sniatyn, formerly a part of the Austro-Hungarian Empire becomes part of Poland.

1919: Chajesrealgymnasium (Samuel's high school) is established at Castellezgasse 35 in the Second District of Vienna as a high school for Jewish students teaching humanism and Jewish tradition. The school is named for Zwi Perez Chajes, the Chief Rabbi of Vienna.

1919/1920: The five members of the Spielvogel family (David, Simon, Jakob, Leo and Chajce) pool their money together and purchase the apartment house located at Beheimgasse 21 in Vienna.

June 13, 1920: Samuel Spielvogel (Susan's father) is born in Sniatyn, Poland.

1920: Eva and David Spielvogel move from Sniatyn to Vienna to live in the apartment house at Beheimgasse 21. Samuel remains behind in Sniatyn while Eva sets up the household. Samuel is left in the care of Eva's sister, Mali.

1922: The British Mandate for Palestine. Great Britain is given the mandate to govern over Palestine and will act as gatekeeper during the Holocaust. A quota is set on the number of Jews who can emigrate from Nazi occupied countries during the Holocaust. Because of the quota, many Jews who otherwise could have been saved are unable to find refuge here. The British require that Jewish immigrants obtain what Samuel calls a "Capitalist Certificate" which specifies that immigrants must prove that they have sufficient funds in the bank to be able to support themselves.

1922: David and Eva Spielvogel bring Samuel to live with them in Vienna. He will live at Beheimgasse 21 until 1939 when he must flee Austria at the age of nineteen.

June 2, 1924: Elsa Spielvogel (Samuel's sister) is born in Vienna.

November 9, 1925: Rosalind Brueck Spielvogel (Susan's mother) is born in Brooklyn, NY.

September 1926: Samuel begins attending *Die Volksschule,* the local public school. Samuel is bullied by a group of anti-Semitic students from his neighborhood walking to school on his first day.

The leader of the bullies is named Josef Brinsky the Younger. He asks Samuel what his name is. Once Samuel tells Josef his name, he immediately realizes that he is Jewish and begins to beat up on him.

October 29, 1929: The Stock Market crashes in New York City, setting the stage for a world-wide Depression.

September 1930: Samuel begins to attend school at the Chajesrealgymnasium. It is because of the bullying at the public school that Samuel's father, David, decides to send his son to a Jewish school.

January 30, 1933: Adolph Hitler becomes Chancellor of Germany after being appointed by President Paul von Hindenburg.

The Holocaust begins in Germany under Hitler's rule. Discrimination and persecution of the Jews is now openly accepted and legal.

Under the Nazis, laws are passed forbidding Jews to:

-hold public office

-work for the press or radio

-The Nazis tell the German citizens to boycott Jewish owned shops

-The Nazis begin to burn books by Jewish authors

1934: Hitler declares himself Fuhrer, or absolute leader of the German nation.

September 15, 1935: The Nuremberg Laws are passed.

Jews are now forbidden to have the same civil rights as German citizens.

Under the Nuremberg Laws, a Jewish person is now defined as a separate race under "The Law for the Protection of German Blood and Honor" which forbids Jews and Germans to intermarry.

Over time, 120 laws strip Jews of every right that a German citizen has. Germans are defined as someone with pure German blood and defined as a member of the Aryan race. Jews are now labeled as non-Aryans. Anyone with one parent or one grandparent who is Jewish is now considered a non-Aryan.

The Germans use race and not religious belief to define who is a Jew.

March 11, 1938: (Friday) News of the pending invasion of Austria by Hitler and the Nazis spread while Samuel and David are attending services at Telemann Schul, the local synagogue. It is a Friday night. Everyone is talking about Hitler's invasion as much as they are trying to pray. David and Samuel leave the synagogue to go home, passing people in the street who treat the occasion as though it is a night of celebration.

While walking back to the apartment on Beheimgasse, David turns to Samuel and asks, "What will this mean for us Jews?" To which Samuel replies, "The Jews have lived under Nazi rule since 1933. We'll be just fine."

David and Samuel return to the apartment to listen to the radio to hear of Hitler's impending invasion and the resignation of the Chancellor of Austria, Kurt von Schuschnigg.

This is the last time that Samuel will ever set foot in Telemann Schul.

March 12, 1938: (Saturday) the Anschluss. Hitler's troops enter Austria riding in tanks. The Anschluss (also called "The Annexation") of Austria has begun. Austria is now referred to as "Ostmark" meaning "Eastern Boundary" as it is now the eastern boundary of the Third Reich. The currency is changed from schillings to Reich Marks.

March 14, 1938: Hitler arrives in Vienna in a motorcade along the Ringstrasse cheered on by a happy crowd. He makes a speech from the balcony of the Hofburg. In the crowd is Frau Habel, a neighbor who lives across the street from the Spielvogels on

Beheimgasse. Frau Habel shouts so loudly cheering Hitler that she cannot speak for the next three days.

Shortly after the Anschluss, Samuel observes all the pomp and pageantry, the banners with swastikas hanging from public building, even the Votivkirche, a medieval church. Overnight, stickers with swastikas appear all over the city, attached to kiosks, lamp-posts, etc., apparently imported by the Germans to ensure every-one know that Vienna is now under Nazi rule. Samuel listens to the radio as Goering makes speeches about a Jew-free Vienna. The speech is so impressive that Samuel has to think twice that a Jew-Free Vienna means one without him in it.

Shortly after the Anschluss, signs such as *Juden Verboten* (Jews are forbidden) are painted onto shop windows telling Jews they are not allowed to shop there. Signs saying *Achtung Juden* are painted in the windows of shops owned by Jews telling Aryans not to shop there. Samuel's response is to go into those grocery shops in the neighborhood owned by Aryans located a few blocks further away where it is not known that he is Jewish. He proceeds to shop at these stores. He begins to hoard staples such as sugar and tea bags just in case there will be a shortage later on. After a while, he has hoarded many pounds of tea bags and sugar.

March 1938: The Night of Street Washing: Shortly after the Anschluss, Jewish citizens are forced to get down on hands and knees and scrub the streets of Vienna in what is called "The Night of Street Washing." David Spielvogel is forced by Josef Brinsky the Elder to clean the street outside of the Brinsky Gaststube on Syringgasse. He is also forced to wash Brinsky's car which is parked outside the bar.

David is bullied by Josef Brinsky the Elder, father of Josef Brinsky the Younger who had taunted Samuel on his way to *Die Volksschule* in the 1920s.

Before the Anschluss, the Brinsky's had always been anti-Semitic and freely expressed these views. After the Anschluss, however, they expressed their anti-Semitism even more publicly. Josef Brinsky the Younger goes on to become a soldier for the SS.

May 1938: Property Transfer Office: Laws are passed in Austria requiring that all Jews turn in anything of value to the Nazis establishing the Property Transfer Office *(Vermogensverkehrstelle)*. Five hundred people are hired to "promote the Aryanization of Jewish economic assets." Among these five hundred employees is Herr Wolff who occupies David's office at the lumberyard. Herr Wolff takes a percentage of David's sales to give to the Nazis. David is left with a modest percentage of the sale of lumber in order to support his family. Herr Wolff is caught later on for skimming the profits that were supposed to go to the Nazis, keeping it for himself. He is arrested and is sent to a concentration camp.

May 1938: A plainclothes detective arrives at Beheimgasse 21 to arrest David and Samuel. The detective does not inform them that they are being arrested. Instead, he tells them that they are to appear at the local police station to answer some questions. Samuel talks his way out of having to appear at the police station saying he has to go to school. David does not understand what he has done wrong and does not know what questions the police want to ask him, He appears at the police station where he is arrested and taken to an abandoned school located on Karajangasse. He is held there with other Jews for a few days after which he is transported to Dachau.

Shortly after the Anschluss, the Nazis begin to arrest Austrian Jews and transport them to concentration camps. This is done gradually over time. Samuel and David live in the Seventeenth District, a working class neighborhood where fewer Jews live. The majority of the Jewish population live in the First and Second Districts. At first, only the males are arrested, as is the case for Samuel and David. The Nazis never came to arrest Eva and Elsa. Had they stayed in Vienna much longer, however, the Nazis would have eventually come to arrest them, too. Later on, when the Nazis begin to liquidate the entire Jewish population, the Gestapo close off the ends of the streets and go from apartment to apartment arresting Jews and transporting them away in trucks to concentration camps.

April 1938: Florence Hobson sends a letter to Herr Viktor Kellner, Director of the Chajesrealgymnasium School, offering sponsorship for one student for a visa to the United Kingdom.

May 1938: Eva Spielvogel writes letters to Gestapo Headquarters in Vienna located in the Hotel Metropol. In her letters, she requests that her husband, David Spielvogel be released from Dachau.

Rumors in the neighborhood are being circulated, most likely started by the Brinsky's, that David has been arrested because he was passing false checks. David had never had a checking account and had always paid in cash for everything.

June 1938: Samuel graduates from high school from what turns out to be the last graduating class of Chajesrealgymnasium. Samuel does not appear in the senior class photograph because he has to stay home and run the lumberyard in his father's absence.

Chajesrealgymnasium closes its doors. The building then becomes a holding tank for displaced Jews about to be transported away to concentration camps.

August 1938: David Spielvogel is transferred from Dachau to Buchenwald where his prisoner number is: Block 15, Prisoner 9707.

August 1938 Jakob and Lusia flee from Vienna to Antwerp were they settle at Kreeftstraat 27.

November 9, 1938: Kristallnacht.

On Kristallnacht, also called "The Night of the Broken Glass," many synagogues in Germany and Austria are set on fire or destroyed. Jewish businesses and homes are also looted. Many Jews are taken away to concentration camps.

Herr Rosenberg, owner of a clothing store in the neighborhood in the Hernals District is the only victim of Kristallnacht personally known by Samuel. The Nazis smash the glass of Herr

Rosenberg's store and steal clothing, packing up the loot in the truck they have brought in for this purpose.

After Kristallnacht, Jewish students are no longer allowed to attend public schools.

Samuel's sister, Elsa, who attends the local public school, is no longer allowed to attend school. From now on, she must stay at home.

Jews, including Samuel, must have their passports stamped with a large letter "J" for *"Jude"* in red ink.

December 2, 1938: The first Kindertransport arrives in England. The Kindertransport is established to transport refugee children (separating them from their parents) who live in Nazi occupied countries to Great Britain. The British government allows children ranging in ages from infancy to seventeen to be included in the Kindertransport. Most of these children will never see their parents again. Most of their parents will die in concentration camps. The Kindertransport leave from Vienna, Berlin and Prague. During this time, Austrian and German children from the Kindertransport arrive at Millisle Training Farm in Northern Ireland located outside Belfast. The last boat of the Kindertransport was on May 14, 1940 from the Netherlands, the day the Dutch Army surrendered to the Nazis.

April 1939: Samuel's visa for Great Britain is finally approved and issued by the British Consulate in Vienna. It takes one year for the visa to be approved.

April 9, 1939: Samuel escapes by train from the Westbahnhof of Vienna. Samuel is accompanied to the train station by his mother, Eva, who has come to send him off, not knowing if she will ever see her son again. Her parting words to him are *"Gehe mitt Gott,"* "Go with God."

Despite having sponsorship for a visa, Samuel is caught on the train at the German-Belgian border when a stormtrooper asks to see his passport. Since his passport is stamped with the letter "J" in red, the stormtrooper hauls Samuel off the train in order to arrest him. Samuel notices the train is about to leave the station, so he makes a mad dash back to the train. The stormtrooper follows him in close pursuit, but the train takes off so fast that the Nazi loses his footing and falls to the ground. Samuel successfully makes it across the border into Belgium.

April 1939: Samuel visits Jakob and Lusia in Antwerp, unaware that this will be the last time that he will ever see his aunt and uncle.

April 1939: The trunk arrives in London. The trunk is then transferred to long term storage with ACME Transport.

April 1939: Prior to escaping from Vienna to Palestina, Eva Spielvogel commissions a giant wooden crate to be created from wood form the lumberyard. The "Lift" as it is called is too big to fit inside the building, so it stands outside in the street. The "Lift" is filled with the entire contents of the Spielvogels apartment at Beheimgasse 21: all the furniture, the credenza, the kitchen set, the built in beds created expressly for the space in the *Kinderzimmer*, even the family's piano are all loaded into the "Lift." Despite the mandate from the Property Transfer Office requiring all Jews to turn in their possessions to the Gestapo, Eva takes everything with her, saying she will not leave anything behind lest if fall into the hands of the Nazis; even if it was a built-in, created to fit the space of the rooms in the apartment and might not fit anywhere else.

April 1939: Hertha Handel, Eva's sister-in-law, remains in Vienna and oversees the loading of the "Lift" to be sent to Palestina. It is her signature that appears on the paperwork.

The exact fate of Hertha and Yankele Handel remains unknown.

April 1939: Samuel's immediate family escape to Palestina by way of train to a port in Italy where they take a boat called the "Italia." They arrive at a refugee center near Tel Aviv.

Because the family has obtained a "Capitalist Certificate" required by the British government, they are able to enter Palestina.

Because of the British Mandate, Samuel must be separated from the rest of his family since he is now considered as an adult male over the age of eighteen (he is nineteen) and does not have enough money of his own to acquire a separate Capitalist Certificate.

April 1939: The Spielvogel family has no other choice but to leave the apartment building at Beheimgasse. Herr Schumacher, an Austrian citizen from the neighborhood begins to occupy the building and run the lumberyard from which he derives an income for himself. He feels entitled to do so because Hitler said, "Aryans are now allowed to own all Jewish property."

April 1939: Samuel arrives at Florence's home in Carnalea, County Down located outside Belfast. She calls her cottage *Firenze,* the Italian word for Florence. Samuel stays with Florence for a short while until he transfers to Millisle Farm.

April 1939: At Florence's suggestion, Samuel moves to Millisle Farm, a refugee camp built to house Kindertransport children located nearby. Millisle Farm was established in Northern Ireland by the Jews of Northern Ireland and financed with the funds from the Jews of Southern Ireland. Millisle Farm is both a refugee camp and a training camp; training the children in farming with the idea that one day they will immigrate to Palestina.

Samuel remains at Millisle Farm while attending university and helps out with the electrical wiring in the dormitory building. Samuel's roommate is named Jakoby. He is older than the other refugees (he is in his fifties) at Millisle Farm and also comes from Vienna. Most of the refugees at Millisle Farm are from the Kindertransport and will never be united with their families. Because of Florence, Samuel is able to keep in touch with his family who has left for Palestine along with her address.

April 1939: The Spielvogel family arrives in Palestina where they move into an apartment in a settlement outside of Tel Aviv. They live among other refugees who have fled from Germany and

Austria. The other refugees, who had to give up all their valuables to the Nazis and have fled with the clothing on their backs and little more, are somewhat puzzled how Eva manages to escape with a crate of all her belongings, including the family's piano.

September 1, 1939: Hitler invades Poland. This officially starts World War II in Europe.

Shortly after the invasion, Polish Jews are forced to relocate into Ghettos. Jews have curfews forbidding them to be out after a certain time. The major ghettos are located in Lodz and Warsaw.

Jews are forced to wear yellow Stars of David in public.

Those relatives who live in Sniatyn are transferred to other locations.

Samuel's great-grandfather Joachim and other family members from Sniatyn are transferred to Shubertgasse in Kolomea. Eventually all family members from Sniatyn are transported to concentration camps with the exception of Eva's sister, Mali, who escapes with her family to Switzerland.

May 1940: Hitler invades Belgium.

May 18, 1940: Antwerp (where Lusia and Jakob are now living after their escape from Vienna) capitulates to the Nazis.

September 7, 1940 to May 21, 1941: The London Blitz. The Blitz is the systematic bombing of London and other cities in Great Britain by German bombers. London is attacked from the air 71 times by the Germans during this period.

It is during this period that Samuel, who is in Belfast at this time, grows concerned that the trunk may be destroyed in a bombing raid over London. He listens to the broadcasts on the radio about the bombings and decides at this time to make arrangements with Acme Transport to have the trunk sent from London to Florence's house in Belfast. The trunk is successfully sent and arrives safely in Northern Ireland where it is stored in Florence's garage. Fortunately, because of Florence, Samuel has a location where the trunk can be stored at no expense. There are many letters back and forth regarding the rental fees at Acme Transport. Jakob has been paying the rental fees to Acme up until this time. However, after he is arrested and deported, he no longer has the ability to pay the rental fees. The trunk would have been lost to history if the rental fees went unpaid, and Acme Transport would have been within their right to sell the trunk and its contents.

September 1940: Jakob is arrested from the apartment on Kreeftstraat in Antwerp to a prisoner of war camp in Recebedou, France.

October 1940: Jakob begins to write a long series of letters from the camp at Recebedou. He continues to write his letters to Samuel for the next year and a half until he is transported to Auschwitz. In his letters, Jakob writes about the trunk and how to care for its contents. He also tells Samuel to take care of himself and oversees his education and progress from afar. Because he is classified as a Prisoner of War and not as an inmate of a concentration camp, Jakob is permitted to write letters to family members including Samuel and Lusia.

1941: The Nazis begin systematically killing Jews en masse. Later on, death camps were built to kill Jews in a systematic way using gas in gas chambers.

The major concentration camps are located in Poland and were Auschwitz, Treblinka, Belzec and Sobibor

Living conditions in the concentration camps are horrific. Food is scarce and is rationed.

December 7, 1941: Pearl Harbor. Surprise bombing of the US naval base at Pearl Harbor, Hawaii. Up until this time, the United States has remained neutral.

December 8, 1941: The United States declares war on Japan.

December 11, 1941: Hitler declares war on the United States.

The United States officially enters World War II.

January 1942: The Wannsee Conference. Reinhard Heydrich, an SS official gathers Nazi officials to the conference where he presents the "Final Solution" to the Jewish problem. Although concentration camps and the killing of Jews has occurred for several years now, this represents the beginning of Jewish genocide with mass production techniques of transporting Jews to concentration camps and killing them in large numbers.

Approximately half of Europe's Jewish population (estimated to be six million Jews) is exterminated. The rest flee and relocate all over the globe. The Holocaust sets the stage for the establishment for the State of Israel.

August 12, 1942: Jakob Spielvogel is transported to Auschwitz.

September 1, 1942: Lusia Spielvogel is transported to Auschwitz.

1944/1945: Vienna is bombed by American and Russian bombs. The building at Beheimgasse 21 is damaged by shells that destroyed the apartment building across the street where Frau Habel lives. The roof of the building at Beheimgasse 21 is damaged in the shelling. Frau Habel, the woman who cheered Hitler on when he rode into Vienna by motorcade in March 1938 is killed in the bombing, According to reports; she is killed because she did not go into the basement along with the other tenants in the building.

1944: Samuel receives a B.Sc. in Engineering from Queens University, Belfast.

April 30, 1945: Hitler commits suicide in his bunker in Berlin, along with his companion, Eva Braun.

The Holocaust ends.

May 6, 1945: Samuel receives a postcard from Eva Spielvogel's cousin, Itzhak Handel in France telling him that his Uncle Jakob was transported in 1942 from Recebedou to the "Cannibal Land."

May 8, 1945: Victory in Europe Day. The War ends in Europe.

August 6, 1945: The Atomic Bomb is dropped on Hiroshima.

August 9, 1945: The Atomic Bomb is dropped on Nagasaki.

August 15, 1945: Victory in Japan Day. Japan surrenders after the dropping of the bomb on Hiroshima and Nagasaki.

September 2, 1945: Japan signs the surrender document officially ending World War II.

1946: Samuel receives a Diploma in Town and Country Planning from the University of Edinburgh, Scotland.

1946: Simon Spielvogel returns to Beheimgasse 21 after the War to reclaim the family's apartment building and David's lumberyard. According to family reports, he was an inmate at a concentration camp, possibly Auschwitz and made his way back to Vienna after the War. Despite opposition from Herr Schumacher, the Nazi sympathizer who had taken over the building and lumberyard during the war years, Uncle Simon successfully reclaims the building and begins to earn a living running the lumberyard.

1946: Samuel arrives in America to attend graduate school at Yale University.

1947: Florence sends a letter to Samuel discouraging him from sending the trunk to America. Instead, she tries to encourage him to donate the clothing to the needy.

1947: The Trunk is sent to the United States.

May 14, 1948: Israel becomes a state, ending the British Mandate.

1953: Samuel receives his MA from the Yale University School of Art and Architecture.

1950's: Eva and Elsa travel back and forth between Israel and Vienna. They settle in Vienna permanently in the late 1950's, re-establishing their lives there.

1969: The "Troubles" begin in Ireland (Also referred to as "The Strife")

The Troubles refers to the friction in Northern Ireland between the Protestants and the Catholics. The Protestants are unionists and want to stay under British rule. The Catholics are nationalists and want self-rule. This causes numerous incidences of violence between the two factions including car bombings and riots. The

British government responds with riot police trying to quell the uprisings.

August 8, 1969: Bulmer Hobson dies.

January 1972 Susan and her family open Lusia and Jakob's trunk to reveal its contents.

March 29, 1972: First night of Passover. Samuel breaks down during the family's Seder and tearfully recounts the events surrounding his escapes from Vienna on April 9, 1939. It is the first time he has told his family about these events.

July-August 1972: Samuel returns to Vienna to reunite with his mother, Eva and sister, Elsa and her family. Susan accompanies Samuel on this trip. Although Florence is still alive at this time and has remained in constant contact with Samuel, it is decided that because of the "Troubles" it is deemed unsafe to visit Belfast on this trip. Samuel brings Lusia's Persianner coat back to Vienna and presents it as a gift to his sister, Elsa.

August 26, 1972: Summer Olympics begin in Munich. This is the first Olympics in Germany since the 1936 Olympics which were overseen by Hitler. Germany wants to put its best foot forward and make amends for its past, hoping that the games would help to heal history's wounds.

August 28, 1972: Samuel and Susan arrive in Munich by train from Vienna. They spend one day there. The Summer Olympics are in full swing.

While in Munich, Susan wants to go to the museums. It is Samuel's decision to visit Dachau because that is where his father had once been an inmate.

September 5, 1972: Samuel and Susan return home from their trip to Vienna by way of London.

September 5, 1972: Tragedy strikes at the Summer Olympics. 11 members of the Israeli Olympic Team are kidnapped and held hostage by the Black September faction of the Palestine Liberation Army. The entire world watches the live television broadcast as the horror of the day unfolds, hoping the events will end peacefully. By the end of the day, all eleven Israeli athletes are killed by the terrorists.

June 1974: Susan graduates from the Hopkins School.

1975: Samuel starts a newsletter for his classmates (referred to as "Chajesniks") from the Chajesrealgymnasium. The newsletter connects and updates all the surviving students from school who are now scattered all across the world. The newsletter continues for three and a half decades.

February 15, 1976: Eva Spielvogel passes away in Vienna at the age of 79.

1977 Dedication of the New Haven Holocaust Memorial in Edgewood Park. The monument is the United States' first Holocaust memorial built on public land. The monument stands in a corner of Edgewood Park where Susan used to play as a child.

1992: The first graduating class of the Chajesrealgymnasium after it reopens its doors in the same building at Castellezgasse 35. It is the first class to graduate from the school since 1938.

1998: The "Good Friday" Agreement ends the Troubles in Northern Ireland.

August 2008: Susan returns to Vienna to visit her family. She retrieves Lusia's Persianner coat and brings it back to the United States, reuniting the coat with the rest of Lusia's objects from the trunk.

December 14, 2012: Samuel Spielvogel dies at the age of 92.

ABOUT THE AUTHOR

Susan Spielvogel was born in New Haven, Connecticut where she graduated from Hopkins School. She is a graduate of Barnard College/ Columbia University where she majored in Art History.

All her life, Ms. Spielvogel had wondered what was inside the trunk which stood in her family's dining room. In 1972, at the age of fifteen, the trunk was opened to reveal its contents. Aspiring to be a writer since the age of four, Ms. Spielvogel was inspired to write the Trunk Trilogy in 2000 when she began to ask her father, Samuel, those hard questions about the fate of the trunk's owners.

Ms. Spielvogel's father, Samuel had lived in Vienna with his parents and his sister, Elsa, until he was eighteen when the Nazis invaded in 1938. By a quirk of history, Ms. Spielvogel's family was split between America and Austria. While Ms. Spielvogel's father escaped to Ireland and then came to the United States, the remainder of his immediate family escaped to Israel. They returned to Vienna after the War to reclaim the family home and business, the lumberyard located at Beheimgasse 21.

During the summer of 2000, Ms. Spielvogel travelled to Vienna and Antwerp to gather testimony from relatives and research locations associated with her family's past. Using original photographs, documents and letters from her family's archives, Ms. Spielvogel began to write the Trilogy. She owes a debt of gratitude to her father, Samuel and to her first cousin, Dalia, who currently lives in Vienna for her assistance in the research, translations and the writing of the Trilogy.

Although Ms. Spielvogel never had the chance to meet Tante Lusia, "the woman of the trunk," she was fortunate enough to personally meet and get to know her grandmother, Eva, who lived in Vienna. She was also fortunate enough to be in contact through correspondence with Florence Hobson, the woman from Belfast who had rescued her father in 1939. Miss Hobson remained in constant contact with the family until she passed away in the late 1970s.

The Trunk Trilogy reflects on these three powerful women in Ms. Spielvogel's life and introduces them to the reader.

Book One: *Seeking a Common Thread*-Lusia Spielvogel-Renewal
Susan is a fifteen-year-old teenager attending Hopkins School in Connecticut in 1972. All her life, she had wondered what was inside the trunk that stood in the corner of her family's dining room. Her father, Samuel, who had once lived in Vienna had always been secretive about his family's past. Because of this, Susan has never really felt as though she were a part of her family. *Seeking a Common Thread* intertwines the story of Susan, with the story of Tante Lusia of Vienna, the mysterious "woman of the trunk" and how through the items in the trunk Susan discovers a connection to family and a sense of herself.

Book Two: *Connecting Threads:* Eva Spielvogel: Defiance (release date TBA)
The narrative of *Connecting Threads* goes back and forth in time as the reader follows Susan as she accompanies her father, Samuel, on a trip back to Vienna during the summer of 1972 to visit his mother, Eva. The narrative then goes back in time to 1938 when Eva must choose between fleeing Vienna with her daughter, Elsa, or attempting the unthinkable, trying to free her husband, David who has been arrested and transported to Dachau. Over the course of the narrative, Susan learns the real fate of her grandfather.

Book Three: *Celtic Knot*-Florence Hobson: Hope and Kindness (release date TBA)
Celtic Knot intertwines the story of Florence Hobson, the Righteous Gentile who rescued Samuel from the Nazis; the story of the refugee camp in Northern Ireland where Samuel stayed along with the children of the Kindertransport and Susan's experiences as she returns to Hopkins School for the Fall semester after her summer trip to Vienna.

Ms. Spielvogel has now become the caretaker for Lusia's trunk and its contents. She defines herself as a Connecticut Yankee of Austrian descent. Ms. Spielvogel currently resides in the Northeast.

www.ingramcontent.com/pod-product-compliance
Lightning Source LLC
Chambersburg PA
CBHW071248250626
47163CB00002B/369